THE WOR[LD OF] DARKN[ESS]

THE SILVER CROWN

William Bridges

A novel based on **RAGE,**
the collectible card game
from White Wolf Game Studio

The Silver Crown is
A product of White Wolf Publishing.

For information write: White Wolf Publishing, 780 Park North Boulevard, Suite 100, Clarkston, GA 30021.

Cover Illustration: Chris Moeller
Cover Design: Michael Scott Cohen

PRINTED IN CANADA

Dedication

To my brother John.
And to my father.

Acknowledgments

Thanks to Joshua Gabriel Timbrook for Albrecht and Mari, *and to Daniel Greenberg for setting the stage.*

And like a dying star is every work of your virtue: its light is always still on its way and it wanders — and when will it no longer be on its way? Thus the light of your virtue is still on its way even when the work has been done. Though it be forgotten and dead, the ray of its light still lives and wanders. That your virtue is your self and not something foreign, a skin, a cloak, that is the truth from the foundation of your souls, you who are virtuous.... And some who cannot see what is high in man call it virtue that they see all-too-closely what is low in man....

— Nietzsche, *Thus Spoke Zarathustra*

Great innovators never come from above; they come invariably from below, just as trees never grow from the sky downward, but upwards from the earth.

— C.G. Jung, *The Spiritual Problem of Modern Man*

PROLOGUE

Mad Luna was in hiding when King Morningkill held the feast. It was ordained that all the tribe should be there, under the new moon, regardless of excuse or mission otherwise. Tonight, before all, Morningkill would reassert his kingship over the Silver Fangs, the North Country Protectorate, and all the Garou of North America. Even if only he believed such claims anymore.

Greyfist growled low, an almost inaudible rumbling in the back of his throat. The horse beneath him whinnied and rolled his eyes, nostrils flaring as his instincts told him to flee from the predator he heard and smelled so close. Greyfist came to his senses and laid his hand on the horse's neck, patting it calmly and reassuringly. "There, there, Tyre. Nothing to get worked up about."

The horse quit its nervous prancing and stilled itself at Greyfist's calm words. Greyfist steered the mount forward to continue his inspection of the bawn, the boundary between the Court of Jacob Morningkill and the world outside. He cursed himself for letting his rage get the better of him.

Damn it all if he, of all the Garou at court, could not control himself! It did no good to get worked up over things you could not change. Things other Garou — better Garou — before you had tried and failed at. No, griping would not change the king's mind and clear it of its years-old madness.

There. It was said. Mad. No other Silver Fang would dare admit that the king was mad, but that's what it surely was. *Eccentric*, they would say. *But mad? Certainly not. That is the talk of fools outside the tribe, envious of our position and state. Denied Gaia's divine favor, they grumble and gnash their fangs, desperate for the Fangs' divinely ordained glory. They would have to earn through hard labor the honor to which the Fangs were born.*

Greyfist spat in disgust. It was such thoughts, such arrogance, that had brought the tribe low, that had allowed a madness like Morningkill's to go so long ignored.

But to think as Greyfist did was treason.

Then gut me for a traitor, he thought. *Ah, how easy it is to speak so boldly in your own mind. But to act out this heroism? No, not I. I shall go on heeding the king, acquiescing to his strange demands. It is the way. It has been so for more years than humankind has built cities. Who am I to question such tradition? The king's seneschal. But not the king himself. Only he can change the ancient laws. Only he can revive the tribe.*

But Morningkill…? His damn jealousy and paranoia had driven away all worthy successors. Was it to end with him? The great royal line, the ancient family of the House of Wyrmfoe? The family that had bred such heroes as were not seen in the world today? Such Garou as Aleking Axeclaw? Gorak Rules-by-Right?

The horse halted and reared back, whinnying in fear. Greyfist gripped the reins to avoid slipping off and again patted the horse's neck. "Calm. Calm. I'm at it again, fuming with anger. Doesn't do you any good, though, does it? I'm sorry, Tyre. Calm down."

But the horse still rolled its eyes and backed away from the trail. Greyfist sighed and dismounted, holding the reins to keep the horse from bolting. He stood still and slowly pulled the animal to him. The horse stopped its shying and settled, looking left and right fearfully, and finally let loose a loud sigh and stood still. Greyfist again patted its neck.

"There. That's better. What's a Garou doing riding a horse, anyway? You deserve much better. Not easy to train a horse to let a wolf crawl onto its back. But Morningkill likes horses. Morningkill demands horses. And so, we Garou ride horses. Royal pageantry. How vain. And you pay the cost."

Greyfist looked about as he stood, still rubbing the horse's neck. It was dark, with no moon to light the night. The landscape was a mass of black shapes on black shapes, vaguely formed into trees. He had reached the far northern edge of the bawn and was now surrounded by the trees, huddling in on all sides except where the trail cut through the deep wilderness. Thanks to the laws that protected it from human despoiling, this was wilderness even humans avoided, as was much of the Green Mountain range of Vermont. The North Country Protectorate covered much of southern Vermont, but Greyfist knew that it had once stretched from Manhattan Island to the Canadian border, long ago when the Silver Fangs had first arrived on the continent to carve their territory from the native lands. From the native's hands.

Greyfist listened. Before he'd left on his patrol, he had used the Gift taught him by spirits to see, hear and smell with the senses of a wolf without actually shifting into wolf form. The only sounds he heard were those natural to the night. Insects buzzing off in the woods, the slight rustle of trees in the breeze. Somewhere farther off, the faint chattering of a brook. Nothing unusual or dangerous here.

Greyfist climbed back onto the horse and turned it around, setting off down the path, back toward the court where the feast was already starting. As he rode, he tried to still his anger. He was used to these tirades when the frustration was too much for him. He realized that he overreacted much of the time. Morningkill did have his moments, after all. He was a scion of the royal house. You could only fall but so far from that kind of pinnacle.

But Greyfist remembered Jacob from younger days. There had been trust between Jacob and Greyfist then. Even today, Morningkill trusted none among the Silver Fangs so much as Greyfist. But why then did he not listen to his counselor's advice more often? Why did he insist on listening to Arkady, vain Arkady? He was enamored of the young hero, Greyfist supposed. The Garou son Morningkill had never had, perhaps. At least a son who lived up to all the traditions, not like Morningkill's real grandson.

Greyfist shook his head. He loved Morningkill dearly, remembering the man he used to be and might become again. If the king could shake off the madness. Where did this paranoia of his come from? Why were so many in the tribe cursed these days with such worries? Had the line really fallen, as the Shadow Lords claimed? No, Greyfist could not accept that. *Start thinking that way, and Harano follows.*

But then... there was the dream. The dream he had had but three nights ago. The dream which had kept him awake almost every night since, thinking it over, fighting to remember every detail of it. Was it a dream or a vision? Misinterpreting such things could be dangerous, especially considering the portents this one revealed. But after hours of consideration, Greyfist believed his dream had been sent by Falcon, the totem spirit of the tribe. But he still could not say what the dream meant for him, for Morningkill and for the tribe.

A dream of fallen kings and ones newly crowned. Of battle and pain. Of an oppressively dark, cathedral-like chamber where a single unblemished band of silver glowed bright.

Greyfist sat up in his saddle and looked ahead. Enough ruminations. He had no idea what the dream meant: It was a scattered play of images, and he did not have enough clues yet to figure it out. He thought instead of the security of the caern. While he was not the Warder, as the king's seneschal it was his duty to ensure that the moot was safe and that the king was not threatened. So he had taken it upon himself to patrol the outlying regions, leaving the defense of the center to the Warder. Besides, he thought it best to cool his rage well away from the court happenings.

He was confident that the Warder could handle the duty, even though she was still healing a bad wound suffered on one of Morningkill's quests. The King had sent Regina to fetch a tribal fetish from the Get of Fenris in the Adirondacks, and she had had to challenge one of their heroes for it. She had won, but still felt the pain of her wounds.

In addition, she now had to play Gatekeeper, at least until young Eliphas Standish could be ordained. The previous Gatekeeper, Garrick Batell, was dead, killed a week ago on a hunt. He had been lured into the Umbra alone and assaulted by a Bane; his body had been found by a wandering tribe of Fianna. That had been humiliating, watching them bring back the body. It wasn't right for a Silver Fang not to be brought home by his own pack. But Garrick had been stupid, and that was exactly what a Garou could not afford to be, with the Wyrm always waiting for just such an opening.

Greyfist rode back into the large clearing that formed the caern and court of the North Country Protectorate. He quickly surveyed the field. Tents were erected in a pattern across the meadow: Those to the north were for the Lodge of the Sun, while those to the south represented the Lodge of the Moon. The northern tents were white with gold pictograms; the southern tents black with silver pictograms. Underneath both tents, and to the east, were huge wooden tables and high-backed chairs, each marked with the crest of its owner. Propriety demanded a seating order at court. The eastern table, out in the open and under no tent, was for the Armies of the King, all the Silver Fangs and court retainers who were not a part of either Lodge. The food had not yet been brought from the nearby mansion — the Morningkill estates — although the youngest from the Kin families were setting the tables in preparation.

But none were seated yet, as it was still the introductory stage of the feast. Garou and Kinfolk mingled on the field, taking part in the courtly game of greetings and gossip. Some Silver Fangs rode horses, dressed in regal display to impress the king, who dearly loved equestrian pursuits. They all wore finery, which for some meant sharp suits or elegant gowns; for others, bone fetishes or gold-laced robes. An odd mix of modern and primitive.

And at the nexus of all this activity, all the comings and goings, greetings and blessings, was the Grand Oak, the ancient tree where the throne of King Jacob Morningkill had been carved among the mighty roots. And on the throne, surrounded by both Garou and human Kinfolk of noble blood, was Morningkill himself. The king was dressed in the brightest of finery, his robe stitched in silver with ornate pictograms illustrating his family's great lineage. His arms displayed gold bracelets handed down from the treasuries of ancient human kings who, unknown to their fellow men, had been Kin to the Silver Fangs and had served only through the graces of the noble Garou. And on Morningkill's head was the crown, carved from wood and studded with jewels won from realms in the distant spirit world by previous kings.

But under all this glory was an old man with a bitter face, whose eyes darted about, watching for potential treachery from the sycophants swarming around him.

Greyfist shook his head in shame.

Kin families had the king's ear and were making full use of the opportunity. Apparently there was a dispute between the Rothchilds and the Albrechts, for Darren Rothchild and Warren Albrecht both argued before the king. Greyfist was always disgusted by such petty displays, but he had to forgive the Kin. They did not share in the full renown of their parents or children and so had to erect a pecking order of their own. The Kin were important, for they carried the blood of future Garou, but they mimicked the Fangs' own noble bureaucracy too well for Greyfist's taste. Theirs was a life of indentured servitude and arranged marriages.

But where was Arkady? Where was the King's Own Pack, his personal guard? Greyfist looked over the field, searching for any sign of them. Inconceivable that they would be late to the king's moot. Yet Greyfist had not seen them before he left on his patrol, and they were not in sight now. He would have words with Arkady when he finally arrived. He was damn tired of Arkady's irresponsibility, always off chasing renown. His place was here, damn it! There was glory and honor enough in serving the king, and Arkady would have to learn to live with it.

Greyfist's horse suddenly screamed and broke into a run, throwing Greyfist off. He hit the ground hard and heard the snap of his collar-bone, followed quickly by sharp pain. He ignored it and stood up, looking for his horse, which he spotted quickly disappearing into the woods. Damn it! Was the animal so easily spooked? His anger hadn't been so harsh that time—

Four sharp knives raked into his back and he fell, grunting in pain. He looked over his shoulder to see a Garou in Crinos form standing behind him, his claws dripping blood — Greyfist's blood. The werewolf grinned wide, a sick grimace. Spittle poured from his mouth as if it welled up from deep within his throat, beyond his control. His fur was terribly mangy, and patched with greenish blotches. The ears were not those of a wolf, but rather resembled a bat's. A Black Spiral Dancer, a werewolf of the tribe of the Wyrm. He looked past Greyfist. Toward the throne.

The creature leaped over Greyfist at a run. Greyfist tried to stand, but the pain hit him hard, causing him to gasp for breath. The king! The king was in danger! He concentrated hard, trying not to panic, and began to shift forms. His muscles grew bigger and his bones followed suit, changing shape and size, forming wolfish features. Now in Crinos form, the form of battle, Greyfist stood.

All about him, a war raged. Silver Fangs fought with other Black Spiral Dancers. The insane creatures gibbered and roared, throwing themselves maniacally at the startled Silver Fangs. Court finery was stained with ichorous blood and gore as the surprise-attackers tore into the Silver Fang warriors.

Greyfist took all this in as he loped toward the throne, moving as fast as he could. He screamed to himself to run faster, but his legs wouldn't respond correctly. Blood still oozed down his back, but his collarbone had reknitted itself as he had changed.

Before him, Greyfist saw his Black Spiral assaulter fighting savagely with Regina, the Caern Warder. She had lost an arm but had cost the creature two or three ribs, which lay bloody on the ground. Its rib cage was gaping open, spilling viscera, but it didn't seem to notice. It had the upper hand and was battering Regina badly.

Behind them, sitting on his throne and staring dumbly at the fight, was Morningkill. The Kinfolk who had been clamoring for his attention not five minutes ago were nowhere in sight. Greyfist couldn't blame them. What human wouldn't flee from a Black Spiral Dancer?

Greyfist drew his klaive and rushed up behind the tainted Garou. Before the thing could hammer another blow onto the fallen Regina, Greyfist thrust the silver sword into its spine. It reared back its head and screamed, dying an instant later.

Greyfist pulled the weapon out of the steaming body and limped over to Morningkill. "Are you all right, my king?" he cried.

Morningkill looked at him, dazed. He then shook his head as if to clear it and stared at Greyfist, his eyes clear and bright. "Yes. I am fine. You have done well, Greyfist. A Half-Moon succeeded where none of my Ahrouns could." He looked over at Regina, who slowly pulled herself to her feet.

"She did her best, my lord," Greyfist said as he limped over to her.

Regina nodded a silent thank-you to him. She picked up her severed arm and held it to the stump. "Do not worry about me," she said. "We must get the king to safety."

"No," Morningkill said. "I will stay on my throne. The moot is about to start."

Greyfist stared in shock at Morningkill, who stood resolutely before the oaken throne. "My king, the moot is over! The Black Spirals have invaded the court! We must flee to safety!"

Morningkill seemed confused and looked out over the meadow. Greyfist also scanned the area and saw, far out on the field, five Silver Fangs finishing up the battle. The King's Own Pack. Arkady had finally arrived. On the field were six Black Spiral bodies, not including Greyfist's attacker. Two horses lay dead, as did three Kinfolk retainers.

Greyfist looked at Arkady, who sauntered across the field, dragging the body of one of the Black Spirals behind him as a trophy. *So cocky and confident*, thought Greyfist. *Why wasn't he here earlier?*

"You see?" Morningkill said. "My guard is here! Arkady has come! There, out on the field! The battle is over. We have won the day!" He began to laugh, but it was choked off in his throat as a figure leapt from the branches above. It hurtled into Morningkill and both of them went down in a heap.

Greyfist ran to the throne and slashed at the Black Spiral Dancer, severing its head with one expert sweep of his klaive. He quickly pulled the spasming, headless body off the king.

Morningkill lay staring at Greyfist, as if he recognized him for the first time in years. The king's guts were spread out in his lap; his blood seeped into the ancient oak. He breathed chokingly, trying to say something.

Greyfist screamed in anguish. "Healers! Healers! Damn it!" He fell to his knees and cradled the king in his arms. Morningkill whispered low and Greyfist, tears streaming down his furred cheeks, bent his ear to the king's weak words.

"My... grand... son...?" Morningkill said, his eyes rolling up to meet Greyfist's. "Bring him... home." The king's eyes shut and he slumped into Greyfist's arms, letting go his last breath.

Greyfist cried, clutching the king close to his breast. "Jacob. Jacob. Why like this? Why?"

Greyfist heard frantic footsteps approach and a sob of anguish. He looked up to see Arkady, staring at the dead king. His face bore shock and grief at once, but also a look of disbelief, as if what he saw could not be true.

"The king? Dead?" Arkady said, almost in a whisper.

Greyfist gritted his teeth and suppressed a growl. "Dead. The king is dead."

Regina fell to her knees, her head bowed, her hand dropping her severed arm before she could heal it. Other Silver Fangs now gathered round, as did Kinfolk of the court. All stared in shock and dismay at Morningkill's body.

One of the Kin cried out, beginning a wail which quickly spread throughout the crowd. Arkady threw back his head and let loose a howl. All the Silver Fangs followed, their heads back and eyes shut with grief. Greyfist joined in, and their howl mixed with the Kin's mournful wailing and was carried out across the woods to the nearby towns, where people clutched their bedsheets in terror and dug themselves deeper into their beds, trying to shut out the fearful sound.

Greyfist laid Morningkill on the ground, wrapping the king's arms across his chest in a regal pose. He rose and walked over to Arkady, who stood two heads taller than him. Arkady was an imposing figure of pure white fur and black leather battle armor. Nonetheless, Arkady's grief was no equal to Greyfist's anger.

"Why weren't you here?" Greyfist yelled. "You were his guard, the King's Own!"

Arkady looked at Greyfist and narrowed his eyes in anger; Greyfist knew something was not right. He saw into the large Garou's eyes and knew that the grief which he now threw off was a blanket easily discarded, that his sorrow over Morningkill's death was not so genuine as his howl had made Greyfist first believe.

"We tried to get here, my pack and I," Arkady said in his thick Russian accent, stepping forward and forcing Greyfist to look up to his height. "But we were attacked outside the bawn by Black Spiral Dancers. By the time we finished them and arrived, the battle had already begun."

"But how? How did they get past the guards?"

"Look! There across the field!" Arkady spun and pointed to the meadow. "See? Holes from the ground. They came from beneath us. Who knows how long they had been burrowing there, secretly and silently so that none of us would know. This was planned, yes? They knew well when to attack."

Greyfist stared at the three holes in the earth. *So that's what spooked Tyre*, he thought. *It wasn't me. He sensed those damn things moving beneath us.*

"So Garrick the Gatekeeper was killed on purpose, to make sure our defenses would be low," Greyfist said, still staring at the dark entrances into the earth.

"Yes, Seneschal. That must be it," Arkady said.

Greyfist wondered how long they had been under there, planning their attack. When he turned back to Arkady, the Garou had stepped up to the throne and was beginning to address the assemblage.

"My friends," Arkady said. "This is a great tragedy we suffer tonight. Our king is dead. But he will live on in our songs!" Silver Fang warriors cheered at that, desperate for some hope to come out of their grief. "In two nights, when the moon is crescent, we shall give him his death rite so that he may join the kings before him in our tribal spirit lands. Always will he be remembered and spoken well of."

Greyfist nodded as other Silver Fang cheered again. *Yes, Morningkill must be remembered. For his good qualities, not his bad.*

"But it is time we consider our new king!" Arkady yelled.

What is this? Greyfist thought, narrowing his eyes in anger. *This is too early! Morningkill's body still lies warm and Arkady speaks of his successor?*

"Yes, I know it is hasty, but the enemy has found us in our very court! We must swiftly have our new king!"

Greyfist stepped forward. "This is too soon! We must review the ranks. Morningkill left only one successor to the first family—"

"But he is in exile, Seneschal!" Arkady yelled to be heard. "He is unworthy, and thus a member of another royal family must rule."

"But there are no other royal families in North Country. It would take too long to summon one from another protectorate!"

"Ah, but here is where you are wrong, Seneschal. Peter, my packmate!" He gestured to a Garou in the crowd. "Tell them what we have discovered on our latest quest!"

Peter walked forward and stepped up to the throne. He was well-known here, a member of the King's Own Pack and thus highly honored. He put his hand on Arkady's shoulder and looked out over the crowd.

"We all know Arkady's story, how he came to us after traveling Europe, homeless. How he barely escaped the horrors of his mother country, Russia, when he was a small child, before his First Change. How the Kinfolk man who smuggled him from that dangerous land was thought lost and dead. But no. We have found him, the man who was a father to Arkady!

"He was old and feeble, still hurting from the wounds he

had received long ago trying to defend little Arkady from the Wyrm spawn. He had told Arkady to run as the creature attacked him all those years ago, throwing himself in the way to defend the little boy, who was not yet Garou. The man had traveled ever since, trying to find Arkady again, to tell Arkady of his heritage. And all the while, Arkady had believed him dead.

"He finally found Arkady but two nights ago, and on his deathbed revealed this great news: Arkady's great-grandparents were of the Clan of the Crescent Moon! Arkady is of the Seven! He is royal, and is thus the next to succeed Morningkill to the throne of the North Country Protectorate!"

The crowd broke out into a massive howl. This was wonderful! A royal had been found, and he was one of theirs! Their own Arkady was to be king!

But Greyfist did not howl with the rest. He stepped away from the throne, where Arkady smiled jubilantly as the Silver Fangs sang his praises. Greyfist knew this was wrong. Oh, he believed Arkady was royal, all right. Who wouldn't believe it, with fur like that and that bearing of his? But Greyfist suspected that Arkady had been aware of this heritage all along, that it was not some newly discovered secret. No, it wasn't right: there was another who was in line for the throne before Arkady. There was another of the House of Wyrmfoe, the first family of North Country.

Greyfist pulled Eliphas Standish out of the crowd and walked him away from the gathering. Eliphas looked annoyed, and kept peering back at the throne, not wanting to miss anything. But he knew better than to ignore the orders of the seneschal, who was king until Arkady was crowned.

"What is it?" Eliphas said. "What is so important that we miss Arkady's announcement? This is a great moment."

"Still your slobbering tongue, cub," Greyfist said. "I want

you to go to New York City."

"What? But I am to be made Gatekeeper next week. I have many duties—"

"Next week! Not yet. You are to go to New York and bring Lord Albrecht back with you."

Eliphas stared at Greyfist. "Albrecht? I can't do that! He is in exile!"

"No longer. It was Morningkill's last request, stated with his dying breath. Are you to deny the king's final commandment?"

Eliphas looked down in shame. "No, of course not. If the king declared the exile over, then...." He raised his head and looked at Greyfist, worried. "But what about Arkady? If Albrecht is no longer denied the court, then he is next in line, not...."

Greyfist nodded. "Exactly. And Morningkill knew that. So, go and do not say a word of it to anyone. You are to speak of this only to me and Albrecht. Just so you know how important this is, I'm declaring it a Court Quest. Do you understand?"

"Yes!" Eliphas said, realizing it would mean honor for him if he succeeded. "I'll be back with him tomorrow."

"Go then." Greyfist watched Eliphas leave immediately; the boy did not even bother to say good-bye to anyone at court. That was good. The young one knew how to follow a court dictate.

Greyfist looked over at Arkady, who was now staring back at him with a frown, obviously wondering what Greyfist was up to. Greyfist smiled and nodded at the newly revealed Duke. Arkady smiled back, but it was a weak smile, full of uncertainty.

CHAPTER ONE

Albrecht was in one of his black moods. He walked down the wet street toward the triangular park two blocks away. He looked up at the gray sky, still dark with the new dawn, and blinked at the rain. *The sky is crying,* he thought. *A slow, mournful drizzle of rain falling on the city, spattering the streets with a sheet of tears. Warped reflections of our world stare up at me from the still water — a mirror, shattered with every step I take.*

God, you're really full of it today, Albrecht said to himself. *What's the big deal? It's just another rainy day.*

Then why do I feel like shit? Bad feeling, like something I'm not going to like is coming down the pike. Never been much for omens, but they seem to like me an awful lot, judging from the past few months. Even an Ahroun can get premonitions now and then. But premonitions of what? I don't have a clue. Just feels wrong, that's all. Is this what a wolf feels like before stepping into a trap?

Albrecht turned the corner and stopped to look at the small park across the street. It was not a very large park, but by city standards it was big enough. It gave Albrecht and his small pack a place to meet besides Central Park, which was crawling with too many other Garou for Albrecht's taste.

He was early by almost half an hour to meet his pack here today, but that would give him time for a smoke or two. Evan didn't like cigarette smoke, and while Albrecht normally didn't give a flying fuck, he had agreed to compromise when with the pack. Mari didn't like the smoke either, but she never said anything about it. Just fumed in that way of hers, and found other ways to attack Albrecht. She still hadn't gotten over that fight they'd had a few years ago. *Just a damn flesh wound*, Albrecht thought. *Deal with it, already*.

Albrecht crossed the rain-slick street and walked onto the wet grass. Standing on the grass was frowned upon by the law, but he didn't care. It was what grass was for, wasn't it? He walked deeper into the small, two- to three-block square park. When he got to the usual bench, there was a man sleeping on it with newspapers piled over him. Albrecht sat down next to him and lit up a cigarette, pretending the guy wasn't there.

He leaned back and let out a cloud of smoke. That felt better. Nothing like a good smoke. Oh, sure, some Garou said it would kill him one day, that he would be devoured by Hoga, Urge Wyrm of Smog. But he just nodded and smiled at such folly. Hell, Indians had been smoking for years before the Wyrm ever got to this continent. Yeah, their tobacco had been a lot purer, and Albrecht wasn't really sure just who owned the cigarette brand he smoked, but he figured there was no reason to worry about it. Wasn't as if his lungs didn't clean themselves out just fine, what with the regeneration and all.

He took another long drag and smiled, holding the smoke in for a few minutes and then letting it out slowly. *Screw 'em*, he thought. All the moral prigs. They had skeletons in their closets, all right. At least Albrecht wore his faults on his sleeve, where everyone could see them. Well, some of them. He knew he was prone to depressions that were not always obvious to others. Mari missed them half the time, although Evan seemed to understand. Albrecht had always had them, although there had been a real bad spell a while back, after his exile, which had ended only when he formed his own pack a few months ago.

The pack. That was something. Something Albrecht hadn't thought he'd ever be a part of again, not since his first pack all up and died fighting the Wyrm. He'd gotten famous with them, but that hadn't stopped them from getting themselves killed and leaving him all alone to face the renown and expectations heaped on him. It was worse when you were the grandson of King Morningkill and the scion of the House of Wyrmfoe.

But that crap was behind him now. Had been for years. He'd been kicked out of the protectorate by Morningkill, accused of hubris and lack of deference, the breaking of the Litany and so on and so on. The truth of it was that Morningkill exiled anyone who displayed genuine ability, anyone who might expose Morningkill's own faults. Albrecht wasn't the first. Loba Carcassone had that honor. And there'd been more after Albrecht, although he didn't know their names.

Albrecht ground out his cigarette on the benchback, shaking his head. Christ, but he was melancholy this morning.

"Huh? What?" The newspapers moved and fell away, revealing the man underneath, now blinking blearily and craning his neck around to look at Albrecht. "Who the hell...?"

Albrecht smiled. "You're sleeping on my property, pal." He pointed at a carving in the wooden back which read *Lord A*. "That's me. I don't mind you sleeping here, but once the dawn cracks, this bench is mine."

The man growled and sat up. He was dressed in an old army field jacket and torn jeans. He rubbed his face and then looked over at Albrecht. "That's kinda rude, don't ya think? This ain't exactly yours: it's public property."

Albrecht frowned and showed his teeth. The effect was

more dreadful than merely that, however, as his rage bled out a little from his eyes. The bench sleeper looked terrified and stood up quickly.

"All right, all right. I'm gone." And he walked off, hands in his pockets, but looking back at Albrecht as if trying to figure out just what it was he had seen.

Albrecht frowned. He knew better than to do that. You never knew when you were accidentally putting the scare on somebody important. Not that a park-bench bum was important, but in this city he might have friends in low places, and low meant power in New York. The city was crawling with Leeches — vampires — who pulled the strings of many important officials from their sewer dens. Sure, some of them lived in high-rises, but the dark alleys and sewerways were their meeting places and hunting grounds.

Albrecht looked over at the two guys entering the park. They were talking to each other as they looked right at him and slowly headed his way. Albrecht wondered what the hell this was about. He didn't recognize the two. These guys had suits on underneath their trench coats, but designer suits, not federal-agent style. Businessmen? If so, what the hell did they want from him?

The two walked up to the bench and looked down at Albrecht. They looked nervous, as if unsure what to do. Then the taller of the two spoke. "Albrecht?"

"Lord Albrecht, yeah," Albrecht said, standing up. He stood about half a foot taller than the one who had spoken. The two men moved a bit closer. "What do you want?"

The tall one looked at his partner and some unseen signal passed between them. They both erupted into action, pulling long, sharp knives out of their coats and jumping toward Albrecht, swinging the knives at his throat.

Albrecht leapt back and onto the bench, then vaulted over it in a somersault. One of the knives caught his coat, tearing a foot-long rip in it, but now the bench was between them.

Klaives! Were these Garou? Albrecht turned to face them, and they split up to move around the bench, one on either side, moving carefully now, as if they were zoo-keepers trying to tranquilize a tiger.

Albrecht growled and shifted forms. In an instant he was nine feet tall in his Crinos wolfman form. His fur was white, the sign of pure blood among Garou. The attackers also began to shift, smoothly flowing into Crinos forms themselves. Their fur was also white, although mixed with faint flecks of gray.

"You're Silver Fangs!" Albrecht yelled in the Garou tongue. "What the hell is going on?"

They said nothing as they came at him from both sides. Albrecht pulled his own klaive from his coat; his was nearly bigger than both of theirs combined. A Grand Klaive, a much rarer and more potent weapon.

Seeing the large silver sword, one of the Garou hesitated, but the other lunged forward, his klaive aimed at Albrecht's guts. Albrecht stepped to the side and parried the knife, but quickly twisted his own blade and swiped it at the attacking Garou. It sliced across his opponent's arm and drew blood. The Garou yelled and jumped back just as the other one came forward.

Albrecht stepped back and met the charge with his klaive in thrusting position. The oncoming Garou barely managed to twist away, although the Grand Klaive still tore a chunk out of his side. He quickly recovered, and slashed at Albrecht.

Albrecht was startled at this one's skill with a blade, and he couldn't parry in time. The klaive sunk into Albrecht's left thigh and stuck there. Albrecht screamed in rage and leapt back.

The other Garou was ready and met Albrecht from behind, slicing into his back. The pain flooded over Albrecht and he felt himself losing control, giving into the anger and pain and rage. But he willed himself to calm down, to ignore the pain. The last thing he needed now was to frenzy.

He ducked down low and spun in a circle, holding the blade out, surprising the Garou who had struck him from behind. The sword bit into his legs, hacking cleanly through one but just grazing the other. The Garou fell, a howl escaping as he hit the wet ground.

Albrecht was up and moving before the other Garou could close in. He backed off as the other picked up his fallen comrade's klaive and moved after him. But the attacking Silver Fang had something in his other hand, something Albrecht couldn't see.

"Damn it, explain yourself! I am Lord Albrecht, of the House of Wyrmfoe! Heed your better, you bastard!"

But the Garou just kept coming forward, warily. As Albrecht moved left, the Garou followed and quickly wove to the right, gaining ground. Albrecht backed up against a tree and knew he had to make a stand.

The other Garou waved his hand at Albrecht, and Albrecht shut his eyes to ward off the sand which flew into his face. *Damn!* He raised his klaive to parry whatever came at him, fighting blind. But the blow came low, slicing into Albrecht's already wounded thigh.

And that was it. Albrecht had had enough and couldn't control his anger any longer. He succumbed to his rage and opened his mouth wide to let out a roar. He opened his eyes to see his assailant drawing back for a thrust, but Albrecht stepped forward with blinding speed, dropped his klaive, and wrapped his clawed hands around the Garou's face.

The Garou brought his blade up but wasn't fast enough to deal with the berserk Albrecht, who dug his claws into the Garou's head, raking furrows in his scalp. Albrecht's weight brought the Garou to the ground, and Albrecht immediately began savaging his captive with his rear claws, stomping the Garou's legs and raking away strips of flesh. The Garou screamed and hit Albrecht repeatedly with the klaive, all weak and ineffective blows with no leverage. In seconds, the Garou was dead.

Albrecht, totally lost to anger, crawled forward on all fours, slapping through the mud, still partially blinded from the sand in his eyes, heading for the smell of the other enemy. But there was another smell there now. A familiar smell. Not threatening.

"Albrecht! Calm down! It's over!" the source of the new scent yelled.

Albrecht circled around defensively, sniffing all about him for foes. None. Only the familiar smell. The non-threatening smell. The smell of a packmate.

Albrecht sat down and looked at Evan, who stood before the other Garou as if defending him from Albrecht. Evan looked like a fourteen-year-old boy, which he was. But he was also a Garou, and fourteen wasn't so young when you were one of Gaia's chosen. He was wiser than his years, thanks to spirits who favored him and taught him special powers. Evan was of the Wendigo tribe, even though he didn't look remotely Native American.

Albrecht frowned. Then he shifted back to human form. *Shit*, he thought. *Lost it. Damn.* He looked around and saw the dead Garou behind him, now a human form bleeding across the wet grass. He looked back at Evan. "That was not fun."

"Who are these guys?" Evan asked, leaning down and looking at the wounded one, still in Crinos form but moaning in half-consciousness, his severed leg lying a few feet away from his body.

"Silver Fangs. Beyond that, I have no idea. Can you fix him up?"

Evan looked over at the leg and then at the Garou's stump. "Yeah. Help me out here. I need you to hold the leg to the wound while I concentrate."

Albrecht gripped the klaive still stuck in his thigh and wrenched it out. The pain was incredible, but Albrecht was used to this kind of hurt and forgot it quickly.

He went and picked up the severed leg, then walked over to the wounded Garou. He dropped to his knees and held the leg up to the bleeding stump. Evan placed his hand over both and sat silent for a minute. Then the flesh around the stump and the severed leg began to grow, to reknit and pull itself back together. There would be a scar.

When that was done, Albrecht stood up and looked around. He wondered what kind of toll this fight had taken on the local residents. For all he knew, a cop or two had come running only to see three wolfmen duking it out. Of course they wouldn't remember it that way. They'd rationalize it away as anything else. The Veil.

As if to confirm his thoughts, Albrecht saw a police officer sitting on the grass near the edge of the sidewalk. He had his head buried in his hands and was muttering to himself.

Not exactly standard behavior for the NYPD, thought Albrecht. He turned to Evan. "We gotta clean this up and move out before that pig wises up again."

Evan looked over at the police officer. "I know. I saw him on my way in. I think he'll be okay." He looked at both the bodies. "Uh... you can carry this one, and I'll get the dead one." Evan began shifting into a larger form. His muscles grew wide and broad and his face took on a chunky, dumb-jock look — a sort of Mr. Hyde to his previous Dr. Jekyll. He walked over to the dead body.

"What the hell is going on?" someone yelled.

"You're late, Mari," Albrecht said. "You missed the action."

Mari walked around the bench, over to the scene of the battle. She was a wiry, muscled and intense-looking woman, a Hispanic-Italian from the Bronx. Her attitude alone could stop fights, but her physique and martial skill ensured that she could back it up with blows. Mari helped teach street-tough skills to battered women. It was a religious cause for her, and she never took kindly to Albrecht's mocking her "coddling of humans." But Albrecht knew that now was not the time to start sparring.

"Two Garou," Mari said, surveying the scene. "One dead, the other half-dead. Who attacked whom?" she said, turning to look Albrecht in the eyes.

"Don't start," Albrecht said, glaring back at her. "I didn't ask for this. These are Silver Fangs, damn it! I don't go carving up my tribe for the fun of it!"

"Then why?" Mari said, stepping closer to him. "Why would they attack you? What have you done now?"

"Me? This is my fault? These two just walk up and start slicing away, and you think I had something to do with it? Lady, get a clue: I am *not* out to make enemies."

"Come on," Evan said, looking at both of them, with the dead Garou on his back. "We'd better enter the Umbra. No way we're going to get these two to Central Park without being noticed."

Albrecht turned away from Mari and picked up the wounded Garou, who still moaned in pain and delirium. "Well, who's leading the way?"

"All right," Mari said. She walked over and picked up Albrecht's Grand Klaive. Holding it up over the street and positioning it to catch the reflection of the rainwater, she concentrated, staring into the depths of the mirror world. Evan and Albrecht moved up next to her and touched her shoulders. Then the world changed around them as Mari reached into the spirit world and pulled them into it, warping the Gauntlet around them.

The streetlights fell away and the rain stopped. They still stood in the park, but it was now five blocks long, and the buildings surrounding it were older than in the real world. The streets were empty of pedestrians, although occasional spider webs could be seen, almost hidden in the alleys.

Evan began walking in the direction of Central Park; Albrecht followed him. Mari looked around, double-checking to make sure they weren't followed by anything, then fell in behind them.

"The wounded one will surely tell us what this is about," Mari said.

"He better," Albrecht said.

CHAPTER TWO

Fengy wandered through the park on his daily rounds. He stopped diligently at each and every trash can, gathering up whatever leftover food he found there, regardless of its condition. A day-old candy bar or a week-old hot dog — it didn't matter to him. It was food.

He was digging into the can by the small pond where the turtles lived when he heard voices from behind the bushes. He looked carefully into the brush. He hadn't heard anyone a second ago, so he wondered where the voices were coming from.

Albrecht walked out onto the sidewalk, still carrying the wounded Silver Fang. Fengy jumped back in surprise, shocked by the sudden appearance of the Silver Fang lord. Albrecht was followed by Evan Heals-The-Past and Mari Cabrah, his packmates.

"That ain't right, ya know," Fengy said, startling Albrecht now. "Steppin' out in front of a fellow with no warning. Yer from the Umbra, right? That must be it, cause Fengy didn't hear ya before."

Albrecht looked annoyed. He had never liked Fengy. The rat was always hanging around, trying to get information or a free meal. The Bone Gnawers had no shame, and Fengy epitomized the worst qualities of his tribe.

Albrecht knew it was uncharitable of him to think that way. The Bone Gnawers of Central Park had welcomed him when he had had no home, and allowed him into their moot rites. But still, he couldn't get over their apparent lack of self-esteem. He knew the pot was calling the kettle black, but he couldn't help himself.

"Yeah, Fengy," Albrecht said. "We just had a jaunt through Umbral Manhattan. You should check it out sometime. Give you a sense of history. Where's Larissa?"

"Mother is on her errands, like any good Gnawer," Fengy said, knowing when he was being condescended to. "She's got mouths to feed, ya know. Some of us work for a living."

"Yeah, yeah. Look, we're heading over to the caern center. Let her know I'd like her help when you see her."

"Sure. I'll do it. Them some wounded friends ya got there?"

Albrecht ignored him and walked down the path. Evan and Mari followed. Mari turned to call back to Fengy as she walked off: "Enemies, Fengy. Enemies. Silver Fangs."

Fengy furrowed his brow in confusion. If they were Silver Fangs, and Albrecht was a Silver Fang, how come they were enemies? He scratched his head and then continued his duties, reaching deep into the trash can for the fast-food burger wrapper he had spotted at the bottom.

The pack arrived at the caern center, a small grove in the middle of the park, hidden from the eyes of any passersby on the paths that surrounded it. The trees grew in such a way as to provide good sound-proofing, so most conversations couldn't be heard by anyone outside.

Albrecht laid the wounded Fang on the ground. Evan

placed the dead one nearby and put his jacket over the Garou's face.

"Well, Albrecht," Mari said. "What now?"

"I want Larissa to look at this one," Albrecht said, pointing at the wounded Garou. "If she can revive him, I'm going to find out what the hell he thought he was doing."

"*If* I can revive him?" an old, gravelly voice said, coming through the trees, followed seconds later by an old hag of a woman, dressed in thrift-store chic and smelling like she'd been bathing in dumpsters. "Course I can revive him, if he's not dead. Now, what's this all about?"

"Mother Larissa," Evan said, smiling at the old lady. "It's good to see you."

"And you, Evan," Larissa replied, smiling back at him; then she looked at Albrecht and grimaced. "But I knew there'd be trouble as soon as I heard the high-and-mighty lord here. Trouble follows him like white on rice."

"Good morning to you, Mother," Albrecht said with obvious sarcasm. "I would appreciate it if you could wake this guy up so I can beat the crap out of him again."

Larissa waddled over to the Garou and bent down, examining his wounds. "What's he done to you? He looks like a Silver Fang. This some sort of family quarrel? 'Cause I don't want no part of it!"

"I don't know what this is about. That's why I need him awake."

Larissa sighed and put her hands on the Garou's chest. She concentrated, singing an old song to herself, low enough that the others couldn't make out the words. Then she pulled her hands back and stared sadly at the Garou, shaking her head. She pulled her dirty shawl from around her shoulders and placed it on his face.

"Didn't want to live," she said. "He didn't have the strength to go on. Whoever he was, he was hurting bad before you tore into him. Not from any wound, but from inside."

"What do you mean?" Albrecht said. "What are you talking about?"

"She means Harano, Albrecht," Mari said, staring at the dead body. "'A weeping from within, crying for that which is not yet lost.' It seems to hit your tribe a lot these days, although they always want to deny it exists."

Albrecht looked down at the two dead Fangs. The enormity of it all finally hit him. He had killed two of his own tribemates. It had been self-defense, but nonetheless, two Silver Fangs lay dead. He let out a deep sigh and sat down, staring at the grass beneath him. The ground was still damp from the earlier rains, but Albrecht didn't care. Tears again, he thought. The world is still crying, but now I'm crying with it.

"Hey, Mother!" Fengy suddenly poked his head around a tree. "There's a Silver Fang out here to see you, real regal like! Something's up!"

Larissa looked at Albrecht with narrowed eyes. "I'll be right there to see him," she answered Fengy, and then pointed a bony finger at Albrecht. "You stay here until I see what this is about."

"What if this one wants to kill me, too?" Albrecht said.

"Not in my caern, he won't!" she said and pulled herself up. She hobbled over the way she had come and then squeezed her way out between the trees.

"Whatever this is, Albrecht," Evan said, coming over and sitting down next to him, "we're with you."

Albrecht looked at Mari, who looked back at him. "Both of us," she said.

"Thanks," Albrecht said and leaned back. He tried to listen to what was going on outside the grove. He couldn't hear anything but the general background rumble of the city. *Another Silver Fang*, he thought. *Is this one here to finish the job these two started, or is he here to warn me about these two?*

The answer came soon enough when Larissa pushed her

way back in between the thick bushes, followed by the visitor.

The man was of medium height, but his posture and the way he looked at everyone told of someone used to getting his way with other people. He was young, though; perhaps no more than eighteen. He wore an expensive trench coat and leather riding boots, as if he'd just come from a horse show, and his hands were snugly fitted with leather driving gloves. He pulled off his sunglasses, revealing bright blue eyes. He looked straight at Albrecht.

"Lord Albrecht?" he asked.

Albrecht stood up and met the other's gaze. "Yeah, that's me. And who are you?"

"I am Eliphas Standish, soon to be Squire of the Lodge of the Moon and Gatekeeper for the North Country Protectorate and the Court of... of...." He seemed confused at this last statement, as if he had forgotten the name of the court.

"Morningkill. You're from Morningkill's court. You can say it here. It's not a dirty word, no matter what passed between me and my grandfather."

Eliphas' eyes widened as he looked past Albrecht at the two dead Garou. The newcomer walked past Albrecht and pulled the shawl and jacket off their faces. He looked down at them with his head bowed and then replaced the coverings. He turned back to Albrecht.

"I... I don't understand why they attacked you. Larissa told me what she knew."

Albrecht stepped up to Eliphas and stared him in the face. "Do you know who they were?"

Eliphas looked straight back, used to being treated in such a manner at court. "Yes. One was Alphonse Grayling and the other was Justin Beauchamp. Both were exiled two months ago from Morningkill's court."

Albrecht's eyes widened and he stepped back. "Exiles? Like me? Then why did they attack me?"

"I'm not sure. It may have something to do with succession

rights...." He looked down at the bodies. "But how could they have known so soon?"

"Known what? Succession rights? What are you talking about?"

Eliphas looked up again and straightened his posture, his bearing becoming rather ritualistic in the process, as if he were performing a sacred duty. "I am here to bring you back to court."

"At whose order?" Albrecht said, somewhat incredulously.

"King Morningkill's. The late King Morningkill. Jacob Morningkill is dead."

CHAPTER THREE

Albrecht stared out the window at the passing landscape. The sun had broken through the clouds and bathed the trees in a golden glow. The still-damp leaves reflected the light back in intense, rich greens, oranges and reds. Autumnal Vermont was beautiful. Albrecht hadn't seen his home country in nearly three years. He realized, watching from the speeding car, that he missed it greatly. More than he had allowed himself to recognize. These colors were his colors, burned into his soul from early childhood. Gaia was everywhere, the Garou said, but Albrecht believed that she loved this land more than any other.

Albrecht turned and looked at Eliphas, who stared ahead down the road as he drove. This kid was pretty cocksure, Albrecht thought. It was obvious that he'd been born with a silver spoon in his mouth, as the humans would say. He was so privileged, he had no clue about just how well-off he was. Albrecht shook his head. This was exactly what pissed him off so much about the Fangs. They were all born to privilege, but had no humility about it.

Albrecht looked back out the window. *Of course, I used to be just like that*, he thought. *That's why I hate it so much. It reminds me of what I used to be. A vain, regal ass.*

He had noticed the way Eliphas kept staring at him when he thought Albrecht wasn't looking. The expression on his face betrayed what he was thinking: He was utterly confused about the Garou lord who sat in the car with him. A street-tough, uncouth Fang. Oh, Albrecht had the features of the Fang ideal, all right: well-chiseled face, fine blond hair. But it went down from there. Five-o'clock shadow, a near-perpetual frown, a torn and filthy trenchcoat, ripped jeans, etc., etc. What in the world had created such a creature as this? Eliphas was surely thinking. What could have brought him so low?

Albrecht sighed. He knew the routine. He'd thought those same thoughts once, whenever he'd met members of the other tribes. So wrapped up in his own glory, he couldn't understand how they could lead their lives dwelling among the scum of humanity. He knew differently now. He'd lived among the scum for some time, and had discovered that most of them were far nobler than the so-called heroes of his tribe. He'd quickly learned that appearance and economic status were the least hallmarks of character. The low-born, as his tribe called anyone of lesser status than they, had perhaps more virtues than a whole sept of high-and-mighty Silver Fangs.

Take his pack, for instance. He'd stand by them no matter the odds well before he would defend the honor of his tribe. Evan was a good kid, a better person than Albrecht was, that was for sure. He was decent, and always thought of others before himself. But the Fangs would consider the young Wendigo a half-breed and always look down their snouts at him, no matter what deeds he accomplished. And Mari. Boy, they would not take to her at all. She was too feisty, too ready to pick a fight with anyone, regardless of their station. No, the Fangs would not approve of Albrecht's new pack.

Well, screw them. His pack had proven many times how, no matter what feud was going on amongst themselves, they'd stand behind Albrecht. When he'd told them they had to stay behind in New York, that he had to go alone to the court, they'd pitched a fit. Mari had torn into him about Silver Fang assassins, and how Eliphas could be fooling them all and really have been sent to lure Albrecht off to kill him. Evan had downplayed the paranoia factor, but still mentioned that the court might not have Albrecht's best interests in mind when summoning him. What if they were trying to accuse him of a crime? On their home turf, he wouldn't stand a chance of justice.

Albrecht had thanked them for their concern, but made it clear that this was something he had to do alone. In a time like this, so soon after caern security had been breached, the Fangs would not allow any non-tribe members near the bawn, let alone the caern proper. As he got into Eliphas' Lexus, Mari had told him that, if they hadn't heard from him in two days, they were coming to get him, and just let any Silver Fang try to stop her. He'd smiled at this but hadn't said anything.

Mari sometimes really had it in for him, but when it came to issues of pack unity against an outside force, she could come off like his personal guardian and protector. She was the same way with Evan.

"Can I ask you something?" Eliphas said, bringing Albrecht out of his reverie. Albrecht looked at the road ahead and saw they were approaching a town. Middlebury. And past Middlebury, near the foot of the Green Mountains, was the Morningkill estate. They were almost there. Almost to the court.

"Sure, go ahead," Albrecht replied, sitting back and looking straight ahead.

"Why were you exiled?"

Albrecht was quiet for a while, looking out at the white birches they passed, ghostly blurs at this speed. "I guess you don't know. You're young enough not to understand what really went on. Morningkill and I didn't get along too well.

He didn't like the idea of any Garou who could threaten his power, one who might make a better leader than him or who could point out his failings to others. Me? I was too big for my own britches. I pushed his button one too many times. I had come back from nearly getting my ass trashed by a Wyrm creature — the Vssh'krang, I think it was — and I did it alone, too. My pack was dead by then, so I was sort of a free agent waiting to make a pack of my own.

"Anyway, I dragged the thing's carcass back to the caern and presented it before the court, demanding they shower me with honor and glory and all the stuff heroes deserve. But Morningkill had gotten tired of these shows of mine. Yeah, I proved I could kick butt good, but Morningkill thought maybe I was too good. He aimed to feed me a fat slice of humble pie. I wasn't having any of that, and he knew it. So, for insolence before the king, he kicked me out."

"That doesn't seem right," Eliphas said, his brow furrowed in worry. "He was the king. He's supposed to reward us when we do our duty to Gaia."

"Yeah. So? The world ain't fair in that respect. It throws us all kinds of curves, like a mad, paranoid king who kicks the best and the brightest out of court."

"But all the other exiles? Surely not all of them were exiled out of vanity?" Eliphas looked very worried now.

"Who? Loba Carcassone? She opened her mouth about the Defiler Wyrm's plots once too often. Morningkill didn't want to hear that crap. If he listened to her, then he'd have to do something about the Wyrm, wouldn't he?"

"But everyone knows Carcassone is crazy, with her talk about the Wyrm hiding in little children, and some sort of generations-long conspiracy to corrupt humans—"

"Is she crazy? I'm not so sure about that. You get out of the caern more often and you'll see some truly weird shit. And as for the other exiles, what about those two who attacked me? What's the story there?"

"They were plotting against Morningkill. Arkady revealed the plot and personally chased them from the caern after Morningkill declared their punishment."

"Arkady, huh? I never liked that guy. That air of his, like he's holier than Gaia. And you said he's the one trying for the throne? Did you ever think that maybe he had those two kicked out because they discovered his kingly aspirations and were going to tell Morningkill? After all, Morningkill wouldn't abide anyone who wanted to be king in his place. Arkady would have wound up on the outside, like me and Loba. Hell, maybe he and I are in the same boat together, and he just wanted to save the Fangs from Morningkill's madness."

Eliphas didn't say anything. He drove on in silence, staring straight at the road ahead.

"Don't get me wrong," Albrecht said. "Morningkill and I used to be real close. I'm going to miss him, even after all he did to me. Hell, he was my grandfather, and he was damn proud that his grandson was a Garou. It used to be good between us. But he just kept getting more and more paranoid, and I just got cockier and cockier. There's nothing to be done about it now, though. He's dead and that's that."

They drove on in silence. Soon Eliphas pulled onto a side road, and about a mile or two down he pulled off onto a one-lane road. They passed an open gate and Albrecht saw two men in the rear-view mirror watching them as they drove past. They were dressed in black and wore long knives in their belts. Garou guards with klaives.

Albrecht looked ahead and saw the mansion through the trees. Cars were parked to either side of the drive. As they pulled into the cul de sac in front of the house, Albrecht saw that every space was taken.

"No one has left yet," Eliphas said. "From the moot, that is. Everyone is needed for the caern defense."

"Makes sense," Albrecht said, looking about. No others were in sight. "Just let me out here. I'll find my way around.

Thanks for the ride."

Eliphas nodded and Albrecht got out of the car. Eliphas turned the car around and drove down the lane looking for a parking space. Albrecht walked around the mansion, staring up at his childhood home.

It had been a long time indeed, he thought, looking at the large house. The two-story, two-wing mansion stood large in his memory, and loomed over him now. It was exactly as he remembered it. Nothing had changed. The maple trees in the yard were older, but that was the only proof that time had passed. Morningkill had not liked change. He certainly made sure that it did not come to his house. At least, judging by the looks of it. But things would certainly change now.

Albrecht walked around the south wing of the house, looking in the windows. Same old rooms with the same old furniture. Classic antiques. No one was inside. He came around to the rear of the house and looked out over the large field.

The first thing to catch his eye was not the group of Garou out on the field, working to cover what looked to be tunnels. Or the empty tents, still standing from the aborted moot. The thing which caught his eye and drew his breath away was the tree. The Grand Oak. A huge, towering mammoth of an oak. And at its base was the throne. The king's throne.

But something was wrong, or rather, something was not exactly right with the throne. Albrecht had not seen it in years, but he knew it well from his youth, and he knew that the bloodstains did not belong. They were alien, intruders in the court. A sign that all was not right with the world. Standing and staring at the dried blood of his grandfather, Albrecht knew that this was going to be harder to deal with than he had thought.

He looked out over the field to the Garou who performed rites by the holes in the ground. *The Black Spiral Dancer tunnels*, thought Albrecht. The Garou were plugging them with dirt and shovels and using the secrets taught them by spirits to add more dirt where necessary. Albrecht figured that more Garou were in the Umbra, the spirit world, likewise using spirits to seal up the rents in their territory. Rites of Cleansing would also be performed, to remove any lingering taint of corruption left by the deformed Garou's passage.

The workers were looking at Albrecht now, some with unreadable expressions, others with looks of anger. One Garou, whose back was to Albrecht, turned to see what they were staring at. He was an older Garou, with black hair going gray and a strong physique. He saw Albrecht and his face broke into a smile. He walked quickly over to Albrecht and embraced him.

"Hello, Greyfist," Albrecht said. "It's been a while."

"Damn. I'd wondered if I'd ever see you again," Greyfist said, looking Albrecht over. "Here you are."

"Yeah. Here I am," Albrecht said, watching the Garou workers, who all stared at him in uncomfortable silence.

Greyfist looked at the workers. "Hurry up! Get those breaches sealed! What are you waiting for? Another attack?" He turned back to Albrecht. "Come on. We can talk in my office."

"Your office? Since when have you had an office?"

"Since Morningkill appointed me seneschal," Greyfist said, leading Albrecht into the mansion and down a hall.

"You? Good lord! He really was crazy!"

Greyfist smiled and opened a door into a large room filled with wall-to-wall bookcases. "Have a seat," he said, gesturing toward a couch while he walked to a large desk and pulled a pipe from the top drawer.

"No thanks," Albrecht said, walking around the room. "I've been sitting all morning. It's a long drive here."

"Sorry. You're the one who chose to live in New York." Greyfist lit his pipe and sat in a leather chair behind the desk.

"I didn't choose. The Gnawers were the only ones who

would have me. You're lucky I didn't move to Alaska or someplace equally remote." Albrecht walked about the office, examining it. He looked at the furnishings and the books along the wall. "Pretty posh place you got here."

"It's just an office, Albrecht. But I am glad you're here. We need you."

"We?" Albrecht said, turning toward Greyfist. "You mean the Fangs? What in the world would you need me for?"

"Cut it out, Albrecht. You know very well that you're next in line to be king."

"Hold on there! What about Arkady? I thought he wanted the job — I sure as hell don't! What are you thinking? The Fangs kick me out and then want me to rule over them? Yeah, that's real likely. You saw those stares out there."

Greyfist leaned over the desk and stared intently at Albrecht. "Don't be an idiot. You're Jacob's grandson. You are the first in line. You are scion of the House of Wyrmfoe, the First Family of the North Country Protectorate. Your line *built* this protectorate, damn it! Your position is the nominal head of the entire North American continent, based on rights of precedence set by your family generations ago when the tribe first came to these lands. All Garou are beholden to the king of North Country."

"Listen to you. You believe this crap! Let me tell you something: there's not a Garou in all of the state of New York who buys that! Morningkill has been a joke for years. Oh, sure, they're supposed to listen up when the Silver Fang king speaks, but since when have they ever done that? And who's going to make them? Morningkill dragged the crown down with him. No one respects it anymore."

"That doesn't mean it can't rise again."

"I don't know if it should."

Greyfist stared at Albrecht. "What do you mean? It's the throne, damn it!"

"I mean maybe it's this damn throne and all the authority

that comes with it that's dragging us down!" Albrecht said, raising his arms exasperatedly and pacing about in front of the desk. "You've heard the way the other tribes talk about the Fangs. Well, I get a lot of that where I'm from. 'The Fangs are nuts. They're going to bring us all down with their silly dictates.' Maybe it's time the other tribes lived without the Fangs for a while, 'cause either it'll teach them that they can't live without us or, more likely, that they're right and we really are a bunch of inbred fuck-ups."

Greyfist looked down at his desk, rubbing his pipe between his fingers and thumb, thinking. Then he raised his head and looked at Albrecht again. "You can believe that if you want. Hell, I know most of it's true. But we will never become the leaders we are supposed to be if we don't strive for it. Just because others have failed does not mean we should cease to strive. Too much depends on us. Gaia depends on us. The king is needed."

"Then let Arkady be king," Albrecht said, walking to the bay window and looking out over the field.

"Arkady… Arkady is not fit."

"What do you mean? He's royal, isn't he? That's what Eliphas said. A Crescent Moon even! You can't get much more royal than that. Besides, he's obviously more purebred than I am. Everyone's always known he had some breeding."

"But I don't trust him, Albrecht. I think he killed Jacob."

Albrecht spun around and stared angrily at Greyfist. "I thought a Black Spiral did it! That's what I was told. What are you saying?"

"Calm down. I can't prove it. And yes, a Black Spiral Dancer is what killed Jacob. But I think Arkady was somehow in on it. That he knew it would happen."

"That's quite an accusation."

"I know. But it's too damn convenient. Garrick is killed, leaving Regina to take over his duties in addition to her own. And she is still wounded from a mission Morningkill sent her on, one that I think Arkady had something to do with arranging. Arkady's pack — the King's Own, for Gaia's sake — arrives late at the moot, too late to prevent the Black Spiral Dancer from killing Jacob. And Arkady's newfound heritage is announced before the king is even buried. Doesn't it all seem too much to you?

Albrecht looked out the window again. "I don't know. Yeah, it sounds real convenient. But I've known odder things to happen. Maybe it's fate. Maybe Arkady is meant to take the throne."

"It was your grandfather's last wish that you be king."

Albrecht was silent for a while, staring out the window, across the field, at the throne. The bloodstained throne. "Vanity. That's all. Just vanity. Morningkill wanted the line to continue when he should have known better. The line is obviously unfit."

Albrecht noticed a woman and a boy walking out onto the field, toward the tents. He turned and walked to the door. "I've got to go. There's someone I haven't seen in a while."

Greyfist looked out the window and then back at Albrecht, who already had the door open. "They don't like you, Albrecht. Your Kin were shamed at your exile, and suffered for it. They blame you."

Albrecht looked at him, the anger in his eyes softening. He then walked out the door and back onto the field.

CHAPTER FOUR

Margot Rothchild looked around the empty tent. The tables and chairs had already been removed, but the tent still stood. *Someone really should take them down*, she thought. *To stand here looking so forlorn, so abandoned... it just isn't right. Not considering what happened to poor Jacob. Someone really should take the tents down, for his sake.*

"Mother, what are they doing out in the field?" Seth said. The ten-year-old boy stood outside the tent, pointing to the Garou rite participants who worked to seal the holes. "They've got those funny sticks with feathers, the ones no one will tell me about. Are they doing magic, mother?"

Margot looked at her son and felt the fear again: the fear which always gripped her whenever he talked about the Garou. She prayed that it was boyish curiosity and nothing more. Just a boy's fascination with the strange. Not an instinctive yearning. *God, please no, not that.*

"Yes, dear," she said, hiding her fear away again. "Don't bother them. They're very busy."

"But what kind of magic, mother?" Seth persisted, his eyes wide with fascination as he watched one of the Garou raise his staff over his head and let loose a low, almost whispering, howl. "It's a ritual, isn't it? Grandfather says that spirits are always near when the Garou do a ritual. Have you ever seen a spirit, mother?"

"Yes. But it wasn't very interesting. It was just a bird. Just like any bird."

"Then how did you know it was a spirit?"

"It spoke to Morningkill and then flew away into the air and disappeared."

"In plain sight? It went to the Umbra, didn't it?"

"I suppose so. Now, let's get back to the car, dear. Your grandfather is expecting us to be there when he is done with his business." Margot reached for Seth's hand, but he tore it away and stepped out onto the field.

"But I want to watch the rite!" he said.

"Seth! Get back here! Don't go too close!"

But Seth was already running toward the Garou. Margot's fear broke free from the little place within her where she hid it. It would hide no longer. "Seth! Please come back!"

Seth turned to look at her and his eyes widened. He stopped running and stared at her in shock. After a moment she realized he was staring past her, behind her. She turned around and gasped.

He was taller than she remembered, and he stood so close she wondered how she hadn't heard him approach. "Jonas! You... you startled me," she stammered out, her eyes falling to the floor, unable to meet his gaze.

"I'm sorry, Margot," Albrecht said. He looked at his cousin, no longer the vivacious girl he'd once known, but a woman in her thirties, premature wrinkles and worry lines clearly visible. Stress had taken its toll on her face and bearing. She stood with shoulders slumped, unable to look him in the face. "How are things? How's the family?"

"They... they're all right. I...." She turned away, back toward Seth. "My son... he... he's run out. He's going to get in the way...."

"He's fine, Margot. There's nothing he can do to disrupt the rites. I'm sure they want him to watch."

"But I don't! I... I mean, I'd rather he not bother them. It's rude."

Albrecht looked out at Seth, who was now standing still, looking back at Albrecht, curiosity on his face. "Has he shown any of the signs? Do they know yet?"

Margot shuddered. "No. They don't know. They say it may be a few years."

"I hope the heritage is true. Gaia knows we need more Garou."

"I've got to go. Warner is waiting—"

"That's right, Margot," a stern voice said from outside the tent, behind them. Albrecht turned around and saw a middle-aged man in a suit standing and staring angrily at him. "I've been waiting by the car. I think you and Seth should go back there right now."

Margot said nothing and left, walking over to Seth, who had come back to the tent and was looking at Albrecht with awe. She grabbed his hand and pulled him around the tent, heading toward the mansion.

"But I want to see Uncle Jonas!" Seth yelled, his eyes still on Albrecht, who smiled back at him.

"Go to the car, Seth!" the stern man snapped, not taking his eyes off Albrecht.

Seth followed behind his mother, but looked back at Albrecht as he moved away.

"Hello, Warner," Albrecht said.

"Don't even bother, exile," Warner said, the disgust in his voice apparent. "I don't know why you're here, but I want you to leave my family alone."

"They're my family, too. Margot was my mother's friend. Her only friend here."

"I don't care about the past. I am concerned with the present, and you are a bad influence on Seth. If he has bred true, you are the last person I want as a role model for him."

"Oh, calm down, Warner," Albrecht said, shaking his head and looking away from the seething statue of a man before him. "You know my exile was politics, nothing more."

"So you say. But I know that you were banned from this protectorate by the king, and I intend to find out exactly why you have returned. I certainly will not allow you to torment my family!"

"I am here," Albrecht said, gritting his teeth, putting a mental cap on his growing anger, "because Morningkill asked it of me with his last breath."

Warner looked at Albrecht as if he didn't believe him. He then lowered his gaze. "I see."

Albrecht walked over to Warner. As he came out of the tent, Warner stepped back, obviously not comfortable standing so close to him.

"I'm sure you're anticipating Seth's Firsting," Albrecht said.

"Yes. If he is Garou."

"That will be a feather in Henry's cap, to sire a Garou. He'll get some respect for that."

Warner turned away, a look of disgust washing over his face. He then wiped his expression clean, replacing it with a stone-faced stare. "Henry is not the father. Joseph Batell is."

Albrecht narrowed his eyes at Warner. "Was this your doing?"

"I had to. You wouldn't understand. You don't give a damn for the family. But we have a responsibility. We must breed Garou, and Henry couldn't produce a child. I had to ensure the family an heir, so I turned to a Garou. The chances of a true breeding were better."

"You disgust me! You and the whole damn pack of Kin families. Look what you've done to Margot! She used to be strong and proud. But this? Forced to lie with a strange Garou just so she can breed a pup? And how is Henry dealing with this? He's probably a self-pitying wreck, if I know him."

"None of this is any of your business!" Warner said, his face now a mask of rage. "You can't possibly understand the pressures on us!"

Another voice broke in, from off to Albrecht's left, toward the mansion. "Of course he can't! He doesn't understand honor and responsibility. Too damn proud. That's why he got what he deserved and was kicked out!"

Albrecht turned to see an older man working his way toward them, leaning heavily on a cane. It was obvious he was having a hard time of it, but his anger was moving him forward.

"Father!" Warner said, stepping up to the old man and helping him to stand. "You were supposed to be in the car!"

"Margot said he was here. I had to see it for myself. Couldn't believe it. Come back again, huh?"

"I don't want to argue with you, Sutter," Albrecht said. "I'm just here for a short visit."

"Hah! You think you're going to get the crown, don't you? You! A low-bred mongrel! That damn mother of yours — I told her to stay away from my son. But he just had to get mixed up with her! It was a surprise to all of us that she was able to squeeze out a Garou. But when it grew up to be you, I knew I had been right all along. Damn scullery maid!"

"Father!" Warner said, shocked at the old man's incivility. "That's enough. She was his mother, for God's sake."

Albrecht knew Warner wasn't shushing Sutter out of respect for his mother. He could see the fear in the man's face: fear from looking at Albrecht's expression, from sensing the growing anger and the impending loss of control that was a trait of the Garou. No, Warner quieted his father out of fear for their safety.

Albrecht was angry, but he could control the raging within him. This was exactly what he'd expected of Sutter. The old man was his human grandfather, the patriarch of the Albrecht line. The Albrechts were a highly regarded line of Silver Fang Kinfolk whose history with the Garou tribe stretched back to England, and to Holland before that. As such, Sutter was rabidly antagonistic to anyone who stained that line, as Albrecht had done when he was exiled. Jacob Morningkill was Sutter's father, but since Sutter had not bred true — had not been a full Garou — he was a second-class son to the king. When Sutter's son, James, had borne a Garou son — Lord Albrecht himself — Morningkill was considered the boy's Garou grandfather, even though he was technically the great-grandfather. Since Sutter's son James had not been Garou himself, Sutter was doomed to be a mere footnote in the Silver Fang annals, a simple genetic bridge between Garou generations.

And he hated it. But instead of attacking the system, he defended it with all his might, living up to his role in society to an extreme degree. And he had handed these traits to his favored son, Warner, Albrecht's uncle.

"How is my father?" Albrecht asked Warner.

Warner looked down, unable to meet Albrecht's eyes. "The same. A damn fool still possessed by the bottle. He can't get over your mother's death. Fifteen years of misery he's given himself."

"And over what?" Sutter cried. "A girl he had no business with in the first place. She wasn't well-bred by any remote definition of the term!"

"Will you shut up about my mother?" Albrecht said, teeth gritted. He felt the chaotic stirring within his gut, the roiling that warned of a coming frenzy. But he shut his eyes and stilled himself. After all, these were just the bitter ramblings of an old fool.

Sutter looked at him suddenly, worried, and was quiet.

"We must be going, father," Warner said, moving toward the mansion, pulling his father along with him. But Sutter seemed to find his courage again and stopped, staring with eyes narrowed at Albrecht.

"Thank Gaia Arkady is royal! The thought of you on the throne sickens me! Arkady is a real Silver Fang. He is everything we hold high. Not like you. Look at you! A damn tramp. Can't even dress properly to come to your king's court."

"That's about all I'm going to take out of you!" Albrecht yelled, his voice rising. "You want Arkady on the throne instead of me? Tough! That's my right! My crown to wear! You know something? I didn't want the damn job, and I still don't. But if it'll piss you off, then I am sure as hell going to sit on that seat. And you're going to kowtow to me like nobody's ever seen! Or else you're outta here! Kinfolk can be banished too, you know."

Sutter looked as if he were choking on a large rock. His face was scrunched up in rage, red and growing redder by the second. He finally managed to open his tension-bound jaws wide enough to say, "You wouldn't dare! You can't be king! You're not half as royal as Arkady!"

Albrecht stared in utter contempt at Sutter. "Oh? Watch me. You are about to see the fight of a lifetime, old man."

Warner, pale and fearful for his father's health, led the old man away. Sutter continued to stare at Albrecht, unable to speak out of sheer anger. His eyes shone from their sockets like windows into a furnace, but a furnace he was unable to control or cool down enough even to communicate. He hobbled off like that, aided by his son, and soon disappeared around the corner.

Albrecht shook his head. *What have I done now? I don't want the damn crown. Sure, I want to piss that old fart off big, but I don't want to be king just for that. Well, it doesn't matter; it's not like I've announced it before the court. I can always back out.*

He started back toward Greyfist's office but stopped when he noticed that the Garou workers were no longer engaged in their rite. Rather, they were all staring at him. Some with looks of confusion, some with uncertainty and some with disgust and hatred. But some were looking at him with... with pride. And approval. Some of them were nodding at him.

Oh, holy Luna! He was in for it now. Practically the entire court *had* heard him. His declaration was official. The only way out now was to crawl home in even more shame than he had arrived in.

Albrecht gritted his teeth and growled low. He'd be damned if that'd be the case.

CHAPTER FIVE

Greyfist kicked the dirt hard. He nodded, satisfied. It was well packed. The hole was sealed up. It would take a bulldozer to open it again.

He walked across the field to investigate the other two holes. It was hard to believe the Black Spirals had done what they had. Tunneling under the caern for weeks, he estimated. And no one had known. That said terrible things about their alertness. But who would have believed they would come so close, would dare such a feat? And through sheer bedrock, at that! The soil was only eight feet deep here; they had tunneled ten feet under, through solid rock, and then come upwards to break through the soil in the caern field. *It's a wonder they didn't come up under the throne. But then Barktooth, the Shaman of the Lodge of the Moon, said that the Grand Oak's roots were deep and thick enough to prevent that. The Black Spirals couldn't have gotten any closer if they had wanted to.*

Greyfist kicked the dirt around the next hole and found it was as well-packed as the first. He did the same for the third hole and was satisfied there also. He nodded to Regina and headed back to the mansion. Behind him, he heard Regina tell her protectors to get about their duties. They had been pulled from their normal posts this morning to seal the holes, and the outer defenses now needed tending to. Soon, Greyfist would once again feel confident about the caern and bawn defenses. If nothing else, the attack had finally woken up the Silver Fangs and made them realize they were in a war. A war not only for Gaia, but for their own protection.

He heard the Garou talking as they headed off for their posts. The word had traveled quickly and was on the lips of every Silver Fang and Kinfolk in the protectorate: Lord Albrecht was to take his grandfather's place as king. Greyfist smiled. He didn't much care for the Albrechts and the Rothchilds, but they had succeeded where his idealism couldn't. Albrecht was now going to do his duty, and the relief Greyfist had felt when Albrecht yelled his intent for all to hear was greater than any he'd felt in a long while.

Albrecht was the one for the job; of this Greyfist was confident. Albrecht's own sense of self-worth had been worn down over the last few years, but Greyfist felt that was an asset. At least he possessed some humility — a quality lacking among most of the tribe members here. Oh, it would take a while to convince Albrecht that there really was no one better to rule than he, but Greyfist wasn't concerned about that. Detail, details; that's all that was. It was Arkady he was worried about.

The high-bred Garou posed a threat to Albrecht's ascension. Greyfist feared he really did have a claim to the throne, even though Albrecht was clearly next in line. Pure breeding was a wild card in Garou politics, and allowed the high-born to break many rules. Well, it would be decided soon enough.

As he passed by the throne, Greyfist saw the preparations already beginning for the meeting of the courts. In two hours, the Lodges of the Sun and Moon would gather and argue over the tricky issue of ascension to the crown. Ancient records would be consulted and debated, and after a few hours, the

Lodges would come to a decision on just who was eligible to rule the Fangs. The problem was that many of the tribal records had been destroyed. Morningkill, in one of his paranoid fits, had set fire to the library a few months ago, and many documents had been lost before the flames were put out. Many more books had been ruined by the water used to douse the fire.

Of course, all of this precedence nonsense was hardly a problem for the other tribes, who each had their own rules for determining leadership. The Get of Fenris' leaders ruled by might: only those who could successfully defeat them in challenge combat could take their place. The Bone Gnawers valued the eldest among them, or those who had collected the most junk. The Children of Gaia chose the most diplomatic among them — at least, so Greyfist had been told.

But the Silver Fangs, overly concerned with blood precedence and membership in one of the Seven Royal Families, had to nit-pick their way to the crown.

Greyfist entered the mansion and climbed the broad staircase to the second floor. He turned down the north wing and walked to the last door on the left. After a pause, he knocked loudly. When there was no answer, he knocked again. After another pause, he opened the door and walked in.

Albrecht was sprawled across a giant four-poster bed, groggily opening his eyes and looking confusedly at Greyfist. "Uhhhh... wha... what time is it?"

Greyfist walked over to the window and threw back the heavy drapes, flooding the room with sunlight. Albrecht let out a yell as if he'd been hit by a baseball bat. He covered his face with his arm and tried to pull the covers over him. But Greyfist grabbed the blanket and yanked it off the bed.

"Oh, no. You're getting up. Now," he said. A long groan was the only answer from Albrecht. "Your presence is requested at court today. The Lodges will decide on the issue of ascendancy. As you are now a contestant for the throne, you really should attend."

"Do I have to?" Albrecht said in a moan which only happened to sound like words.

"No. But I recommend that you do. If not, those at court who disapprove of you may find a way to deny your claim."

"What's wrong with that?" Albrecht said, sitting up and rubbing his eyes. "That's exactly what I want. I don't want to be king."

"Then why did you scream that you did to everyone in listening range?"

"I was angry. I meant to take it back, but great Gaia, it's now an issue of honor. And I'll be damned if Arkady's going to come out of this shining purer than me."

"So?"

"So if the court says I can't be king, then I can't. It's got nothing to do with honor at that point."

"You think that, when they declare you unable to take your grandfather's place, people won't know exactly why? If you don't stand up and fight for your right at court, everyone will know you're just a blowhard coward. It's easy to claim the kingship, but much harder actually to get it."

Albrecht looked at Greyfist with a surly, smoldering expression. "Thank you, sir. May I have another?"

"Joke all you want. But get up anyway. Come to court. Do it for me, Albrecht, if for no one else."

Albrecht looked away and covered his face in his hands, leaning on his knees. "Okay."

"Okay?"

"Okay! Okay already! Just get out of here. I'll meet you at court."

Greyfist smiled and left the room, quietly closing the door behind him.

A howl resounded throughout the caern. Guards at the edge of the bawn stopped their tasks and looked back toward the field. Even those out of view of the caern center could not help being drawn to the source of the howl. They all controlled the urge, the instinct, to answer the call, to pick up the howl with one of their own. This summons wasn't theirs to answer. The call went out to the aspirants to the throne, the Garou who sought the kingship of the North Country Protectorate. And all the Silver Fangs knew that there were only two who were bold — or crazy — enough to try for that position. All of them waited quietly, some holding their breath to hear better; waiting for the answering howls.

There — there was one from far off, outside the bawn, off to the east. Even distance could not hide its rich, deep-throated character. Arkady. The leader of the King's Own Pack was far from the caern, which meant he would not be coming to court, but he answered the howl anyway. Although surprised by his absence, many Silver Fangs nodded as they heard, proud that, even away from the caern, Arkady would do his duty.

Then another howl, this one closer. Louder, even considering the closer proximity. Not as deep, but angrier, a growling, rage-ridden howl. The howl of Lord Albrecht. The Silver Fangs nodded again, this time more reserved, doubtful. Albrecht had been gone from the caern for a long time, and some were unsure whether they wanted him back. But no one could deny that his howl had been good, had rivalled Arkady's. No matter, though. It was just a howl. Wait for the challenge, they told themselves. The challenge would answer the question: Who would be king?

Eldest Claw, Shamaness of the Lodge of the Sun and Master of the Rite for the North Country Caern, sat down again, taking in a deep breath to recover from her howl. It had been a loud, long howl, as was necessary to summon the claimants. She waited to hear the answering cries. There was Arkady's, from off to the east. Eldest Claw frowned. The distance meant that Arkady would not be at court today. Was this arrogance? Did he not consider it important enough to come?

Then came Albrecht's answer, from much closer, over by the mansion. Eldest Claw's eyebrows rose. A good, hearty howl. Perhaps this cub was more qualified than the old lupus had thought.

She nodded to Barktooth, sitting across the circle from her. The lupus nodded back. They could now get down to business. She looked at Thomas Abbot, to her right, and nodded. The Steward of the Lodge of the Sun stood up and began the recitation.

"Hear ye, all in attendance and Silver Fangs of the court wherever ye be: the Court of the North Country Caern is hereby begun. Absent is our king, the late Jacob Morningkill. Hence, our business this day is the matter of the vacant throne. Two claimants have answered the Howl of Precedence. One, Lord Albrecht, grandchild of Jacob Morningkill and scion of the House of Wyrmfoe, the First Family of the North Country Protectorate. Two, Arkady, scion of the Clan of the Crescent Moon and purest of blood. We are to consider: which of the two claims is greatest? Which of the two shall inherit the throne?

"Ruling the court this day, as the matter of worldly leadership is determined, is the Lodge of the Sun. Leader of the Lodge and eldest among us is Eldest Claw, Shamaness of the Lodge. The court is begun...."

Abbot sat down, and all nodded their approval. Eldest Claw looked about the court. They were gathered in a circle at the foot of the Grand Oak, at the base of the empty throne. The sun shone down upon them; a good sign, considering the precedence of Lodge at today's court. If it had been cloudy, a gloomy fate would have been predicted. It was the Lodge of the Sun's position in court to decide on worldly matters, as opposed to the more spiritual concerns of the Lodge of the Moon. This was why the moot was taking place during the day.

On one side of the circle sat Eldest Claw's Lodge: herself, Abbot and Mountain Runner, the Squire of the Lodge. Across from them sat the Lodge of the Moon: Barktooth, the Shaman; Shining Outward, the Steward; and Eliphas Standish, the new Squire and Gatekeeper.

Gathered about them, as witnesses to the court, were Greyfist, the Seneschal; Regina, Caern Warder; and other, lower-rank Garou such as Pale Sire, the leader of a small Silver Fang pack which often roamed northern Vermont, away from the caern and away from politics. Also gathered were members of the Kinfolk families: Warren Albrecht, Desmond Rothchild, Cynthia Batell and a few from lesser families.

Eldest Claw sighed. This would be a long moot. She hoped they could finish at a decent time so they could all prepare for Morningkill's funeral that night. She looked up at Barktooth and began. "The debate shall begin with Arkady. What is his claim?"

"He is scion of the Crescent Moon!" Shining Outward said, standing and looking at all gathered. "Is that not enough?"

"No, it is not," Abbot said, also standing. "The Crescent Moon is not the First Family here. That honor belongs to the House of Wyrmfoe. Arkady is thus not eligible."

"But he has the purest blood of any among us," Barktooth said. "He is a Duke, the only representative of the Second Family. With his breeding, he is more than eligible."

And so the arguing went....

Greyfist shook his head. So much red tape! A sense of security and tradition was important, yes. But to drown in rituals and little laws such as those they argued here — it was too much. It was a sign that the Silver Fangs had lost touch with their primal, more flexible nature. What needed to be resurrected in the Fangs was the lost touch of the Wyld.

All the talk of the Seven Royal Families sometimes made his head swim. What a bog of lineage! It was a hobby of just about every Silver Fang to be able to trace the intricacies of his or her lineage down to the last Kinfolk as far back in time as possible. Some Silver Fangs could keep track better than others, either through good record-keeping or the active participation of their ancestors' spirits. The families that had the strongest hold on tradition and breeding were known as the Seven, for these were the seven families whose Garou blood was considered strong enough to rule a protectorate.

Legends said that there were once thirteen families, but six of them had been lost over time. Elaborate stories were told about the doom of certain royal families.

It was said that the thirteenth family, whose name no one remembered, came to an end in the War of Rage — the ancient war they had called and waged against the other werecreatures of the world. Successive births over the years following the war were never able to revive the line, and it eventually ceased to be.

The twelfth had been largely of lupus stock: those Garou who are born to wolves. It was said that this line had died out over time due to lack of proper breeding partners. Their name was also lost.

The eleventh family, the Conquering Claw, died due to massive infighting. A well-told epic about their fate served as both a marker to their glory and a morality tale against fighting amongst family members. Although a member of this lineage had been known to be born once in an age or so, thanks to the recessive Garou gene, none had owned a protectorate within historical memory.

The tenth family was not spoken of, and their name had

been struck from the tribal records. They had gone to the Wyrm. Those born of this blood were either killed by their Silver Fang parents or stolen by Black Spiral Dancers before the parents could act out their duty.

The ninth family, the Winter Snow, had seemed to be ominously named once their doom became clear: the entire family had succumbed to Harano, the great depression which few Garou could throw off once trapped within its gloomy embrace. Any new births of this lineage also succumbed to the curse. The source of their fate was a mystery to the tribe.

The eighth family was the most mysterious of all, however. Known as the Golden Sky, the entire family had disappeared in the Middle Ages and was never seen again. No new cubs had been born to this lineage since that time. Most Garou believed that the family went into the Umbra.

The seventh family was the Clan of the Crescent Moon, the premiere family among Silver Fangs; for they controlled the legendary Caern of the Crescent Moon in the Russian Urals, rumored to be the first caern created by the Garou back in the dawn of time. This was Arkady's family.

The sixth family was the House of Wyrmfoe, Albrecht's line and the founding family of North America. They were the first Silver Fangs to create a caern in the New World, and had ruled over the entire continent since then, although almost no one outside the tribe still upheld this claim.

Of the other families, the Austere Howl was strong in Britain; the Wise Heart ruled in the Mediterranean and parts of the Middle East; the Blood-Red Crest held a protectorate in Asia; the Unbreakable Hearth could be found in various regions, but especially in the American mid-west; and the Gleaming Eye was powerful in Europe.

Each of these families favored flocks of Kinfolk with whom they preferred to breed, ostensibly to keep the lines pure. For the House of Wyrmfoe, this included the Albrechts.

Greyfist turned his attention to the court again and

listened for a while. They were wrapping up their discussion of Arkady, and their decision seemed to be exactly what Greyfist had known it would be: Arkady, due to his breeding, was eligible for the kingship.

Greyfist looked around him. Where the hell was Albrecht? They would discuss him next, and he really should be here to defend his name if they tried to besmirch it; which he knew they would.

"Is he coming?" Regina asked, leaning over from her place to his right. She still nursed her arm, the one which had been severed two days earlier by Morningkill's assailant. It was reattached to her shoulder, but it would be a while before she could again use it fully.

"He's supposed to," Greyfist said, looking around the field. "He damn well better, or he'll find *me* challenging him instead of Arkady!"

Regina looked over toward the mansion. "Well, he needn't worry about that. There he is."

Greyfist followed her gaze and saw Albrecht slowly wandering his way over to the circle. He had a cigarette in his mouth and appeared to be enjoying it. Greyfist met his eyes and glared at him. Albrecht took a long drag on his cigarette, threw the stub on the ground and stomped on it. Smiling, he shrugged his shoulders at Greyfist and walked over to sit next to him.

"How goes it?" Albrecht said. "Can I be king yet?"

"They're just getting to you now," Greyfist said. "Arkady, by the way, is eligible. So, if they decide in your favor, you'll have to fight him."

Albrecht pulled out a pack of cigarettes. "So I figured. So everybody figured. Hell, they're looking forward to it here like it's bigger than a Foreman versus Tyson match. Maybe Arkady'll chicken out and disappoint them."

"Ha! Don't count on it. Seriously, though, you should worry. He's damn good."

Albrecht looked at Greyfist, smiling and shaking his head as if he couldn't believe what his friend had just said. He pulled out a cigarette and lighter and lit up. "Yeah. So? I'm better."

"Look, you haven't seen Arkady in three years. You have no idea what he's learned in that time."

Albrecht took a long drag on his cigarette, putting the lighter away. He then breathed the smoke out. "He hasn't seen me, either. I've been in New York. He's been here. So maybe he's knocked off a couple of Black Spiral Dancers and some Bane-possessed deer. I've fought fucking Sabbat vampires. Now who are you going to bet on?"

"I think the odds on that bet are closer than you think. Did you know he killed a Nexus Crawler last year? Not by himself, of course. The King's Own Pack was there to help, but he led the battle and took very few wounds."

Albrecht frowned. "He did, huh? Hmpf. How'd his pack fare, though? I bet he let them get cut up while he coached from the sidelines."

"It's true that they took more wounds, but the tale they tell is that he threw just as many blows as they, and that his all connected and cut deep."

"Ahh, they're just talking. Trying to beef up their pack leader."

"You're an arrogant ass, you know that? When will you concede that he may be your equal in combat, if not your better?"

Albrecht shook his head. "Yeah, right. You don't win battles by thinking your opponents are better than you. You win by being better than them, and knowing it."

Greyfist sighed and turned back to the court. They were talking about Albrecht now. Barktooth was arguing against him, since Albrecht was, after all, an exile. Abbot stood up for him, letting it be known that Morningkill had rescinded the banishment with his dying breath. Greyfist looked at

Albrecht, who seemed oblivious to all this talk about him, although it was clear he was listening.

"So his exile is over?" Barktooth said. "What does that matter? He's obviously unfit for the throne! Look at him!" Barktooth gestured with his snout toward Albrecht, and all eyes fell on him. Albrecht simply puffed on his cigarette. "Does he look like a Silver Fang to you? The evidence is in his breeding. His mother was low-born."

Albrecht frowned.

"But his Garou blood is royal," Abbot cut in. "That is all that matters."

"I disagree," Barktooth continued. "Breeding is everything to the Fangs. We are not mongrels like the other tribes. Gaia ordained that we would carry the blood of the first Garou with us until the end. From the Dawn to Apocalypse, we shall remain pure. Letting Albrecht, the son of a low-born human woman, take the throne is to ignore Gaia's will."

"I don't know what kind of brick got stuck up your ass," Albrecht said, standing up. "But I am the grandchild of Jacob Morningkill, your king up until two days ago. Is your memory so short? I've got enough royal blood to stain your fur. And I am sick of hearing everyone here dis my mother. She was a damn fine woman. She may not have been a member of one of our dysfunctional Kin families, but that's a virtue in my book."

Barktooth looked coldly back at Albrecht. "My memory is not short. It's long enough to remember your exile, called for by your own grandfather."

Albrecht stepped forward, staring hard into Barktooth's eyes. "Yeah? Well he ended it, in case you didn't hear Abbot over there. If you've got a problem with that, maybe you and I should work it out here and now."

Eldest Claw stood up and shouted, "Enough! Sit down, Albrecht. This is not the place for unfettered anger. Sit down, I said."

Albrecht looked at the elder, then walked back to take his seat. Greyfist put a hand on his shoulder, but Albrecht ignored it.

Rather than staring with anger at Albrecht, Barktooth smiled. Albrecht had won the respect of the lupus, as Greyfist had known he would. That's why he had wanted Albrecht here. The lupus did not judge people the way a homid did. Blood was important to him, but so was rage and the ability to respond to an insult. He judged people who stood flesh-and-blood before him, not simply the rumors and tales about a person. By losing his temper, Albrecht had managed to convince the holdout of the court, the last one to resist Albrecht's claim.

"I say that Albrecht has proven himself strong enough to bear the crown," Barktooth said, sitting down. His debating opponent, Abbot, seemed surprised. After a confused moment, he also sat down.

Eldest Claw looked about. "Is there any other who disagrees?" When no one answered, she said. "Then it is done. Albrecht is worthy. Albrecht and Arkady are the claimants to the throne." She let out a howl, similar to her earlier cry, but longer and quieter. The Howl of Confirmed Precedence. She then got up on all fours and walked off. The other court members also stood up and walked away, some in Lupus form, others in Homid.

The court witnesses stood and departed, although Warner Albrecht gave his nephew a scowl before leaving.

"Is that it?" Albrecht said. "What now?"

"The challenge," Regina said, standing up and rubbing her arm absently.

"The fight. So, when does it happen? I'm itching to get it over with."

"As soon as you challenge Arkady," said Greyfist, standing up and stretching. He took a few steps into the circle.

"Me? I have to challenge him?" Albrecht said, standing

up now himself.

"More likely he'll challenge you." Greyfist turned to look at Albrecht.

"When do you figure that'll be?" Albrecht said, reaching for another cigarette.

"Tonight. During your grandfather's funeral," Greyfist said.

CHAPTER SIX

The crescent moon haunted the night. The pale white birches stole its bare sliver of light, gleaming bright in the night while the rest of the landscape disappeared into black darkness. Except on one hill, removed from the Morningkill mansion, where torches burned. They were placed on poles every few yards, leading up a small path to the crest of the hill. Their red and orange flames danced at the top of the poles, throwing the shadows of the mourners marching up the hill into a chaotic frenzy.

At the top of the hill were Lord Albrecht, Greyfist, Regina and Shining Outward. They watched as the line made its way toward them, led by Eldest Claw, who loped forward in Lupus form. She was immediately followed by the King's Own Pack, who bore the body of King Jacob Morningkill wrapped in its ceremonial raiment. All of the Pack were in Homid form, including Arkady. Behind them were the rest of the Garou of the protectorate, and finally the Kinfolk families.

Albrecht looked about as he waited for the mourners to reach them. Trees, rocks, grass and dirt were all around him. This is what any human might see if he stumbled onto this isolated hill. But Albrecht saw it differently, as any Silver Fang would.

The odd scratching on that tree was a marker, a pictogram carved there to declare who was buried beneath it: Henry "Woundgiver" Standish. That rock covered the grave of Lord Batell, the "Eye of Gaia," as was made clear by the wolf paw and circle pattern depressed into it. The mound of dirt he was standing next to was a fresher grave. The small rocks scattered about its edges marked it, and declared that Gregory Breaking Heart lay here. A member of Arkady's pack, killed in service to the king a year ago. Albrecht wondered if it was the Nexus Crawler that had brought him down. The cemetery, known as the Grave of Hallowed Heroes, was even more obvious in the spirit world, where the markers could not be missed and were often guarded by spirits.

Eldest Claw came over the rise; the mourners had arrived. They quickly spread out to take their places in the small clearing while the King's Own Pack marched forward to the hole. The bearers paused over it, and then lowered the king's body into the earth.

Albrecht watched Morningkill disappear into the ground. It was hard to believe the old man was finally gone. He had been seventy-five years old, long-lived for a Garou. Garou could certainly live longer, with their advanced healing abilities, but they usually died in battle before then. It wasn't that Morningkill hadn't been able to fight — hell, when he was young, no Garou on the east coast, perhaps the entire continent, could have bested him. So it was said, at least. Albrecht believed it. He had the scar to prove it.

He had been only one year into his Firsting, and fresh from his Rite of Passage, when he had gotten into a heated argument with his grandfather. Being new to his powers, Albrecht had believed he was the toughest thing to walk the earth. Morningkill had proved him wrong, but it had taken a scar to convince Albrecht of it. It was still there, a deep claw mark on his left shoulder. It even hurt sometimes, when it rained heavily.

Damn it, though, he was going to miss the old king. His scar was a mark of humility, a lesson Morningkill had meant him to learn for his own survival. Regardless of all the years and the enmity that had passed between them, Albrecht couldn't hold a grudge against this man. He had been the ideal at which Albrecht had long aimed. But that goal was as dead as the man.

The King's Own Pack moved aside from the grave to let the line of mourners pass by. They moved behind Albrecht, and he watched them as they passed. They were pretty tough-looking all right. Even that Ragabash — what was his name? Peter — looked like a bruiser. But Arkady looked meaner than all of them. The Garou did not look at him as he passed, but Albrecht paid attention to the way he walked. Confident, supple. This was a werewolf whose economy of movement showed he knew his body well. His stance was ready to assume a battle pose at an instant. Albrecht knew this because he had once tried to cultivate those moves himself. But it wasn't his style.

Albrecht turned back to the grave and watched the mourners. They all looked genuinely grief-stricken. Most of them were old enough to remember Morningkill in better times, before the king had become… eccentric. He saw Garou whom he hadn't seen in years, and a few Garou from far protectorates, come to pay respect to the dead king.

But Albrecht noticed that Loba Carcassone was not among them: Her exile had not yet ended. He would have to do something about that when he became king. He also wondered about poor Alphonse Grayling and Justin Beauchamp, the Silver Fang exiles who had attacked him and whom he had been forced to kill. The mystery of why they had attacked him was still not solved. But their bodies had not come back to the protectorate with him and Eliphas. They had been exiles, and thus were denied a proper burial among their fellow tribe members. Albrecht felt a pang of guilt. If he'd been able to control his rage, they might be alive today. He was sure their attack had been just a misunderstanding of some sort. Of course, if he hadn't frenzied, maybe *he* wouldn't be alive today.

The Garou had all gone past, winding their way back down the hill. The Kinfolk families were coming through now. There was Sutter, followed by Warner. They threw dirt on Morningkill's grave and walked on, not looking at Albrecht. Behind them was Warner's wife Daphne and her two daughters, the haughty and ugly Lenore and the quiet Margot, who pulled Seth along behind her. Margot looked at Albrecht but then looked away, nervous and shamefaced. Seth stared at him, though, obviously proud to have Albrecht as his uncle.

Albrecht shook his head. The kid really had no clue, did he? Albrecht was no role model to follow. Well, it didn't matter. If he didn't get the crown for some reason, he wouldn't be sticking around anyway.

James Albrecht walked up to the grave alone. He looked down sadly and threw a handful of dirt into the grave. Then he looked up at his son. Albrecht felt his throat tighten. The man looked terrible. He was only in his late forties, but years on the bottle had aged him badly. His eyes bore right into Albrecht's, swimming with tears, a look of pain and loneliness on his face. Albrecht looked away.

After all these years, he thought he had finally forgiven his father for being weak, for not being man enough to stand up to his own father and brother, for not defending his wife or son to them. Albrecht had borne great resentment for the man. He had grown up humiliated, called "low-born" and "mongrel" by other boys of the protectorate, most of whom had not bred true as Albrecht had. But their words had stung him nonetheless. He had thought the pain of the past was gone, but all the hate and anger came back as he saw his father here in the flesh again.

James Albrecht lowered his head and moved down the hill. Albrecht fought to keep from stepping forward, from calling out to his father to give the man some sort of word or sign that his son cared. His anger — no, his pride — was too great for that. He could forgive Morningkill, who had banished him from home, but he could not go to his father. The pain of that broken pride was greater than exile. He looked away from the gathering, trying to hide his self-loathing at his failure to forgive.

After the Rothchilds and the Batells and the other families had passed, the King's Own Pack came forward again. They carried shovels and began to throw heaps of dirt into the grave, onto Morningkill. Albrecht wanted to leave. He had to get out of there. But tradition demanded he stay. He was the closest family; he had to stay until the end.

He must have begun fidgeting or something, because Greyfist looked over at him and gave him a frown. He looked back at the seneschal and shrugged his shoulders. *Man*, he thought, *what I would do for a cigarette now.*

The pack worked quickly, though, and soon enough the grave was covered and the dirt packed. Albrecht noticed that some of them had shifted into Glabro form — the near-human form — to work faster with the added strength. Shining Outward and Regina stepped forward, carrying a marble headstone between them. It was sheer vanity to use such a thing, and it would do nothing to hide the graveyard from humans, but Morningkill had insisted on a headstone for his grave.

They placed it on the ground and drove it in with their bare hands, shifting to Crinos form for the brute strength required. When it was solidly placed, they shifted back to Homid and stepped away, looking at Albrecht. He sighed and walked forward. Stopping at the foot of the grave, he looked down.

Well, he thought, *this is for you, Granddad. I hope you like it, wherever you are.*

He shifted into Crinos form, his bulk and height increasing greatly. He drew in a deep breath, held it for a moment, and then let out a long, mournful howl. He was joined by the others, who had shifted to Crinos or Lupus, and they all hung their heads back to the sky, crying out their sorrow to Gaia. Albrecht carried the howl for minutes and minutes as others dropped out, unable to continue. Finally, only one other was left howling with him: Arkady.

Albrecht frowned and a note of anger crept into the howl. Arkady was trying to make a contest out of this, when he knew that it was Albrecht's right to begin and end the Dirge for the Fallen. He felt his anger rise as Arkady also matched the growling note Albrecht had introduced. Now he was mocking him. Albrecht turned to look at Arkady, and saw that the wolf had been watching him all along, a smirk in his eyes. Albrecht's howl became a growl which choked off out of anger and frustration. But Arkady carried the original howl on for a few more seconds.

This was too much! That Arkady would dare such an insult here, at the funeral rites of his grandfather! Albrecht couldn't have cared less about Arkady's aspirations to the throne before, but this was personal now!

He marched forward on all fours in Crinos form. Arkady was already in Lupus. He matched the wolf's gaze and stared, growling deep and low, waiting for Arkady to back down. But the wolf stepped forward, staring up intently into Albrecht's eyes. It was now a contest to see who would break first, who would look away or who would lose control to rage.

Albrecht's vision narrowed. Only Arkady existed for him now. His vision grew red as his anger rose, a roiling furnace of molten bile in his gut. He longed to leap forward and throat the damned bastard before him, the wolf who met his gaze and did not flinch. Indeed, whose eyes bore deeply into Albrecht's, searching for some sign of weakness, some breaking point.

And then Arkady said one thing, all the while his gaze never wavering. One word spoken in the Garou tongue: "Charach."

Albrecht roared and leapt forward, faster than even Arkady had anticipated. The wolf tried to step aside, but Albrecht's fangs snapped shut on his right rear leg, causing him to howl in pain. He lunged at Albrecht, burying his snout into Albrecht's shoulder. But Albrecht was consumed with rage and ignored it, savagely chewing Arkady's leg. The wolf shifted into Hispo form — the prehistoric dire-wolf form — and then straight to Homid. In the second in which Albrecht's fangs opened wide to accomodate the larger leg and, before they could crash down again on the smaller human leg, Arkady pulled free.

Albrecht howled in anger and ran at Arkady, but was hit from the side and thrown a few feet away. This confused him for a moment. He smelled someone other than Arkady standing over him — Regina, the Caern Warder. Her face hovered over his, growling low and threateningly. Albrecht didn't know what was going on now. He had no desire to fight Regina, and so he bowed his head and shut up. When she saw his submissive gesture, she stepped back.

Albrecht looked up and saw that Shining Outward stood over Arkady, likewise cowing the Garou into submission. It was not hard; Arkady was obviously hurting badly and was only too glad to give up.

Albrecht stood up, shifting to Homid form, and began dusting himself off. "What's the deal? Why'd you stop me? That bastard insulted me! Here, at Morningkill's funeral!"

"That's exactly why we stopped you two," Regina said. "How dare you challenge over Morningkill's grave! Such a disrespect for the dead! I am appalled."

"I started nothing!" Arkady said, now standing in Homid form and limping over to his pack. His leg was badly mauled, but one of his pack members bent down and began to call on a Gift to mend it. "You saw it! This mad one attacked me!"

"Shut up, Arkady!" Greyfist said. "You know very well that you provoked it. I consider it a challenge."

"Ah, but Seneschal, I am Master of the Challenge at this caern. It is I who decides what is a challenge and what is not."

"Not in this case," Regina said. "Since you are a claimant to the throne, you cannot act in your normal caern position until the claim is resolved. Another must be declared Master of the Challenge in your place."

"Since you are the Caern Warder," Greyfist said to Regina, "doesn't the position fall to you?"

"I believe that is the standard etiquette," Shining Outward said, dusting the dirt that had been kicked up by the fight off the headstone.

"Well, then?" Greyfist said to Regina. "Is Arkady considered to have challenged Albrecht for the throne?"

"Ha!" Arkady said. "I did no such thing! I simply carried the howl longer than his weak lungs could."

"You asshole!" Albrecht said. "That wasn't your right! It was my right to end the howl. You stepped on my territory!"

"Albrecht's correct," Regina said, looking at Arkady. "You disrupted his grandfather's death rites. As a member of House Wyrmfoe, it was Albrecht's duty to lead the howl, but you took it over. I consider that a challenge."

"Pah!" Arkady said. "How silly. It does not matter, though. It was only a matter of time until he challenged me."

"Yeah," Albrecht said. "But *you* challenged *me*, so I have choice of weapons."

Arkady glared at him angrily. "So? What do you choose?"

"Klaives."

"Then I will carve you from chest to groin and hang your pelt on this tree!" Arkady said, pointing at a nearby birch.

"Hold on there," Regina said. "I haven't set the time or place yet. I decree that it will be tomorrow night before the Grand Oak. Be there by midnight, or forfeit your claim."

Arkady nodded and gave Albrecht a sneer. He then walked off, his leg now fully healed thanks to his packmate's magic. The King's Own Pack fell in behind him, and they soon disappeared over the ridge of the hill.

"King's Own Pack, huh?" Albrecht said. "We'll see whose pack they are once I'm king."

"Your temper is as bad as it's always been," Greyfist said, walking past Albrecht.

"Hey!" Albrecht said, following him. "You saw that. He provoked me. And why'd you break it up? I almost had him."

"You weren't close, Albrecht," Greyfist said. "It was clear that as soon as he got over his surprise, he would have won by out-thinking you. The way he slipped from your grip showed that."

"He got lucky on that one."

Greyfist stopped and spun around to face Albrecht. "Damn it! When are you going to wake up? Arkady can beat you. You walked right into his challenge — don't think he didn't plan it this way! He's a master of the klaive. He really will carve you up! You could have chosen Gamecraft to best him, a contest of wits. You're not particularly smart, but you could have overcome him at that at least!"

"Don't talk to me like that," Albrecht said. "I'm sick of it. In case you aren't aware, I am also a master of the klaive. And mine's bigger than his, besides. I've seen his klaive. It's nice, but it's no Grand Klaive. I think House Wyrmfoe's family heirloom is going to wind up flaying his ass."

Greyfist turned around and walked off down the hill, fuming. "Your ego is going to get you killed, and then the dream will be dead for good."

Albrecht watched his friend march off down the hill. Dream? What the hell was he talking about?

CHAPTER SEVEN

Mari hit the punching bag again. And again. One hundred, one hundred one, one hundred two.... After one hundred and ten blows in succession, she took a break and jogged around the one-room gym. She had broken a sweat but wasn't breathing heavily yet.

She ran past Evan, who sat at the small desk by the door looking bored, staring out the window onto the streets of New York. He turned from watching the passersby outside to watch Mari as she ran past. He yawned.

"Look, I think we should try to get in touch with Albrecht," Evan said.

Mari did not answer him. She kept running until she finished her lap. She then took a deep breath and sat down on the blue mat that stretched from wall to wall.

"Tomorrow," she said. "I gave him until tomorrow to let us know what's happening."

"Yeah, but that could be too late."

"He can take care of himself. I'm sure we would have heard something by now if he were in trouble."

"Not necessarily. Little word gets in or out of that place.

Those Silver Fangs are true New Englanders: secretive and shut-mouthed."

"Well? What do you want to do? We don't have a phone number and I'm not sure exactly where the caern is."

"But Mother Larissa would know. She'd surely tell us."

"She's been bothered enough in this affair—"

The phone rang. Evan looked at it, then reached over and picked it up. "Cabrah's Self-Defense. This is Evan speaking."

"Don't you have school or something?" Albrecht said.

"Albrecht! Where the hell are you?!"

Mari stood up and walked over, her hand out for the phone. "Give me that. I've got a few things to say to him."

Evan turned away from her, covering the receiver. "Wait a minute. Let me find out what's going on." He uncovered the receiver and leaned back in his chair. "So what's happening? Do you know why those guys attacked you? Is the king really dead? Who's going to be the next king?"

"Hold on," Albrecht said. "One at a time. First: A whole hell of a lot is happening. Second: No, I don't know why those two attacked me yet. Third: Morningkill is really dead. His funeral was last night. Fourth: I'm fighting someone tonight to become king of the Silver Fangs."

"What? You're joking, right?"

"Nope. The guy's name is Arkady and he's a real asshole. But I can take him."

"But… king? You?"

"Hey, don't sound so surprised. I thought I'd get some support on this from you at least. Of course, king! I've told you my heritage before."

"Yeah, but I thought you had given up on that. I never thought you'd actually… you know, become king."

"King?" Mari said. "Albrecht?!" She reached out and snatched the phone from Evan. She yelled into the receiver, "What do you mean, king? You can't be king!"

Albrecht chuckled. "Yeah, that's what some of these guys

tell me. But I say otherwise. What's the matter? Don't like the idea of ol' Albrecht lording it over all the tribes, including yours?"

"The day you 'lord it over' the Black Furies is the eve of the Apocalypse, Albrecht. Don't even joke about it. Are you serious about this? What are you thinking? We have a pack."

"Yeah, so? I can be king and member of a pack at the same time. It just means that you guys might have to help me out with official duties and all. Big-time stuff. Lots of renown in it."

"Shove your renown, Albrecht. I don't like the idea of you as king at all. Why can't another be king?"

"Because the only other contender is too big of a jerk. I can't let him have it. Hell, I'd never hear the end of all that talk — 'The Silver Fangs are going down.' 'The Silver Fangs can't rule.' 'The Silver Fangs blah, blah, blah.' No, I'm not going to contribute to more of that."

"Really? What do you think people will say when they hear that Albrecht, lord of drunks, is taking the throne?"

"Hey!" Albrecht said, getting angry. "That's not called for. That was a long time ago."

Evan grabbed the phone back from Mari, who frowned at him but walked across the studio to the hanging punching bag. She began to throw a series of blows at it.

"It's me again," Evan said. "Don't worry. She's just surprised. We're behind you."

"Is that noise in the background what I think it is? Is she hitting the bags again?"

"Yeah."

"She's awfully weird for a Theurge, kid."

"Well.... Hey, what do you want us to do? How can we help?"

"I'll call you tomorrow and let you know how the fight goes." There was a pause. "Of course, if I don't survive, I probably won't be calling you."

"You said you could take this guy!"

"Well, yeah. But you never know. I'll see you! Bye!" Albrecht hung up.

Evan placed the receiver back in its cradle. He looked at Mari, who stopped punching the bag to look back at him. "He's in trouble."

"Of course he is. But he doesn't want us involved. We've got to respect that."

Evan looked out at the street, at the dirty buildings crowding in. "I guess." He didn't like it, though. Not at all.

Albrecht left Greyfist's office. The call was exactly what he had expected: Evan curious and concerned, Mari ready to tear his head off. He knew she was just as worried as Evan, but she hid it well.

He had spent most of the day practicing with the klaive. He wasn't out of shape by any means, but after that fight in New York, he wanted to make sure Arkady didn't slip any blows past him. He concentrated on his defense, since his offense was not in doubt.

He also did meditation exercises to help calm himself down. He did *not* want to frenzy against Arkady. Greyfist was right about one thing: If he frenzied, Arkady would win. So Albrecht worked to calm himself with meditation.

But Mari had pissed him off anyway.

He should have called them earlier, and then exercised. But he knew the hours she kept at her gym, and he was guaranteed to reach her in the afternoon.

He walked back up to his room to meditate again. He was confident that Greyfist would alert him well in time for the combat.

The crowd was already gathered and waiting when Albrecht went out to the field. Regina's caern protectors had marked off the combat arena with small, white rocks placed one after the other in a large circle. The Grand Oak stood at the western edge of the circle.

There were no bleachers or raised seats, so spectators had arrived early to get the prime viewing spots. There weren't that many Garou or Kinfolk at the caern, so the circle was probably big enough that there would only be two rows once the battle began. But those rows would encircle the entire marked space.

Albrecht walked onto the field and examined it. Torches on poles surrounded the field, providing the only light besides the crescent moon and stars. A layer of dirt had been laid on the field and packed down, with all the rocks and pebbles cleared away. The field was clean and open, with no depressions. A good, fair playing field. That was in Albrecht's favor. He had never been one to rely on tricky distractions. He was a straightforward fighter, and this was his kind of field. From what he'd heard of Arkady and his fighting preferences, Albrecht would have the advantage.

He went over to the Grand Oak. Greyfist had set up a chair there, along with towels, a bucket of water and a first-aid kit. Thomas Abbot was also there. He had volunteered to act as healer for Albrecht.

"Hello, Thomas," Albrecht said to the older Garou as he sat down in the chair. "By the way, I want to thank you for standing up for me yesterday in the moot."

Abbot smiled and shrugged. "Certainly. I was only defending my views. You are Morningkill's heir, therefore you should be king."

"I get the idea you don't think much of Arkady."

Abbot sneered. "I suppose it shows too much, then. Well, if he does win — perish the thought — we will need a gadfly against his policies. I will be happy to fulfill that role."

"And if I win?"

Abbot smiled at Albrecht. "As long as you're on the up-and-up, you have nothing to worry about. Act like your grandfather, however, and you'll be in for some disappointments from the court."

Albrecht nodded. "Of course."

He looked out at the field again. Across from his position, the crowd had cleared away to make room for Arkady's chair. The King's Own Pack were carrying it over. Arkady's packmate, Peter, was to act as his healer.

Albrecht glanced at his watch. Quarter till twelve. He knew it was too much to expect that Arkady would be late. It appeared the fight was on.

A murmuring went through the crowd and Albrecht looked up to see Arkady in the circle, checking it out the same way Albrecht had earlier. He was frowning, as if he was disappointed with it. Albrecht smiled. *Good, you schmuck. I'm glad you hate it.*

Arkady went and sat down in his seat. He stared across the distance at Albrecht, smoldering. Albrecht smiled and nodded at him, and Arkady returned the nod, smiling also. *Bastard,* Albrecht thought. *Facetious bastard. Of course, so am I.*

"I just don't get it," Greyfist said. "Why does this sort of thing always come down to combat?"

Albrecht chuckled. "Wake up. We're Garou. It always comes down to two guys bashing each other's heads in."

Regina walked onto the field and surveyed it. She then took her place at the throne, to Albrecht's left. She addressed the crowd.

"Since both combatants are here, we can begin. The challenge combat has been declared: klaives. The conditions are, as always, to fight until an honorable surrender. If none is given, then to the death. I would remind both combatants to heed the Litany concerning a surrender. I will be harsh with any who disregards it."

Albrecht nodded, as did Arkady.

"Then let the combatants take the field."

Albrecht stood up. His armor was strapped over his trench coat: a small breastplate and epaulettes, carved with ornate pictogram sigils, and vambraces on his arms. He sauntered out into the circle and stopped, taking his place just inside the marks.

Arkady also rose, walking into the circle. His battle armor was more impressive than Albrecht's — black with an ornate breastplate and vambraces. Thick, black leather covered the rest of him. He was an impressive-looking warrior.

"Draw your weapons," Regina said.

Albrecht pulled his Grand Klaive from the sidesheath in his trench coat. The crowd recognized it and began murmuring. It was a well-known family heirloom, having been used by Morningkill in his youth, and by his Garou predecessors before him.

Arkady drew his blade; not a Grand Klaive, but one which he handled well. He swished it around in a circle and seemed to be perfectly at ease with it.

"Fight!" Regina yelled.

Albrecht immediately crouched low and moved forward, his klaive out before him, ready to parry any blow. Arkady walked toward Albrecht, his klaive swinging slowly in an arc from right to left. Albrecht began to slide to the right, trying to circle Arkady, but Arkady moved to his left, cancelling out Albrecht's move.

"Well, Arkady?" Albrecht said. "Why don't you come at me?"

"I will act when I feel like acting," Arkady said, still swirling his klaive. "Not when you prefer it. Why? Are you afraid to take the initiative?"

"Ha! I just want to make this last, to give the crowd a show. If I started first, this would all be over in seconds."

"You are such a braggart," Arkady said, moving slowly and

carefully forward. Albrecht stood his ground, his large sword out before him. "Why do you not back up your words with action?"

"I like watching you swing that thing around. Ever thought of taking up tennis? 'Cause that's what you look like, a wussy tennis player swinging a racket."

Arkady growled. "You had best take Crinos form, Albrecht. It will hurt very badly for you otherwise."

"You first, Rusky."

Arkady leapt forward, dropping down as he reached Albrecht and stabbing his knife up from below. Albrecht took one step back and easily parried. He then stepped to the right and swung his sword down, but Arkady rolled away and stood up straight again.

"Temper, temper, Arkady. I saw that coming a mile away."

"I was simply stretching," Arkady said, standing in place and swinging his klaive in an arc again. "I did not get all my exercises done earlier."

"Oh? Too busy jacking off?"

Arkady's face contorted into a grimace. He began growling and his shoulders grew broader, his arms bigger and his legs longer. He was shifting to Glabro form.

Albrecht shook his head. "Tsk, tsk. Can't even stay in Homid form long enough to throw a few taunts, huh?"

Suddenly Arkady was in Crinos form, a towering wolfman who came hurtling at Albrecht with incredible speed. His klaive whirled in a blur, one Albrecht could barely keep track of. But instead of stepping back on the defensive, Albrecht lunged forward, stabbing his sword into the whirling arc of Arkady's klaive. Arkady was taken by surprise and his klaive was knocked from his hand. He jumped back, dodging Albrecht's slashes as Albrecht closed the distance between them.

Arkady then slipped to the side when Albrecht least expected it and reached out with a claw to slice at Albrecht's shoulder beneath the epaulette before he could bring his klaive up to block it. Blood sprayed forth. Arkady had scored first blood.

Albrecht stepped back, bringing his klaive up and calming himself, ignoring the pain. It was just a scratch. But the distraction allowed Arkady to run off and pick up his klaive.

He's good, Albrecht thought. *He's more flexible than I am. I thought I had him, and even though he was surprised, he escaped pretty quick. I've gotta be a bit more careful. Ready for anything.*

Arkady was now smiling, his klaive again circling in his hand. Albrecht growled and began to shift forms, growing into Crinos. He was huge in Crinos, although he and Arkady were almost equal in height. Albrecht's fur was white, but Arkady's was even more purely white, the sign of superior breeding.

Albrecht stomped forward toward Arkady, tired of playing around. He wanted to get this over with. He had never been much for taunting in combat, and he didn't know why he had wanted to do it earlier. Had he been scared? Trying to test Arkady's boundaries? Screw that! Time to kick butt.

Arkady slowly backed away as Albrecht came closer, but Albrecht didn't hesitate. He kept coming. Arkady tried to slip to Albrecht's left, but Albrecht stepped over and cut him off. He was in range now and began to swing his klaive wildly at Arkady, with such powerful blows that Arkady knew he couldn't parry them and was forced to dodge.

But he didn't dodge. The Russian Garou stepped forward, past Albrecht's reach, and thrust in with his klaive. It slid down Albrecht's breastplate and sank into his stomach. He barked in pain and tried to step back, but he couldn't bring his large klaive up quickly enough with Arkady so close. But the other Garou moved in closer, twisting his knife in Albrecht's gut. The pain was incredible! Albrecht shut his eyes and forced himself not to lose control. He dropped his sword and grasped Arkady's head, driving his thumbs into his opponent's eyes.

Arkady screamed and pulled back, leaving his klaive in Albrecht's stomach. One of his eyes had been put out by Albrecht's claw, but Albrecht had missed the other one, managing only to scratch the eyebrow. Blood poured down Arkady's face, blinding his good eye. He ran back, trying to get clear. Albrecht ran forward, picking up his klaive and swinging it at Arkady's torso.

It was a clean shot. Arkady was in for it. The fight was almost over.

But Albrecht tripped and fell to the ground. The klaive in his stomach hit the dirt first, driving deeper, exiting the other side, barely missing his spine. He yelled in pain, coughing up blood, stunned and unable to move.

Arkady ran over, wiping the blood out of his good eye. He slashed at Albrecht with his claw, tearing through the back of Albrecht's trench coat and ripping a layer of muscle off. He drew back for another blow, but Albrecht leapt up and knocked him off balance. Rather than taking advantage of it, however, Albrecht ran to the edge of the circle and pulled Arkady's klaive out of his stomach. Blood poured forth from the wound and Albrecht clutched it tight. *Nothing worse than a gut wound,* Albrecht thought. *Hurts like hell.*

He looked at Arkady, who cautiously came at him. Arkady was barely hurt, and Albrecht was almost dead. Albrecht wondered how that had happened. He had had a clean shot, damn it! How had he tripped? There was nothing on the field! He had checked it out himself.

He raised his klaive at the last minute to parry one of Arkady's rakes. Arkady didn't seem to expect it and couldn't pull back in time, and the klaive cut through his forearm to the bone. Arkady gasped and pulled back. Albrecht stumbled forward, trying to take advantage of the surprise. He slashed upwards and then quickly to the side. The blade caught Arkady on the right shoulder, slicing through the battle armor and the bone. Arkady's arm fell to the ground.

Arkady screamed in rage and clutched his shoulder, running to the far side of the field. Albrecht tried to follow right behind him, but the pain kept him from running too fast. Arkady spun around then and ran right back at Albrecht. As Albrecht stopped and pointed his klaive forward to receive the charge, Arkady leapt into the air. He flew past Albrecht, who tried to duck, but Arkady's claw caught him on the scalp, tearing out a chunk of hair and opening a large gash.

Albrecht fell to the ground, stunned again. He tried to stand and turn, blindly swinging his sword behind him at the foe he knew must be there. He was right. His klaive connected and Arkady grunted, but the klaive was now stuck in Arkady's left thigh. Arkady stepped back to take a breath, obviously fighting to control his rage.

Albrecht blinked and wiped the blood off his forehead before it could run down into his eyes. He readied himself for Arkady's attack as Arkady pulled Albrecht's klaive from his thigh and smiled. He began to swing it around in a circle as he approached Albrecht.

Albrecht felt dizzy watching it. He was suffering from massive blood loss and a concussion, he was sure. And now Arkady had his klaive and was going to carve him up with it. Sure, he had cost the Garou an eye and an arm, and given him a big wound to the thigh, but he was still coming on while Albrecht felt like he was about to faint.

Arkady came near Albrecht and pulled the sword back to slash at him. Albrecht fell down and the sword cut empty air over his head.

Albrecht, too weak to continue, drew in a deep breath and said, "I surrender, Arkady."

Arkady didn't seem to hear him. He stepped forward and drew the sword back again.

"Damn it, it's over. I surrender," Albrecht said, barely able to sit up.

Arkady's eyes narrowed and he began to swing the sword.

Albrecht shut his eyes, but the blow never landed. He opened his eyes, blinking from the blood running into them, to see Arkady, sword poised in mid-swing, staring past Albrecht at Regina, who was giving him an angry stare. Albrecht could barely hear her deep growl from here. Her message was clear: *You can kill him, Arkady, but king or no, I will make you pay for it later.*

Arkady stood there, seeming to weigh his options. He then dropped Albrecht's klaive and turned away, limping back to his chair. "Get out of here, Albrecht. You will be gone by tomorrow. And you won't return to my protectorate."

Albrecht sat there, staring at Arkady's back. He then shut his eyes and cursed himself.

CHAPTER EIGHT

Albrecht stared up at the night sky and the crescent moon stared back at him. He breathed heavily, wincing in pain with each exhalation. Thomas Abbot moved his hands over his stomach and concentrated. The wound began to seal up. Albrecht breathed more easily as the pain subsided.

"Turn over," Abbot said.

Albrecht rolled over onto his side. Blood ran down his back, staining the dirt. Abbot touched the torn muscles and again concentrated, calling on the healing power of the spirits to reknit Albrecht's ripped flesh. He then healed the scratch on Albrecht's shoulder. Albrecht felt much better, but he knew he would be sore for a while.

"Now, sit up," Abbot said, and Albrecht groaned as he obeyed. He almost fell back down as a wave of dizziness came over him. Abbot felt his forehead and then healed it. The blood stopped flowing and the wound closed up.

Albrecht smiled at Abbot. "Thanks. I feel like a million dollars."

Abbot didn't say anything. He just stood up and walked away. "Try to get some rest."

Albrecht sighed. He got up and looked around. Most of

the spectators had left, following Arkady and his pack. Arkady's wounds had been healed and he had declared a victory party by the edge of the bawn. Most of the Garou had gone to celebrate with their new king.

Greyfist and Eliphas stood nearby, talking quietly between themselves. Eliphas looked worried, and Greyfist was frowning. Albrecht walked over to them.

"Hey, no need for long faces," he said. "I'm fit as I ever was. And you won't have to put up with me as king now. You should be celebrating."

Greyfist looked gravely at Albrecht. "We need to talk. In my office."

Albrecht looked at Greyfist as the Garou walked off to the mansion. He turned to Eliphas, who had begun to follow. "What's up with him? Sore loser?"

Eliphas stared at Albrecht as if he couldn't believe what the man was saying. "I think you need to hear this," he said and followed after Greyfist.

Albrecht pulled out a cigarette, lit it, and followed. As he entered the office, Greyfist was standing by the window and Eliphas sat on the couch. He closed the door behind him.

"So what's up?" Albrecht said, getting a bit worried now.

Greyfist didn't turn from the window as he said, "Arkady cheated."

"Oh, come on now," Albrecht said. "You saw it. You were right all along; he really is better than me."

Greyfist turned around. "No he's not. You had him dead by rights with that one blow. Then you fell."

Albrecht flushed with humiliation. "Yeah, well...." He puffed on his cigarette. "Do we have to have a blow-by-blow? I know my mistakes. He got lucky on that one and was able to turn the tide from there."

Greyfist looked solemnly at Albrecht. "Eliphas, tell Albrecht what you told me."

Albrecht turned to the young man, who seemed very

worried. "What? What is it?"

Eliphas leaned back on the couch, not meeting Albrecht's eyes. "I... I was given my accouterments as Gatekeeper yesterday. But I have not completed the training yet, so I can't be sure—"

"Don't bandy words," Greyfist interrupted. "You know the fetish was correct."

Eliphas nodded, swallowing nervously. "Yes. It can't be wrong, can it?"

Albrecht sat down next to Eliphas. "What can't? Tell me what the hell happened."

Eliphas looked at him now. "I have a fetish, the Spirit Ward of the caern. It has been used by every Gatekeeper of North Country for three centuries now. Its purpose is to alert the Gatekeeper to intruder spirits who enter the caern. It detected one during the fight. There was an alien spirit on the field. That was what tripped you."

Albrecht leaned back, his mouth open and his head shaking. "You mean Arkady brought in a spirit to cheat?"

"That's not all," Greyfist said. "It was a Bane."

Albrecht growled. "No. That can't be. Not even Arkady is that stupid."

"But the fetish does not lie," Eliphas said, exasperated. "When it warned me, I didn't know what to do. I've only just become the Gatekeeper, and Garrick is not around to train me. I went into the Umbra to see it with my own eyes, but it had fled by then. However, the area... stank of the Wyrm. It had left the scent of its corruption behind."

"Wait a minute," Albrecht said. "That could have been the smell of the Black Spiral Dancers from a few days ago."

Greyfist shook his head. "No. Rites of Cleansing removed those yesterday. Regina saw to it personally. This was a new scent."

Albrecht shook his head, staring into the corner of the library.

"Why is this so hard for you to believe, Albrecht?" Greyfist asked. "I've suspected for some time that he was behind the Black Spiral Dancer attack. He's obviously made allies among the Wyrm."

"That bastard," Albrecht said, gritting his teeth. "I would have won. I would have had him."

"Quit being so damn selfish!" Greyfist snapped.

Albrecht looked at him, surprised. "What do you mean? He caused me to lose the fight."

"Don't you understand what this means? Arkady is king now! He has brought the taint of the Wyrm onto the throne!"

Albrecht shuddered. His guts turned. It was his fault. If he'd been able to beat Arkady, the throne wouldn't be in danger of corruption. He had to do something. Albrecht stood up, heading for the door.

"Where are you going?" Greyfist said.

"To take this up with Arkady," Albrecht said, reaching for the doorknob.

"You can't!" Greyfist yelled. "You've just lost a challenge to him. You can't challenge him again; he doesn't have to accept it. The others would turn against you, and your accusation would be assumed false."

Albrecht stopped and looked down at the floor, thinking. "We've got to reveal this! He can't get away with it."

"I've already thought through all the options," Greyfist said, turning toward the window again. "Eliphas cannot bring forth the accusation because he is too new at his position, too low in rank. He has no tangible proof by which to accuse the sept's Master of the Challenge, only the faint evidence of the spirit's tracks, and no definite connection between that spirit and Arkady. Arkady is fresh from his victory and has many allies. The sept wants a king, and he has proven his right by combat to be king. Arkady would ridicule Eliphas, and force a physical challenge." Greyfist paused. "No. I have to challenge Arkady."

"What?" Albrecht said, walking back to the center of the room, staring at Greyfist's back. "You will do no such thing!

He'll tear you to pieces in seconds. Hell, you know I can beat the crap out of you, and if he can get me, you don't stand a chance. Besides, what if he cheats again?"

"There is always Gamecraft. I can easily best him at that."

"But you are the one bringing the challenge. The form of resolution will be his choice. He'll choose klaives — you know it."

Greyfist sat down at his desk. "You're right. We have a treacherous secret and we can't even reveal it. Damn this whole system of rights and challenges! If only the mighty rule, then the mighty can bring us down."

"But only the mighty can protect us from the Wyrm," Albrecht said, "Or so the theory goes."

They all sat in silence for a while. Greyfist looked out the window and seemed to be struggling with heavy thoughts. Then he looked at the other two. "There is one hope."

Albrecht looked up at him. "What?"

Greyfist looked down at the desk nervously. "It... it's a bit preposterous, really. It came to me in a dream. I've been struggling to figure it out over the last few days. It's made me think a lot about our tribe's situation."

"A dream?" Albrecht said. "What makes you think this one was special?"

Greyfist looked straight at Albrecht. "I believe this dream was sent by Falcon."

Albrecht didn't say anything, but looked back at Greyfist, waiting for him to continue.

"Have you ever heard of the Silver Crown?"

Albrecht frowned. "It's an old legend, isn't it? Something about the first crown worn by a Silver Fang king? Back in the Dawn Times?"

"I have heard the story," Eliphas said. "It's the crown of kings, the true test of rulership. It is said that only those worthy to rule the tribes under Gaia and Falcon can wear the crown. The unworthy who attempt to wear it die."

"That's right," Greyfist said. "Many believe the crown is an ancient fetish artifact, not just a myth or a figment of the imagination. I saw this crown in my dream. I saw Morningkill try to wear it and perish. But I saw another — I don't know who — take it up and survive. I believe the Silver Crown still exists, that Falcon showed it to me for a reason. It's our only chance, Albrecht. If you can get the Silver Crown, you can be proven a true king, one fit to rule over Arkady."

"Wait a minute," Albrecht said. "One, you said it kills whoever is unworthy. That could be me. Two, we have no clue that it really exists, and if so, that we can find it."

"I've done some research on this," Greyfist said, "with what little is left of the protectorate's records. I think it's in the Umbra, Albrecht. Waiting in some realm for a true king to come claim it. That king is you."

"Here we go again. What if I'm not worthy? I'm supposed to go off on a dangerous Umbral quest because it *might* be there? And if I get it, it *might* not fry me alive? This sounds a bit farfetched."

"What other hope do we have?" Greyfist said.

Albrecht couldn't answer that.

"I have spoken with Antonine Teardrop, a Stargazer in the Catskills who has extensive records of tribal legends. He claims to know something called *The Lay of the Silver Crown*, a saga composed by a Silver Fang Galliard years ago. He thinks it holds some clues to the crown's location."

"Look, I like Antonine and all — I mean, he saved my butt once — but he *is* a bit cracked. He tends to believe a lot of things just because they're mystical."

"Isn't my dream mystical, Albrecht? We are Garou. We are beings of spirit as well as flesh. You're an Ahroun, so I know you've never paid a lot of attention to spiritual matters; but I have. You need to believe me, Albrecht. The Silver Crown exists. And you must find it. Otherwise, the North Country Protectorate is doomed to corruption."

"All right. I believe you. I've got to get this crown. Hell, I guess I've gone off on crazier quests for less. But where do I start?"

"You return to New York, gather your pack, and then visit Antonine. He will tell you the *Lay*."

"My pack. Great. They are going to love this."

"You need to go now, Albrecht. You have to get the crown and return with it before the cusp of the next full moon. That is Arkady's auspice, and the day he will be crowned. After that, not even the Silver Crown can break a kingship rite."

"So that's... what? Eleven days starting tomorrow? Great. I've gotta trek across the Umbra to who-knows-where, pick up a lost fetish, and get back here in less than two weeks?"

"Yes," Greyfist said. "Eliphas will drive you home."

CHAPTER NINE

Dawn touched the highest towers of New York City, but in the streets below it was still night. In the early morning gloom, Albrecht and Eliphas drove through the awakening streets. People were coming out of their apartments and getting into their cars to head for work. Buses roared by, stopped to drop off and pick up people, and roared off again, speeding to the next block's stop.

Albrecht rubbed his eyes and put his hands back on the wheel. He looked over at Eliphas, asleep in the passenger seat. Albrecht had been too worked up after last night's revelation to sleep, so he had taken over the driving duties. Eliphas had protested, experiencing visions of massive dents appearing on his Lexus, but Albrecht was hard to resist when he was fixed on something. So Eliphas had made the best of the situation and crashed out for the journey.

Albrecht pulled up outside Mari's gym. There was a space open, probably left by someone who had just gone to work. It was a bit tight, and it had been a while since he had parallel-parked, but he was confident. He pulled forward, put the car in reverse, and backed into the space. He was looking back over the seat, doing a good job of swinging the car in, when he heard the sound of metal grinding from the front bumper. *Shit*, he thought. *Scraped the car in front.*

Eliphas sat upright and looked forward. His face fell, an expression of confirmed doom on it. He then sat back again and closed his eyes.

Albrecht straightened out in the space and shut the engine off. "Sorry about that. You took it better than I thought you would."

Eliphas didn't say anything. He just frowned with his eyes shut, looking like he still wanted to sleep.

"That's okay. Just go back to Nod. You wait here while I run in and inform the crew."

Eliphas nodded and rolled onto his side. Albrecht shrugged and got out of the car, then went up to the studio door. The large window next to it looked in on the gym. Painted in large letters were the words: *Cabrah's Self-Defense*. And in smaller letters, beneath it: *Martial Arts Classes for Women. Karate, Judo, Tae Kwon Do*. Albrecht took out his key and unlocked the door. Stepping in, he shut the door behind him and walked across the room.

As he walked, he looked at himself in the full-length mirror that ran from wall to wall on one side of the gym. Gaia, but he looked terrible. Abbot had done a good job of patching him up, but he still had a large bruise on his forehead. His coat was torn and dirtier than usual. He hadn't shaved since the meeting of the Lodges: his stubble was almost a beard. He shook his head, opening the door on the far wall, and walked up the stairs beyond it.

He came into a small hallway with two doors opening off it. He went down to the last door and knocked. He heard someone walking around on the other side and listened carefully. *Let's see*, he thought. *Judging from the sound I'd say it's Evan. Not heavy enough to be Mari.*

The door opened and Evan's face lit up with a smile.

"Hey! You're back!" Evan said. "Come on in! What

happened? How'd the fight... go." His enthusiasm trailed off as he noticed the bruise on Albrecht's forehead and his tattered coat. "I guess it didn't go well. Since you're here so quick and all."

Albrecht stepped past him into the apartment. "You think fast on your feet, kid. I like that. I got my ass whupped."

"That's too bad," Evan said. But then he smiled. "I guess that means you're back here with us now."

"Hold on, now. I thought I said on the phone that just because I was going to be king didn't mean we weren't a pack."

"Okay," Evan nodded, obviously not buying it but not interested in fighting either. That was what Albrecht liked about Evan. He was the only one Albrecht knew who wouldn't immediately jump into an argument with him.

"Where's Mari?" Albrecht said, looking around the small apartment. They were in a living room with a kitchen opening off it. A hallway was to the right, leading to the bedrooms.

"She's out on her morning jog," Evan said, walking to the small table by the window. "Breakfast?" he asked, picking up a box of Cap'n Crunch.

"No thanks. I'm more of a Crunch Berries man myself. When do you think she'll be back?"

"I don't know. Ten minutes, maybe?"

"Well, I've got someone waiting out in the car. I don't—"

"I'm here, Albrecht," Eliphas said, coming in the door. He looked annoyed. Mari walked in behind him, glaring suspiciously at him. "Your friend here did not like me waiting in front of her establishment."

"Do you vouch for him, Albrecht?" Mari said.

Albrecht laughed. "Yeah. He's all right. You can ease off him, Mari."

She nodded at Eliphas, who nodded back. He then rolled his eyes and went to sit down across from Evan, who handed the cereal box to him. He stared at it for a minute, as if he didn't know what it was, then nodded again and took the box.

"So, Albrecht," Mari said. "What's the story?"

"You might want to sit down for this one," Albrecht said, leaning against the wall and pulling a cigarette out of his pocket. Mari's brow wrinkled in disgust, but she didn't say anything or move to sit down. He lit the cigarette and took a drag on it. "On second thought, you better stand. You're a pacer, anyway, aren't you?"

"Just spit it out," she said.

"Well, I lost the fight. I got trashed pretty good."

Mari smiled at that. "The mighty Albrecht taken down? No!"

"Oh, but wait. Here comes the good part. My opponent, Arkady, cheated. It appears that he had a little Bane ally waiting in the Umbra to trip me up. Literally. I had a killer blow on that bastard, but this Bane interceded and screwed it up."

"A Bane? So this Arkady is Wyrm-corrupt. What did the Fangs do to him when they found out?"

"Now that's the really good part. They don't know yet."

"What?" Evan said, still chewing his cereal. "Why not? You've got to warn them!"

"Hold on. It's not that easy. And that's the crux of the matter, really. You see, we can't prove it. And with the laws of challenge the way they are, we don't have anybody who could successfully bust on Arkady."

"Just point him out to me and I'll take him down!" Mari said, her fists bunching up.

"Ah, it's not that easy. Believe me, I really wish I could. But he's guarded by a damn good pack. And if I were found to be siccing my pals on him, that would be considered conspiracy against the throne. You gotta realize, he's king now."

"King!" Mari yelled. "You let a Wyrm-fetid Garou take the throne of the Silver Fangs and the rulership of the thirteen tribes?!"

"Wait a minute here! Just the other day you were singing

a different tune there. Something about the day the Fangs ruled over the Furies being Apocalypse night?"

"That was *you*, Albrecht. I said that the day *you* ruled would be the eve of the Apocalypse. But apparently I got it wrong. You've let a Wyrm ally onto the throne. If that's not a step toward the Final Days, I don't know what is."

"Well, damn it! I'm trying to do something about it! I'm the only one who can take the throne from Arkady. If we just get someone to kill him — assuming they succeeded — the crown might go to a regent, one of his packmates. They could be corrupt also."

"But they might not know," Eliphas cut in, crunching cereal. "We don't know for sure that they are aware of Arkady's treachery."

"That's true. But we have to assume they're just as culpable all the same. Now, here's the plan...."

Mari raised her eyebrows, waiting.

"There's this ancient artifact called the Silver Crown. If I can get it, I can be king. I think."

Mari nodded. "Of course. The Silver Crown. If you don't kill yourself putting it on, you will be proven fit to rule the tribes."

"Yeah," Evan said. "That's a good plan. Do you know where the crown is?"

Albrecht was looking in surprise at both of them, as was Eliphas. "You mean you've heard of the crown?"

"Of course," Mari said. "Who hasn't? It's only the greatest treasure of the Silver Fangs."

"Wait. Wait," Albrecht said, throwing his hands up. "I've only heard vague rumors of this thing, and it turns out you guys know all about it? Is it just me?"

"I have only heard references to it in other legends, myself," Eliphas said.

"Unbelievable," Mari said. "You've forgotten your own treasure! No wonder the Silver Fangs are said to have fallen. Everyone knows about the crown except the Silver Fangs!

And we thought you had it in hiding from the other tribes for all these years! The Furies and the Uktena would do anything to get it. But no one's looked for it because everyone knows it's being guarded by a Silver Fang sept somewhere. But now! Once this news gets out, everyone's going to be searching for it."

"Then it doesn't get out," Albrecht said, glaring at her. "'Cause we're going after it. We've got some clues. We can do this. We *have* to do this."

Mari nodded. "Yes. I wouldn't dare miss such a quest. The renown alone would be considerable, let alone the chance to see this great artifact."

Albrecht's eyes narrowed. "We need to make something clear here. We do this so the Fangs can get the crown, not the Furies. Got that? This crown needs to be among the Fangs, not sitting in some Fury stronghold on a remote Greek island."

Mari glared at him and was silent for a while. "All right. The crown goes to the Fangs. But if I think it will be misused, I will not hesitate to liberate it and place it in the keeping of our crones."

"Don't worry. If I get it, it'll be in good keeping."

"I will judge that for myself when the time comes."

"Guys!" Evan said. "Stop it. Look, Mari, we've got to do this for Albrecht. For the Fangs. For the entire Garou nation. If you can't make that promise ahead of time, it's not in anyone's best interest to involve you in the quest."

Mari's eyes widened as she looked at Evan as if he had just put a knife in her back. "You're taking his side!"

"I have to look at the greater good in this," Evan said. "You know the Furies don't need the crown. Come on. Be realistic. You're letting ego get in the way."

Mari frowned at him and then threw up her hands. "All right! The crown will go to Albrecht."

Albrecht nodded. "Thank you. Now we've got to leave. Antonine Teardrop knows some lore about the crown that'll give us a pointer in the right direction. Eliphas will drive us to the Catskills."

The dome sat on a rise, poking out above the fall foliage. Evan pointed it out to them as they drove along the small back road that wound its way to the Stargazer's home. Albrecht had never been here before, but he had heard about it. Antonine Teardrop lived in one of those weird Buckminster-Fuller-designed geodesic domes. He had telescopes pointing out of windows along the top so he could glean omens from the stars. Albrecht was a bit skeptical about such things, but he knew that Antonine was considered a very wise Garou, albeit one with a foot in the twilight zone.

Albrecht admonished himself for being uncharitable about another tribe again. Antonine had saved his butt. He had saved the entire pack, back when Evan had had his Rite of Passage and the Wyrm had been after him. Antonine had been the only one to read the proper omens and to act to get Albrecht, Evan and Mari to the holy site where the spirits could instruct Evan in his heritage: that of a Wendigo prophet and warrior.

But Albrecht had not seen Antonine since then. The Stargazer stayed in his home for the most part, occasionally showing up at a Garou moot here and there to tell of a new omen. Most of the time, the rest of the Garou didn't like his omens. They were uncomfortable prophecies, pointing out insidious Wyrm plots that no Garou wanted to believe could exist. Lately, Antonine and Loba Carcassone had been working together, realizing that they had both separately come across the same Wyrm plot — if it was a Wyrm plot. Their "plot" was probably the freakiest conspiracy theory Albrecht had ever heard, linking generations of child abuse to a conscious plot by near-immortal Wyrm servitors. To untangle such a chaotic thread and put a cause-and-effect label on it seemed a bit much even for Antonine.

But they did have some scary evidence at times.

Albrecht looked at the dome as they drove closer. Loba's Wyrm plot did not concern him now, however. The crown was what was important here.

Soon they pulled into the gravel drive outside the dome. Antonine was patiently waiting on the porch that encircled the dome, obviously expecting them. He was a middle-aged man, fit and healthy-looking with deeply tanned skin and a face which had seen much of the outdoors. He wore a red-checked flannel shirt, blue jeans and brown leather shoes.

As the pack got out of the car and walked over to him, Albrecht looked around. It was quite an impressive spread. Trees surrounded the dome and grew up right next to it, leaving a nice, shady canopy over the drive and the porch.

"Greetings," Antonine said as they reached the porch. "Hello, Albrecht and Mari. And how are you doing, Evan?"

"I'm fine, Antonine," Evan said, shaking the Stargazer's hand. "I want to thank you again for all your help during my Firsting."

Antonine smiled and nodded. He looked at Eliphas. "You must be Standish. Greyfist told me about you. Congratulations on your new post as Gatekeeper."

Eliphas looked unsure of how to respond. He was obviously a bit awed to be meeting the famed Stargazer. "Thank you. I... I am very pleased to meet you. I have long respected your wisdom."

Antonine's eyebrows raised at that. "Then you are a rare Garou." He turned back to the others. "Why don't you all come in? I have prepared a meal. Standish, I have a bed you can sleep on to rest for your journey home. The rest of you will not return with him. You have another place to go, a journey you must make on foot."

It was evening. The crescent moon was at the end of its waxing, close to becoming a half moon. The Philodox moon. The pack was gathered in Antonine's living room, at the center of the dome. Rooms opened off to the side, leading to bedrooms and a kitchen. Above them, encircling the ceiling, was a walkway. Windows lined it, each with a telescope and a small table with odd devices.

They sat on cushions on the floor, facing Antonine, who had a stack of books and scrolls before him. He had a pair of reading glasses on and was looking through some of the scrolls. The Garou had eaten a fine meal, some sort of exotic Indian dish, the recipe for which Antonine said had been given to him by a friend named Shakar, an excellent cook.

Albrecht wanted a cigarette, but he wasn't about to insult Antonine's hospitality by lighting up inside the dome. He sat back and tried to relax. Antonine seemed to notice his restlessness and put his scroll down.

"Let's begin," Antonine said. "Greyfist and I have spoken about the crown before. Frankly, I was surprised that it is actually lost. I am sure you are aware of the rumors that it has been well-hidden by the Silver Fang leadership?"

Albrecht rolled his eyes. "Uhm... can we just talk about where it is now?"

Antonine smiled. "I have done some reading. It is not easy to find written Garou records, but every once in a while an enlightened Garou scholar emerges who records what lore he can for those of us who are interested. I was sorry to hear that the North Country lost most of its records in a fire. But I believe I have discovered a source, a recent one, relatively speaking, which points to the possible fate of the crown."

Albrecht leaned forward. "Is this the *Lay of the Silver Crown* that Greyfist mentioned?"

"It is indeed. It was written in the late Renaissance by a Silver Fang Galliard...."

"I thought you said this was a recent source."

"I said 'relatively.' Understand that most of the written lore for the Silver Crown is truly ancient, older than Rome. It has fallen into common lore and become the source of many rumors and legends among the other tribes since then. But this *Lay* seems to be authentic and written by the last person to have seen the crown. At least, the last who has told of it. The author's name is Vassily Hearthcenter."

"I have heard of him," Eliphas said. "He is somewhat famous. Wasn't he a chronicler of the Clan of the Crescent Moon?"

"As far as I can tell, yes," Antonine said. "I will read you the *Lay*, but I am going to have to paraphrase much of it. The actual written language is a bit hard to understand if you're not familiar with its idiom. So, in the tradition of oral storytellers, I am going to take his story, mixed with what other lore I have concerning the crown, and tell my own tale. One which I believe aims sure at the truth."

Evan and Mari nodded. Albrecht said, "All right. Let's hear it."

Antonine took off his reading glasses and placed them in a case on the floor next to him. He folded his legs under himself and seemed to be meditating, centering himself for the tale.

"It begins, like all things, in the Dawn Times.... Long, long ago, before humans learned to think and their Weaver tools were but a dream unborn, the tribes of the Garou warred among themselves.

"There were few tribes then, but those there were had only come to their status recently. They had become separate from their brethren through migrations away from others of their kind, and the changes made on them by time and place. There was the blood of the original wolf, the Silver Fangs, and then many children who had strayed. The Children of Gaia spread far and wide and loved all which walked and crawled on and in the earth. The Get of Fenris went to the chill north to mold themselves into Fenris' hammer. The Fianna moved to the west, following the faint but beautiful music of the fae. And so on with the other early tribes.

"But it happened that they began to fight among themselves, either for right of territory, right of breeding flock, or simply for glory. They had fallen far from their first ways. The Silver Fangs, leaders of them all even then, tried to stop them, but the others would not listen. The Silver Fangs, purest of the pure, ordained to rule the Garou by Gaia, knew not what to do. They went to their totem, mighty Falcon, and asked of him a solution to their problem.

"Falcon's eyes gazed down at them, judging them. Finally, he spoke. 'One among you must choose to travel the road of sacrifice. On this road are four gates, and at each gate is a guardian who must be passed. If all gates are passed successfully, this one shall be given a boon greater than any given unto a mortal being before. He who bears this gift shall be king over all, and shall command all things of the earth to stay their proper courses, as is the will of Gaia.'

"The Fangs talked among themselves and finally decided that there was one among them who was best suited to travel the road. They went to him and told him of Falcon's words. He thought for a while, and then said, 'I shall undertake this quest. I so choose.' In the morning, he left.

"He walked for a long time, following the portents Falcon laid before him. Soon, he came to the first gate. It was but an opening in a rocky pass, with no portal to bar the way. The Garou looked about and saw no one, so he walked through the pass. But before he could get there, a beast leapt down upon him from the rocks. It was a Garou, a tribeless one, mad and snarling with rage. The Silver Fang shifted forms and fought with the ronin for a while. This was a strong ronin, one who ignored his wounds and kept fighting, as a mad thing with no control. Finally, the Silver Fang killed it, although he was hurt. He left its body there and went through the pass.

"The next day, he came to the second gate. This was a wooden fence with a door between two posts. There was a beautiful woman there, a human female. The Garou had never seen one so pure before, so perfect. He knew that she would birth many Garou if given the chance. Remembering Gaia's desire that the Garou spread their seed across the world, he got down to lie with her. He then saw a falcon fly high overhead, past the fence, and he remembered his quest. He stood up again and walked through the door, knowing that the comforts of hearth and family would not be his as long as the world was in danger."

"Is that really a part of the legend?" Mari said, her eyes narrowed.

Antonine chuckled. "Yes, I'm afraid so. They saw things differently back then, Mari."

"I'm not so sure. I know many legends where the hero was a female and only changed to a male by a later storyteller. This could be the case here."

"Perhaps. But I have no evidence for it. So I shall continue my tale based on what I do know.

"The following day, he came to the third gate. It was constructed of stone, but well made. It was an arch, with a gate under it. A spirit waited at the gate, holding a bag, out of which light glowed. It was looking in the bag as the Garou came up. When it saw the Garou it quickly sealed the bag, shutting up the light. The Garou asked what was in the bag, what the source of the wonderful light was. But the spirit said it was a secret, and that only the truly enlightened could look in to see it; otherwise the secret could destroy the world. The Garou said that he was the representative of his tribe, and thus the most enlightened among them. He asked to see into the bag. But the spirit said that he had to prove his enlightenment first, that he would have to come to the spirit's home and pass an initiation.

"Now, the wonderful glow within the bag had awakened a

great curiosity in the Garou. He desperately wanted to know what was in it. Perhaps it was something that could help his people? Perhaps it was the gift Falcon had spoken of? He had forgotten whether he had been through two gates or three. He was afraid that if he did not take the spirit's offer, he would be denied the special wisdom forever.

"Then he heard, from far ahead down the road, barely audible, the cry of a falcon. And he remembered his quest. He opened the gate and walked past, realizing that he would never know the secret but that others one day might.

"The day after that, he came to a great city. There was a huge portal before him, with two doors which opened outward when a large wheel inside was turned by ten men. Humans could be seen in the windows above, looking down at the Garou as he approached. He looked up at them and asked to be let in. They laughed and said that his kind did not belong there. They told him to go home and chase deer. He persisted, asking what he could do to get in. The humans talked among themselves and then said, 'You must give us your pelt.'

"The Garou was horrified. But he knew his quest. He knew he had taken the road of sacrifice. And so he nodded and said yes. The great doors opened, swinging slowly out at him with a rumbling, grinding sound. The humans came out with silver knives and carefully approached him. They stopped before him and said, 'We can't take your pelt if you have claws. We must cut them off first, to protect ourselves.' The Garou nodded and put out his hands. The humans chopped off the tips of his fingers, leaving him clawless.

"Then the humans said, 'You might still fight back as we take your pelt. You might bite us with your fangs.' He opened his mouth, and they took tongs and pulled out all his teeth. He was fangless. They then began to carve into his flesh, flaying off his hide. Soon, he was skinless and red, exposed to the world.

"They stared at him in awe, however, impressed with his

resolve and wondering at his mission. They led him into the city, closing the great doors behind them. They placed him on a chair and lifted it up, marching it to the center of the city, to a great palace. They walked him up the stairs and led him into a room where the sun shone down from a hole in the ceiling above.

"There, on a dais in the center of the room, was a gleaming crown, made of pure silver. Its brilliance under the sun nearly blinded the Garou, but he knew that this was the gift he sought. He asked the humans if he could have it, and they nodded, motioning him to the crown. He took it in his hands and placed it on his head.

"He screamed with the pain as its silver burned into his raw skin. He tried to yank the hurtful thing from his head, but it would not move. It had burned into him, and become a part of him. He cried in pain, tears blinding him, and he begged Falcon to save him.

"He heard a voice, one commanding him to open his eyes, and he did so. He was standing in a field at night. The city was nowhere to be seen, although he knew that he was still standing in the same place. The pain was gone, and his pelt had regrown, along with his fangs and claws. His head felt uplifted, drawn to the heavens by the lightness of the crown. Falcon stood before him, his wings wide.

"And Falcon said, 'You now know what the Garou must sacrifice to be more than beasts. But you also know that it is a painful sacrifice, one many will not be able to bear. Return to your people and rule them wisely. All Garou will follow you now. Know that the pain of sacrifice is only because your people have forgotten the ways given them by Gaia. Were it not so, sacrifice would not be necessary. Whenever your people forget, remember that one among you must bear the burden of pain to help them remember.'

"The Garou thanked Falcon and returned to the Silver Fangs. When they saw the radiant crown on his head, it was as if they recognized it immediately, and they knew again what they had once known: Gaia's covenants of behavior. The Garou, now known as king, traveled to the other tribes, and the sight of him brought remembrance of the old ways back to them all, and they ceased to fight among themselves and knew the Wyrm for what it was."

Antonine sat back. He shut his eyes and seemed to be resting.

Albrecht coughed. "What was the Silver Fang's name?"

Antonine slowly opened his eyes. "It is lost. He is simply the first king."

Albrecht nodded.

"That's quite a story," Evan said. "Very rich in symbolism."

"Deceptively so," Antonine said. "It seems very simple and obvious at first, but it actually touches some core meanings."

"Is there more?" Albrecht said. "What about the current location of the crown?"

"Yes, there is more. Let me get some drinks and I'll begin again." Antonine stood up and went into the kitchen. Soon he brought a tray of drinks out and placed it on the floor in the midst of them. "Help yourself. It's herbal tea."

Albrecht rolled his eyes. "Don't you have a beer?"

Antonine sat down again. "Yes, but you'll have to get it yourself."

Albrecht got up and went to the kitchen, where he opened the fridge and saw a six-pack of Samuel Adams. *At least the guy has taste in beer*, Albrecht thought. He took one and twisted the cap off, tossing it in the garbage can. He went back into the living room and sat down. "Thanks. Good beer."

"Of course," Antonine said. "Now, I'll finish. There are some other legends that I'll skip because of time. But there's one from somewhere around 300 B.C. or so that I think is important.

"A Silver Fang king named Ranix Hammer Claw ruled over a protectorate in what used to be called Gaul — France, today. He was known far and wide as a terrible leader, one who had squandered many of the treasures of his kingdom. So badly had he ruled, it is said, that even the spirits fled their fetishes when he touched them, fearful of being poorly used. His own warriors stayed away from him unless he commanded otherwise, for they feared his dictates.

"He often sent his Garou off on dangerous quests for little return. While the Wyrm grew all around his kingdom, he was unaware, so busy was he sending his warriors out in search of new treasures. One day, his warriors returned with a chest. They placed it before him, and he looked suspiciously at it, still chewing on the boar's hind leg upon which he was feasting. They said that it was by far the greatest treasure yet seen in any kingdom, and they had been astonished at how easily they had won it.

"They told the tale of its winning, of how they had come upon a dark glade in a sunny wood, and how three beasts attacked them there. One was a chimera, the legendary lion with the head of a dragon and a goat besides its own lion's head. The other was a great serpent with the head of a panther, whose eyes caused fear in all who met them. The third was a falcon.

"The men drove the other beasts off into the woods, but they were afraid to attack the falcon, since it was the child of their totem. It ceased its attack against them and spoke: 'Since you have honored your vow to my father and left me unharmed, I shall give you something.' It led them to a rock in the glade and told them to lift it. When they had it up, they saw a chest in a hole. They pulled the chest out and replaced the rock as they found it. The falcon was gone. When they opened the chest, they were all stunned by what they saw, and knew they had to bring it back to their king.

"The king sat forward on his throne of wood and hide, still chewing on his dinner, and told the warriors to open the chest. They did, and a silver brilliance shone forth from it. The king's mouth dropped wide; his half-chewed meat fell to the floor. He dropped the boar haunch and reached his greasy hands into the chest to pick up the Silver Crown, the long-legendary artifact of his tribe. He knew that if he wore it, everyone would obey him and would have to do as he wanted.

"He cackled and placed the crown on his head. But then he screamed in pain as it welded itself to his skull. And he kept on screaming, for the burning did not stop. His very flesh began to melt about the crown, and he tried to pull it off. But as with the first king before him, the crown was now a part of him, and could not be separated. His flesh ran down his face in molten gobs, and his bones began to burn. The smell of it revolted all the Garou near him, and many fled the tent. He screamed for someone to help him, but none would dare. Soon his body fell to the floor, dead, his head a pool of ashes and sizzling grease.

"The warriors stared at their dead king. The crown was missing from his head, gone. But they remembered what they had long forgotten: Gaia's covenants, the Litany, which included the right to overthrow unfit rulers. They were ashamed that they had so long followed such a fool, and swore they would not do so again."

Albrecht and Eliphas stared uncomfortably at the floor, aware of the parallels to their own situation.

Antonine continued. "The last part of the *Lay* which I will tell you is from Vassily Hearthcenter's own experience. It concerns Dmitri Spiral Slayer, the last known Silver Fang to wear the crown. There had been a terrible Wyrm uprising in Russia. Remember, this is the late Renaissance, probably the late sixteenth century or so. King Dmitri led a pack of Silver Fangs against the queen of the deformed Garou, leaving all his other warriors behind to defend their caern. He admonished them before he left not to follow him, for if the caern fell, their future generations would fall with it.

"Vassily went with the king's pack, to glean the tale of

their heroism. After many harrowing adventures, they fought their way to the throne room of the Black Spiral queen. But the hag fled into the spirit world, and Dmitri followed, alone. He followed her trail through the hell hole that surrounded her Umbral throne and finally cornered her before a pit of bubbling ichor. They fought, tooth and claw, each tearing the other to bloody pieces. Finally, the queen reached out to crush Dmitri's skull. When her hands touched the Silver Crown, she screamed in horror and yanked her hands back, but it was too late: her hands had been burnt to a crisp by the crown, and she pulled back stubs instead.

"Dmitri shoved the surprised and pained queen into the pit of boiling Wyrm's blood. That was the end of her. But Dmitri was sore wounded, and lay dying. He cried, for he knew that he had failed in one thing: the Silver Crown would be lost in this Wyrm place, fallen into the hands of the enemy.

"But then Vassily arrived, having followed the scent of his king here. He had also entered the spirit world, but it had taken him longer to thread the Gauntlet. The king, seeing his loyal vassal, wept tears of relief, and commanded Vassily to take the crown and hide it far away where no evil could reach it. All of the royal line were dead, and there were none of the Seven to take the crown after him. But Vassily hesitated to touch the great treasure, fearful it would burn him. Dmitri put his bloody hand on Vassily's shoulder and said, 'Fear not. You are but its bearer. Do not try to place it upon your head, and you shall not be harmed.' Vassily nodded and removed the crown from his king's head, whereupon Dmitri died.

"Vassily left that place, crying because he had to leave the body of his king behind where it could be defiled by Banes. But he had a duty. He traveled far, searching for a place to hide the crown. After many days, he found it. He hid the crown at the Dawn, in the Wyldest Garden."

Antonine shut his eyes, meditating again.

Albrecht sat up from his slouching. "That doesn't tell us

anything. Where the hell is the Dawn? I've never heard of it as a place. Or of any Wyld garden."

Antonine slowly opened his eyes again. "It is what Vassily left behind. It is his only clue. I think I know what place he is talking about."

"Where?" Albrecht said.

"Pangaea," Antonine replied.

"That makes sense," Mari said. "It is the most primordial place in the spirit world. It has the magic of the earliest times in it. All Garou are said to revert back to an earlier form when they enter it."

"What? Sort of like in the film *Altered States*?" Albrecht said.

Mari scowled at him. "No. I mean that the laws of reality work differently there. Things are more primitive, less formed. The Wyld is stronger, and the Weaver is but a shadow."

"I see. The Wyldest Garden. A sort of Garden of Eden for Garou."

"Exactly," Antonine said. "If you'll remember the first story, it took place in a Pangaea-like environment, except for the Weaver gates and city. I think Vassily was trying to hide it where it had originally come from."

"Don't forget," Mari said, "it's a very dangerous place. The only rule is that everything there is hungry, and there are bigger things on the food chain than Garou."

"Sounds like a challenge," Albrecht said. "So we go to Pangaea. How do we find the crown from there? It's a pretty big place, isn't it?"

"It's huge," Mari said. "As big as this continent, at least."

"Great! We're supposed to spend years finding this thing?"

"These are the only clues I have," Antonine said, standing up. "I believe that you will find the legends I told you instructive along the way. Simply look for the gates. Remember that in the spirit world, things are not as they seem."

"Well, I guess that makes sense," Albrecht said. "Look, thanks for everything you've done. Without you, we wouldn't even know where to begin."

"My pleasure," Antonine said. "I think we should rest now. You're going to need a lot of sleep; you've got a long walk ahead of you. I advise you to leave tomorrow night. The Moon Paths will be faint by day, making travel dangerous."

They nodded and went to the guest bedrooms, each of them reflecting on the tale they had heard. Only Albrecht remained in the living room, stretching out on the floor cushions. There weren't enough guest beds, so he had volunteered to take the floor.

He stretched out and looked at the ceiling as he heard the bedroom doors shut and saw the lights go out. There was a window right above him, and the stars shone clear against the darkness. He hoped he had what it took to wear the crown, and made a silent prayer to Gaia for Her to look favorably upon him. He then rolled over to sleep, but he was plagued by nightmares the whole night. Visions of his hands burning off, or his skull igniting, and a sharp band of pain around his head.

CHAPTER TEN

"You take care of yourself, Eliphas," Albrecht said, looking down at the young Silver Fang who sat in the driver's seat of the car.

Eliphas smiled at him. "Good luck, Lord Albrecht. I hope you succeed. For all our sakes." He turned the ignition key and the engine purred to life.

Albrecht stepped back and waved. "So do I. Don't worry. I always come through in the end."

Eliphas nodded. He accelerated down the gravel drive and drove off into the darkening day as the sun went down. Moments later, he was gone. Albrecht walked back into the dome. The others were gathered in the living room, packing for the journey. They had all brought backpacks, rations and changes of clothes with them. They had been on long jaunts in the spirit world before and knew what they needed to survive. Albrecht went over and sat down with them. Pulling his own pack over, he began taking inventory.

Antonine was walking around the room, searching through the bookcases which lined the walls. He had a stack of books in his hand. When he seemed to have found everything he needed, he went into his study, a room near the kitchen.

"What's he up to?" Albrecht said.

"I think he's making a map," Evan said.

"To Pangaea?" Albrecht said.

"Yes," Mari said. "I have been there before, but it was by a... longer route than we need now. Antonine is trying to put together a good map of signposts to look for."

"Like what?" Albrecht said. "I thought the Wyld nature of the place prevented mapping."

"True, the closer you get to it. But we have a way to go before reaching the realm itself. Any shortcut we can find will help greatly."

Albrecht nodded. "You're the Theurge. I'll trust that."

Mari nodded. "Finally thinking sensibly."

Evan smiled at both of them. He was glad they weren't shouting at each other yet. He knew that would come later, but for now they were getting along.

Albrecht zipped up his pack and placed it before him. "Done. Clothes, sleeping bag, food, water. Do we need anything else?"

Evan was also finishing his pack, and Mari had already finished hers. "I can't think of anything," he said.

Mari shook her head. "I think we've got it covered."

Antonine came out of his study with a parchment. He walked over and sat down next to them, handing the paper to Mari. "This is the best I can do. It's based on some accounts I have of journeys to Pangaea, along with hearsay from friends of mine. You should do okay by it. Remember, though, that you're departing under the half moon, so the Moon Paths will be somewhat faint and incomplete, and the Lune spirits will not be guarding all of them. Travel will be dangerous at times. However, I believe this place here" — he pointed at a spot on the map — "is a Lunae, a crossroads of Moon Paths, where you should be able to rest for the day. You will need to find as many of these as you can along the way. I don't recommend taking shelter in a realm, since you might not know the laws under which it operates before entering. The last thing you need is to get caught in a sub-realm and waste a few days trying to get out. However, it would be worse to stray off the paths; you'd easily get lost without them to guide you."

"Thanks," Mari said. "It's pretty self-explanatory. I can use this. A very complete job in such a short amount of time."

Antonine nodded and stood up. "The sun's almost set. I think it's safe for you to leave now."

The pack stood up and shouldered their bundles. Antonine led them outside and around behind the dome to a small field. He looked about and stopped, turning back to them. "This is a good spot. I've used it many times before. Mari? Do you want to lead us in?"

"Certainly," Mari said, stepping next to him. The others followed her and gathered around in a circle, all touching her. She held a small mirror up and looked into it, moving it about to catch the final rays of the sun peeking through the trees. When she was satisfied with the reflection, she stared into it. She reached out with her spirit to connect to the spirit world. Once she touched it, she pulled herself toward it. Or did it pull itself to her? Many Garou had argued that point. In any case, the Gauntlet wrapped about them and then parted as it passed. They all stood in the Penumbra, the spiritual shadow of the physical world.

The field looked very much the same on this side as on the other. It was darker here, since the sun did not shine at all. The half moon was clearly visible in the sky.

Albrecht looked around and saw part of Antonine's house beyond the trees. It looked different. Webs were spread across it, but in a very beautiful, almost chaotic pattern, as if the spider creating it had had an aesthetic purpose when weaving it. *That is weird,* Albrecht thought. *The Weaver and Wyld in balance. Quite rare.*

"I think that path is best," Antonine said, pointing down a small, one-person-wide path that disappeared into the woods. "If you follow it long enough, it leads to a Moon Path. At least, it used to. In the physical world it leads to a small pond, but I've never found the pond from this side. Just follow any signs of brighter moonlight. The Lune spirits will be there. Remember, stick to the Moon Paths: without Luna's guidance, you may never find Pangaea."

"Thank you again, Antonine," Mari said, shaking his hand.

"Yeah, you've been a lot of help," Evan said.

"Don't think anything of it," Antonine said. "I am doing what is important."

Albrecht walked up to him and put out his hand. "If this crazy plan actually works, then I'll certainly remember your help when I'm king."

Antonine smiled and shook his hand. "Just be a good king, Albrecht. Remember the *Lay of the Silver Crown*. Heed it."

"Of course. I'm kind of fond of my skull."

Antonine chuckled and walked off. "You had better get going. You have little time."

"We're off," Albrecht said, turning to the path. Mari was already ahead of him, and Evan had stepped in between them. Stopping at the edge of the woods, Albrecht looked up at the moon. *Well, Luna,* he thought. *Don't get crazy on me here. Help me out. All right?*

He then turned and walked into the woods, falling in behind Evan.

Greyfist looked up at the half moon and felt the strengthening of his spirit, a gift from Luna on the night of his birth auspice. He was a Philodox, and the half moon was his moon. He thought about Albrecht and his pack. He hoped Antonine had been able to help them. Had they left yet? Were they walking the spirit world now?

There was a knock at the door. Greyfist turned from the

window and sat down at his desk. "Come in."

The door opened and Arkady appeared. He walked into the room and shut the door behind him. "Good evening, Seneschal."

Greyfist was surprised, wondering what the king-in-waiting wanted with him. "Greetings, Arkady."

Arkady walked across the room and stood before the desk, looking around the room. "I have never been here. It is a nice office. You have many... books. Have you read them all?"

Greyfist tried to hide his look of annoyance. Non-readers always asked that stupid question. "No, I haven't. They are mostly for reference. It is what remains of the protectorate's library after the fire."

"Ah, yes," Arkady said, sitting down on the couch. "I had forgotten. It is good you have saved them. You are very loyal."

Greyfist did not respond. He simply looked at Arkady, waiting for him to reveal his purpose in coming.

Arkady sat back and smiled. "You are wondering why I have come? I should not...what? Mince words? I am here to find out what Lord Albrecht's plans are since losing our combat."

Greyfist's eyebrows rose. "Plans? You made it clear that he is no longer welcome. He's gone back to New York, to whatever life he had during the exile."

Arkady looked at Greyfist, not saying anything. Then he sat forward. "You must understand my position, Seneschal. He was a threat to my ascension. I did what I had to. I bear him no personal ill will."

Greyfist opened a drawer and pulled out his pipe. He knew Arkady was lying. A bald-faced lie. As a Philodox, the spirits had gifted him with the insight to tell truth from fiction.

"But I am worried," Arkady continued. "I suspect that he will try to sabotage my rule on the throne."

Greyfist lit his pipe. "Why do you think that? It was hard enough convincing him to try for the throne in the first place.

Why do it again after losing so ignominiously?"

"Yes, why?" Arkady said. "That is what I have asked myself. It makes no sense. There is no way he can take the throne by law. And to break the law is not to be king. So what could he be attempting?"

Greyfist sat back and puffed on his pipe. "I would say that he is attempting to get shit-faced drunk right about now. As he probably did last night."

Arkady's smile disappeared. "I heard that Eliphas Standish drove him back. But Eliphas has not returned yet."

"Albrecht probably dragged him out for a night on the town before returning to the caern."

"I doubt that. The Gatekeeper is a very dedicated young man. I cannot see him willingly forsaking his new duties here for a simple drunken binge."

Greyfist did not say anything. He just puffed on his pipe.

Arkady stood up. "I know that you had both Albrecht and Eliphas in here after the combat. What did you talk about?"

Greyfist's eyes narrowed. "Personal business. Why are you so curious, Arkady? If you have a problem with Albrecht, why don't you go to New York and take it up with him?"

"Because he is not in New York, is he?" Arkady said, stepping forward and putting his hands on the desk. "Where is he? Where has he gone?"

Greyfist stood up. He did not like the looks of this. Arkady was beginning to look flustered. Greyfist recognized the signs of a frayed temper: Arkady was close to losing control of his anger. Was he really so paranoid about Albrecht?

"Get out of here, Arkady," Greyfist said. "Come back when you can control your rage."

"You cannot order me around, Seneschal," Arkady said, leaning forward, eyes glinting.

"Yes I can. I am seneschal, and you are an uncrowned king-in-waiting. You will do as I say, cub."

Arkady stood there, breathing heavily, his shoulders

shaking. He was obviously trying to control his anger. Greyfist walked around the desk, toward the door. Arkady grabbed his shoulder and pulled his face inches from his own.

"You *will* tell me what conspiracy you and Albrecht have thought up!" Arkady said.

Greyfist put his hand on Arkady's and pried it off his arm. "Get out!"

Arkady exploded into action. His fist slammed into Greyfist's chin, knocking the Philodox to the ground. Arkady was in Crinos form before Greyfist could react, jumping on Greyfist, bearing him down. Arkady's weight knocked the wind out of the seneschal, but he concentrated and shifted to Crinos form. Arkady still had leverage and size over him; Greyfist was pinned down. Arkady held his right claw to Greyfist's throat while he reached into his pocket for something with the other hand.

"Get off me, Arkady," Greyfist said through gritted teeth. "Before you bring a rite of censure upon yourself!"

"Shut up," Arkady said, pulling a bug out of his pocket. The creature looked like nothing Greyfist had ever seen. It flexed its tiny, chitinous legs as it dangled from Arkady's fingers. Arkady then grabbed Greyfist's chin and pulled it open. Too quickly for Greyfist to stop him, Arkady thrust the bug into Greyfist's mouth and down his throat. He let the Philodox go, jumping away from him.

Greyfist coughed violently, straining to vomit up the bug. His body began to shift back to Homid form, even though he tried to stop it. What the hell was Arkady doing? What had he put into him? He could vaguely feel the thing moving — crawling — down his throat. He choked out a few words, "You… will… suffer… for this!"

"Tell me, Seneschal," Arkady said, standing behind Greyfist. "What plot are you and Albrecht hatching?"

Greyfist stood up and started to speak, to tell Arkady to go fuck himself. But the words would not come out. Instead, he felt a quivering in his gut, which traveled up his spine and into his brain. He couldn't help himself as he said, "Albrecht is after the Silver Crown."

Arkady's eyes slowly opened wide. "But that is a myth! A legend! No Silver Fang has worn the crown in... in ages!"

Greyfist tried to move toward the door, but he couldn't. His legs wouldn't work. "What... what the hell is this thing?"

"It is a gift from an... ally," Arkady said. "One who knew you would not tell me what I needed to know. Conspiracy against the throne is a very serious charge, Seneschal."

"Damn you! No one has conspired. You are not king yet!"

"Oh, but soon. Soon," Arkady said. "Now, where has Albrecht gone?"

"To Antonine Teardrop."

Arkady's face fell into a frown. "Why did you involve him? He will tell Loba! She is an exile! You are delivering protectorate secrets to outsiders."

"You know that's not true," Greyfist said, feeling dizzy. "You're fishing for accusations. It won't work. You've attacked the seneschal in his own den. I will have a rite against you, Arkady."

Arkady growled. "We will see who wields more power here, Seneschal. Where is Albrecht going from Teardrop's?"

"I don't know," Greyfist said, feeling sick to his stomach. He collapsed onto the floor.

Arkady looked worried. "What do you mean, you don't know? Surely you know where the crown is, if you sent him off for it? Why are you on the floor?"

"I... feel... terrible. What the hell did you put in me?"

Arkady looked very worried now. "Put your finger down your throat! Throw the thing up!"

Greyfist growled in pain, clutching his stomach. "It's a Wyrm creature, isn't it?"

"No!" Arkady said, leaning down over him. "It's just a fetish to make you answer my questions. It had no Wyrm scent on it."

Greyfist looked at Arkady angrily and then growled low and menacingly, looking past the Silver Fang. Arkady turned around to see a large Crinos Black Spiral Dancer step from the Umbra, grinning madly.

"Damn you!" Arkady yelled at the Dancer. "What is your fetish doing to him?"

"Killing him slowly and painfully," the Black Spiral Dancer replied, sauntering over to them.

Greyfist grabbed the fur about Arkady's throat and pulled his head around. He locked eyes with Arkady. "You bastard! You've betrayed the throne to the Wyrm!"

Arkady looked surprised. "No.... No! He was not supposed to come here. I did not intend this!"

Greyfist growled and tried to dig his claws into Arkady's throat, but a sudden pain washed over his body. He grabbed his gut again and howled as blood broke forth from a wound opening out of his stomach. The Wyrm bug crawled its way out of the wound, chewing the flesh around the edges. Arkady stared at it in horror.

Greyfist's eyes rolled up into his head and he collapsed. With the last of his strength, he whispered to Arkady, "You are doomed. Albrecht will find the crown and become the true king."

Arkady stared in shock at the seneschal. He carefully put his hand on the Garou's shoulder and shook it. But there was no response. Greyfist was dead.

Arkady turned around to see the Black Spiral Dancer smirking down at him. "Dagrack! How dare you? We had a bargain! You have betrayed me!" He rose and pointed a clawed hand at the Garou.

Dagrack shrank, assuming Homid form. He stood about five foot eleven, with black hair streaming over his shoulders. He had a long, thin face, but a smile which spread practically from ear to ear. He held up his hands, cautioning Arkady. "Now, now, ally. You misunderstand. I am only helping you in ways you have not yet realized. Did you really think you could interrogate the seneschal like that, and not have to kill him afterwards? I'm only saving you from him."

"But why did you come here? If the others see—"

"Calm down your wayward temper, O king," Dagrack said. "The Gatekeeper is gone, remember? No one saw me pass over. We will now proceed to stage a scene. You came to talk with the seneschal, and things were going just fine, when a horrible Black Spiral Dancer — me — came leaping from the Umbra. Using its forbidden and unholy Wyrm powers, it killed the seneschal. And cut you up badly before fleeing, wounded by your mighty blows."

Arkady clutched his fists and stared angrily at the wall. "No. I do not like this one bit. You think you can take control of me now because we have bargained. It is not so. I will not allow it. I did not wish the seneschal dead. He was loyal! He would have been loyal to me!"

"Untrue," Dagrack said, walking over to Greyfist's body. He reached down and picked up the bug, putting it in his pants pocket. "He was trying to dethrone you before you had even worn the crown! You call that loyal?"

"I will not listen to you!" Arkady shouted.

Dagrack walked up and looked him in the eyes. "Oh yes, you will. Who was it who saved you all those years ago from the fomori slavering for your blood, back in the Motherland? Who helped you escape to this new land, a land where you have built yourself a base of power? You are to be king! And you have gotten here because of my aid. I have told you before, our goals are not dissimilar. It is because of the Fangs' witchhunt against my tribe that we cannot work together to heal the damage to Gaia, to war against her true enemies."

"Stop it! I do not want to hear this. Lies! You think your stupid logic will convince me?"

"If you don't believe it, why have you accepted our aid for so long? It wasn't my Garou who failed to kill Albrecht. If your two exiled flunkies had done their job, you wouldn't be in this mess now, and I wouldn't have to bail you out."

Arkady fumed, silent. He stared at Greyfist's dead body.

"Enough of this," Dagrack said. "We must bloody ourselves, and I must escape, before more Garou come."

"What if I do more than bloody you? What if I kill you and show the trophy to the tribe?"

Dagrack smiled. "Then my packbrothers and sisters will do everything in their power to reveal your treachery against the Silver Fangs. You will become a pariah, worse than your hated Albrecht. No Garou will trust you then. At least Albrecht has the Bone Gnawers to feed him. You... you will feed only with the lost."

Arkady glared at Dagrack as if trying to decide his course. He then lowered his head.

"What do I need to do?" Arkady asked.

"First," Dagrack said, opening his shirt as he walked up to Arkady, "slash me across the chest. And then across the thigh. Oh, and a head wound would be good, too. After that, I'll rip you up a bit, so you'll have some wounds to show for it. I'll drip the blood all over before I leave."

Arkady slashed out at Dagrack, hard and fiercely, cutting open his chest. Blood sprayed forth.

"Oh," Dagrack said, his eyes rolling up with what seemed like pleasure. "A bit more than necessary, but good anyway. Now, the thigh."

Arkady was disgusted. He stepped back from the Dancer. "No. There is enough of your blood here now. They will believe me."

"Not without this, they won't," Dagrack said, reaching his claw out quickly and slashing Arkady across the shoulder. Arkady grimaced, but didn't move. "One more." He slashed Arkady's left thigh, where a scar from the challenge combat two nights ago was still visible. Arkady winced and stared coldly at the Dancer.

Dagrack smiled. "Well, I'm off. Don't worry, I'll dispatch some packs to hunt down Albrecht. He won't get far." The Dancer stared at his spilled blood on the floor, leaning down close, looking for reflections within it. He stared so for nearly five minutes, and then faded out of view, into the Umbra.

Arkady kicked a chair and cursed. He looked down at Greyfist. "I am sorry, Seneschal. I never meant this. Take this condolence: I will not be pushed around so for long. I will turn the tables. It has always been my plan. It is hard to understand, I know. But... you have no idea of the horrors in Russia. How hard it is to escape. Can you think? How many have slipped past the Shadow Curtain besides me? None. I am the only one. But... a bargain was required. I will turn the tables, Seneschal. Believe that."

He then walked to the door, opened it, and howled long and hard. The Warning of the Wyrm's Approach.

CHAPTER ELEVEN

The pack traveled down the curve of the shining road. The Moon Path reflected the radiance of the half moon above them, faint near the edges, but brighter in the center. In certain places along the road, the path actually broke up, forcing them to walk on the dark, nondescript ground between the shards of moonlight. The unformed ephemera — raw spirit — was all that could be seen in every direction around them. Their only marker was the path.

Occasionally they passed a Lune, one of the guardian spirits of the Moon Paths, gliding by on its mysterious errand. The mobile strips of moonlight spun slowly around and around as they moved past, in some unfathomable form of communication. Even Mari, who knew the language of the spirits, was puzzled. Lunes were among the most enigmatic of spirits, especially during a crescent moon. But even under a half moon, the Lunes were strange.

The pack let the Lunes pass and kept on their way. They traveled for hours, each chewing on his or her own thoughts, not sharing them with the others. The Moon Path cut through many small domains, but the pack stayed their course. As long as they remained on the Moon Path, they were relatively safe from whatever spirits laired in the domains into which they trespassed. Safe also from the odd laws of nature which were often different in each domain or realm of the spirit world. Reality was a local phenomenon here, not the shared fact known in the material world.

In one domain — a chimare, a mortal's dream given reality — they saw a man leap from a skyscraper. He fell for a long time — longer than the height should have allowed. His family and friends gathered on the street below, staring up at him and gossiping about his predicament. Before he hit the ground, the chimare unravelled and became featureless ephemera again.

The pack kept walking. Later, after passing through a mountainous mini-realm, Mari stopped and consulted the map. "I think the Lunae is just ahead. Maybe forty minutes at the most."

"I hope so," Albrecht said, pointing to the horizon. "The moon has almost set. It'll be dark in half an hour. I don't want to be out here much longer after that. Once this Moon Path goes, we're lost."

"The paths soak up light, though," Evan said. "This one should hold the light, like one of those glow-in-the-dark toys, for at least long enough for us to get to the Lunae."

"Well, let's get moving anyway," Albrecht said, walking again. "The Moon Paths are our only fixed geography. Everything else here changes so much, we'd never find our way to Pangaea in time without them."

Mari nodded, folded the map, put it in her pocket and moved on, with Evan behind her.

Half an hour later, the moon had indeed set and all was dark, except for a slight radiance from the Moon Path. Albrecht shifted into Lupus form, his backpack shrinking to conform to his new shoulder width. He had performed the Rite of Talisman Dedication on all of his equipment, allowing it to change shape to accommodate his various forms. Mari and

Evan followed suit and each of them walked down the path on four legs. They made better time that way, and soon Albrecht could see a light over the next rise. As he came over it, he saw a large, glowing circle of light. Bisecting it crossways to their Moon Path was another Moon Path. A crossroads.

"This is it," Albrecht said. "The Lunae. Antonine was right."

"Let's go," Evan said, sprinting forward.

"Wait," Mari said. "Let me go first. There may be other spirits there. We don't want to pick a fight by just walking in."

Evan slowed down and let Mari pass him.

"Let us know when it's okay to go in," Albrecht said.

"I will," Mari said, shifting to Glabro form. She stepped into the circle of light, disappearing from view. Albrecht and Evan shifted back to Homid form and waited at the edge. The Moon Path was fainter, as was the other one bisecting the circle, but they weren't worried now. If worst came to worst, they'd step into the Lunae and deal with whatever was there. Regardless of the spirits there, the Lunes would intercede in any fights. But no one wanted that. That kind of intercession could lead to anything: most often the antagonists popping up in some strange realm far away, transported there by the angry Lunes.

Mari, now in Homid form, poked her head out and motioned them in. They stepped into the circle and blinked at the brightness. When their eyes had adjusted, they saw a large, silver-white glade, with a single white tree and a lawn of white grass surrounding it. Three Lunes glided slowly about, like helium balloons set loose on a random course. A crow perched in the tree and cawed at them as they came through.

"That's Ivan," Mari said. "He's a naturae spirit taking haven here for the day while traveling the airts. Don't worry about him."

Albrecht nodded and walked to the base of the tree.

Shrugging his pack off, he sat down, pulled out a cigarette and lit it up. Slowly taking a drag, he leaned back, smiling, then let out a cloud of smoke. *That's the ticket,* he thought. *Nothing like a good smoke after a long walk.*

Evan walked over and dropped his pack. After untying his sleeping bag and spreading it out, he lay down and rolled over. He was asleep in seconds. Mari was watching the Lunes, trying to fathom their movements. She gave up after a few minutes and came over to the tree, sitting down next to Albrecht.

"I haven't done a walk like that in a long time," she said.

"Me neither," Albrecht said, still smoking. "It's hell on the feet. I think we should travel in Lupus more often."

Mari sighed. "I guess. I prefer Homid or Glabro, however. I fight better that way."

"You can always shift if you need to."

"I know, but... I'd like to be ready for anything."

"You're pretty paranoid, aren't you? I don't mean in the conspiracy-theory sense, but in the... distrusting sense. You seem to think there's always someone out there ready to pop you one."

"So? In my experience, there is. The world is cruel to the unwary, Albrecht."

"Yeah, I guess it is. But going around always expecting the worst... I don't know. It seems like a waste of energy to me."

"And sucking in toxic fumes, like that cigarette you have there, isn't? Someone in this pack has to be ready in case of attack."

"Okay, okay. Don't bite my head off. Just trying some small talk is all. I'm going to crash. See you tomorrow."

"I'll take first watch. I'll wake you for the second."

"Watch? We don't need a watch. The Lunes'll warn us if anything dangerous approaches."

"We can't depend on that—"

"Yes we can. We are in a Lunae, Mari. A crossroads of Moon Paths. Luna herself protects these. If something were to happen here, believe me, we'd have enough time to deal with it. So go to bed. And don't wake me up for a stupid watch." Albrecht lay down on the grass. He rubbed his cigarette into the ephemeral dirt and put the stub in his pocket. He then rolled over and was snoring in less than five minutes.

Mari looked around for a while. When she was satisfied that the place was safe, she spread out her bedroll and lay back on it. Even with her eyes closed, it took her a while to get to sleep. Every time the crow on the branches above moved, she started, expecting danger. But she finally forced herself to ignore it, and was soon asleep.

As the moon rose the next evening, they packed up their bags and left the Lunae. The crow was already gone, presumably having left at the first crack of moonrise. They traveled down the same Moon Path, but this time they were in Lupus form from the beginning of their journey. It did make for better time, and they traveled farther than they had expected by the next morning, when the sun rose in the material world and the moon set in their world.

An hour before moonset, they had seen no sign of another Lunae.

"I think we've got to take the next domain we find," Albrecht said. "We can't stay out here. It's too unpredictable."

"And a domain isn't?" Mari said.

"Less so than the barrens between realms with no Moon Path," Albrecht said, looking at her.

She stared back at him. "What do you suggest?"

"The first thing we come upon, that's what," Albrecht said.

"Hey!" Evan called. He was a few paces ahead of them, bending to the ground. "There are some tracks here. Rabbit, I think."

Mari brightened up. "There must be a Glen nearby. I can't imagine a rabbit wandering so far otherwise."

"Let's keep our eyes out then," Albrecht said, continuing on down the road. The others followed him.

Ten minutes later, they saw the Glen. It was thirty yards to their right, off the Moon Path. It was unmistakable. The scent of grass and pollen wafted across the barrens to them. They could see the vague outline of trees from the path. After looking carefully around, they set out for it, stepping off the path, staying close to each other. Soon, they were within the boundary of the Glen, a sub-realm within the spirit world, a pocket reality which followed the laws of nature known in the material world. Of the many geographies in the Umbra — realms, domains, sub-realms, Moon Paths — Glens were perhaps the most normal; a welcome respite from the weird rules of the spirit world.

They all breathed a sigh of relief and looked around. It wasn't a very big place, perhaps five acres square, but it was lush. Trees grew up around a small clearing in the center, and a babbling brook ran across it, entering from nowhere on one side and exiting to nowhere on the other. Albrecht wondered what would happen to something that was placed in the stream. Where would it float to?

Signs of small fauna could be seen, such as rabbit tracks and mouse prints. They walked around the place, making sure that everything smelled right, that the scent of the Wyrm was nowhere to be found. Satisfied with the purity of the place, they gathered in the clearing by the brook.

"I wonder what created this place," Albrecht said. "It's awfully weird to find it here."

"It was planted on purpose," Evan said.

"How do you know that?" Mari said, looking around for signs of intention.

"That tree over there," Evan said, pointing at the largest of the trees surrounding the clearing. "It has a pictogram on it. It says that this place was planted by a traveling pack of Children of Gaia."

"Well, that was awfully nice of them," Albrecht said. "Now we know it's all sweet and cozy here. That explains the cute bunny rabbits."

"Albrecht!" Mari said. "It's because of their forethought that we have a place to rest tonight. They don't deserve your mocking."

Albrecht nodded, holding his hands up toward Mari. "I know, I know. I'm just a cynical bastard, that's all. I'll shut up."

They ate their dinner in silence and then pulled out their packs and went to sleep. This time, however, Mari took the watch. She woke Albrecht in the middle of the day to tell him it was his turn. He nodded and got up, not bothering to argue with her. Surprised, she crawled under her slight covers. Although she was suspicious of danger, she knew she needed sleep for the next leg of their journey, and soon went to sleep. She slept lightly, though, having taught herself to wake at a moment's notice.

Albrecht sat by the brook, thinking about their journey. He had no clue where to start looking once they reached Pangaea. And if the crown wasn't there, what would they do then?

He heard the scuffle of a small creature moving through the underbrush on the other side of the stream. The rabbit came out and stared at Albrecht. Albrecht nodded at it. It quivered its nose and hopped back into the brush.

Albrecht looked up at the sky. He could see stars, which surprised him, although they were faint, as if they were very far off. Albrecht realized that this Glen looked up into the Aetherial Realm, the realm where the sky spirits resided. The place where Moon Bridges crossed. He wondered what Garou were now passing through those stars on their way to caerns all over the earth.

He sat thinking about such things for the rest of the day, until the moon rose again.

They took to the Moon Path again that night. After they had walked for many hours, the path began to curve wildly, and the ephemeral landscape around them started to change. Hills rose up and down; fields rippled and moved under a nonexistent wind. Wisps of cloud floated past them, ephemera that couldn't decide if they were clouds or fog banks.

"We are very near," Mari said. "The signs of the Wyld are all about us."

"How far do you figure it is?" Albrecht asked, looking about nervously. The Moon Path had already broken up twice. He hoped it could stay together far enough to get them to Pangaea.

"Who can say?" Mari said.

They kept walking. The moon was low on the horizon when they came around a large hill, and stepped into sunlight and a primordial jungle. They looked around, surprised. They had seen no sign of the realm, but suddenly they were there, standing in Pangaea. The musky jungle smells overwhelmed them after the day's walk in a largely scentless environment.

"Wow," said Evan. "So this is it?"

"Yes," Mari said, stepping forward to peer through the thick stand of trees before them. "Look here! Between these trees."

They all stepped up and looked. Beyond the trees, the landscape fell downwards, a vegetative cliff face. The vista from here was astonishing. Laid out before them was a land from an earlier time, a primal forest of Jurassic plants. A place humans could only imagine. But here, for the pack, it was real.

Pterodactyls glided far out over the huge sea which encompassed the horizon to their right. Herds of prehistoric antelope could be seen farther off, roaming across a grassland plain. Behind the pack, through the stand of trees that now hid the Moon Path, the land rose up, and they could see mountains with pine forests along their bases. The clash of geographical regions was remarkable.

And the marks of civilization were nowhere to be seen; not a hint or clue of them. No roads, no buildings, no litter. No sound of cars or machines in the distance. Only far-off bird cries and the hum of insects. The thrashing of huge beasts in the forests. Nothing but nature, pure and untrammelled.

"Gaia...." Albrecht murmured. "It's incredible. It really is as amazing as they say." He turned to look at the other two and saw them staring speechlessly at the landscape. Something deep within him — within them, too — was stirring. Something ancient and primal, some deep sense of wonder and belonging. He had a sense that, somehow, regardless of his city ways, he was home. They were all home.

"Do you feel it?" Albrecht said. "I don't know, some sense of... belonging."

"Yes," Mari said. "All my senses are awake, even in Homid form. It's as if all my instincts were alive, as if they had finally found an outlet."

"It's great!" Evan said. "Far more real than any Boy Scout outing."

Albrecht looked at him and shook his head. "If that's all you've got to compare it to, you need to get out more."

"I *am* out," Evan said. "I think I can truly say, as none of us have ever been able to say before, that I am *out*. I am outside!"

Mari laughed. She looked about them, at the trees and the ground. "Look here. Dinosaur tracks."

Albrecht looked and saw what indeed looked like dinosaur tracks, although small ones. *One of those egg-stealers*, he thought. *But if the small ones can be here, so can the big*. "You know, I just thought of something. The legends about this place say there are dinosaurs. Big dinosaurs. Dinosaurs who eat Garou."

Mari and Evan looked at him.

"I mean, we need to be careful. It's fine and dandy to enjoy it all, but we've really got to be on our toes here. This is primal. That means dog-eat-dog. What Mari said about the food chain here is right: we're not the highest point on it."

"Correct," Mari said. "We should not let our guard down. It *is* dangerous here."

Evan looked disappointed, but nodded.

"Now," Albrecht said. "We've got to figure out where in this jungle to look for the Silver Crown."

"I've been thinking," Evan said. "We should start with the legends about this place. What does the Silver Record say?"

"I don't know," Albrecht said. "I thought you were more familiar with that. It's a Philodox and Galliard thing, isn't it?"

"It's our history," Mari said, staring scornfully at Albrecht. "We should all be familiar with it. Especially a king."

"I think there is something," Evan said. "I'm not sure. There's a line about the Litany. How does it go? Uh.... 'A Grand Moot of all Garou was called at Table Rock. All gathered from all over the world in a night's time where they were one Tribe, and the Galliards chanted the first Litany. From sunrise to sundown they repeated the words until all present could remember.'"

"That's pretty good, kid," Albrecht said. "How'd you remember all that?"

"We live in an oral culture, Albrecht. It's our duty to remember these things. Not everyone can keep records like Antonine."

"Well, what do you think it means? I didn't hear a mention of Pangaea there."

"That's just it: there's no direct reference. But that line about 'where they were one Tribe.' At a place called Table Rock. I think that's here. Don't you remember the other stories, the ones that say that all Garou are of one tribe when they enter Pangaea?"

"I've heard those, but I don't believe them. How can we

lose our tribehood? It's inherent."

"But this is the Umbra, Albrecht," Mari said. "Anything can happen here. Landscapes and identities are fluid. Nothing is set."

"Fine. Let's assume Table Rock is here. What then?"

"Well, it seems to me that it would be a good place to hide the crown," Evan said. "If the record is correct, that is the place where Garou civilization began, with the Litany, Gaia's covenants. If it's not there, then surely a clue will be."

Albrecht nodded. "All right. Sounds like a starting point. Where do we go? Where is Table Rock?"

"I don't know," Evan said, looking around. "I don't have the slightest idea of where to start."

"Well," Mari said. "Where would Garou gather? Table Rock has to be someplace hospitable for Garou."

Albrecht looked out across the vista behind them. "Do you see that? Way out there, to the... north, I guess it is? It looks like a pine forest. I think that's where we'll find wolves. And where there are wolves...."

Mari nodded. "Let's head that way."

"How long a walk do you figure?" Evan asked.

"At least a half-day," Mari said.

"Assuming no interruptions," Albrecht said, walking off into the forest.

Their wonder increased as they went. After a while, the woods grew so thick they were forced to take Lupus form to get through the brush.

"Albrecht!" Mari said in the Garou tongue. "What happened to your fur?"

Albrecht looked at his pelt and barked in surprise. It was no longer white, but gray, like a common wolf. "My fur!" He looked at Mari and Evan and saw that their fur had also changed. "Mari, your black pelt is gray! Evan, yours is grayer than usual."

They all looked at each other.

"What's going on here?" Albrecht said.

"One tribe," Evan said. "We're all one tribe. No marks of breed to distinguish us. You're no longer a… a…. I can't remember what tribe you were."

Albrecht thought. "I can't either. I don't even know what tribe you guys are!"

Mari smiled. "Good. Maybe now you'll learn some humility."

"Perhaps you will, too," Evan said. "You're not a… well, you know. You're not your tribe anymore either."

"I don't need my tribe to know who I am," Mari said, and sauntered off ahead into the forest. The others followed.

Even in wolf form, the going was slow. They had to stop many times to get their bearings. The environment changed from hardwoods to pines. After a few hours, Albrecht caught the scent of wolves. He stopped and looked around, sniffing.

"Territory," he concluded, turning to Mari and Evan. "We're in a wolf pack's territory. They've marked it in various spots," he said, pointing to a tree and a rock. "Think we should announce ourselves?"

"I don't think it can hurt," Mari said. "Go ahead."

"What's a good howl? I don't want to scare them off."

"A simple Howl of Greeting will do."

Albrecht sat back on his haunches and howled. A long, one-note howl. He looked about, waiting for signs of approaching wolves. Soon he smelled a wolf off to the left, still a ways off, but approaching them warily. Then, to the right, another smell. Also to the front now. They were approaching from all sides.

Ahead, a wolf stepped from behind a tree, obviously the alpha. Albrecht couldn't believe its size — it was a prehistoric dire wolf, akin to the Hispo form of the Garou. Then, even more surprisingly, the wolf spoke in a broken Garou tongue. It wasn't a wolf; it was a Garou.

"What… want… here?" it said, glaring at the pack.

"We seek Table Rock," Albrecht said. "I am Lord Albrecht

of the… well, a Garou. My packmates are Mari Cabrah and Evan Heals-the-Past."

The alpha cocked his head. "I… Rake-to-Death. Lupus. This my place!"

"We don't want your territory!" Albrecht said. "We just want to pass through, to Table Rock."

The alpha seemed to be torn. He paced around, growling low. Then he turned to them and said, "Follow." He whirled and headed to the north.

Albrecht, Mari and Evan followed. The Garou alpha's pack could be seen and heard running along with them, a few paces away to either side. The land rose up, and they were soon running up a hill, struggling to keep up with the alpha. They finally came to the top of the rise, and looked down into a bowl-shaped valley. In the center of the valley was a large, flat rock, resting horizontally on top of a vertical slab.

"Table Rock," the alpha said, watching them as they came over the rise.

"Thanks," Albrecht said.

The alpha moved back into the woods, and the pack moved down into the valley. As soon as the wolf was out of sight, they all shifted into Homid form.

"I don't think he liked us," Albrecht said.

"We're too civilized for him," Evan said. "I don't think he's native: he doesn't seem like a spirit. He's obviously trying to get back to nature. Our reminders of civilization — our backpacks and all — probably don't help."

They reached the bottom of the valley and walked carefully up to the rock. Painted Garou pictograms adorned it, faded with time, wind and rain. The ashy remains of many fires were scattered about.

"Well, here's a sign of fire at least," Albrecht said, kicking some of the ashes. "That's civilized."

"It's probably the only concession to tool-use we'll find here," Evan said, roaming about the rock, looking into every small fissure he could find. He tried to read the faded pictograms, but few of them made any sense. "These writings are old. I can't make out most of them. Those I can read seem incomplete. None of them has anything to do with a crown, or even leadership."

Albrecht explored the valley, looking for signs of any buried objects or caves. He came back to the rock, where Evan and Mari were searching, and threw up his hands. "Nothing. There's nothing here. We're not going to find anything."

"Don't be so defeatist," Mari said, sitting down. "Maybe we need to wait. Something might show itself."

"Yeah, like a big Tyrannosaurus Rex." Albrecht sat down and fumed.

"Look," Mari said. "Maybe some Garou will show up who know this place better than we do."

"Yeah, real likely. We could be waiting weeks for that."

"I think we should camp here tonight," Evan said, coming over to sit with them. "We can figure out our next step in the morning."

Albrecht looked up at the sun. "It's weird to see the sun again. It's really throwing off my hours. Been used to night travel for a while."

"Look," Evan said. "This place is sort of like a caern. You never know what could show up under moonlight."

"All right," Albrecht said. "We'll wait here tonight. Tomorrow morning, we'll figure out a new plan." He stretched out and looked up at the shifting clouds.

Mari moved her bag to the base of the rock. "I think we should camp close to the rock. There are no animal tracks around here, almost as if they know better than to come here."

Albrecht sat up and looked around. "I hadn't thought of that. Interesting. Now, what could be driving a bunch of wild animals away from here?"

"I doubt it's the rage of the Garou," Evan said. "Maybe it's something spiritual. There may be a ritual in effect here."

"How would we go about finding out?" Albrecht said.

"Normally we'd look for signs of a ritual, such as pictograms. Those are already here. Maybe it's just the strength of successive rituals. Maybe it's the fact that fires have been lit here. That may be bad mojo for the inhabitants. Remember, Albrecht, these animals may act like animals, but they're really spirits."

"I keep forgetting. Seems so real," Albrecht got up and pulled his bags closer to the rock. "Well, I'm going to get some shut-eye. Do you want me to help you light a fire first?"

"We can manage," Evan said. "Besides, I got more sleep than either of you. You should both sleep. I'll stay up for first watch."

Mari nodded and lay down. Soon, she and Albrecht were both asleep. Evan sat for a while, listening to the sounds of the primordial world. He swatted more than a couple of times at some very large insects. *These are going to get annoying*, he thought. He wondered if there was anything he could do to ward them off, but decided that there wasn't. Except for a fire, perhaps.

He walked to the edge of the valley and started gathering what old wood he could find. He found mostly pine, which he knew didn't burn well, but there were few hardwoods in the region. He soon had a stack of wood in his arms. After carrying it back, he dug a shallow fire pit, then walked around again, this time gathering twigs and dry pine needles for kindling. These he brought back to the gathered wood and pulled out a box of matches from the sealed plastic baggy he carried them in. *Be prepared*, he thought wryly. He struck the match and held it to the kindling. It flared into life, catching on the dry twigs and growing bigger.

Evan sat back and readied himself for a long afternoon. He thought about the quest they were on and the metaphors in the fable they had heard from Antonine. He tried to figure out if these things had any meaning for them, on this quest.

Four gates, he thought. *Have we passed any yet?* Or, *more importantly, has Albrecht passed any of them? Does he need to? That was just one story. The other story, about the bad king, didn't have any gates to pass. Is the quest different for everyone?*

The sun was beginning to set. Standing up and stretching, he figured he should wake Mari up and get some sleep himself. The fire was dwindling. Twice already he had had to go in search of more wood. One more trip would probably be enough for the rest of the night.

He walked into the woods again — and froze in his tracks. A loud bellow came from beyond the grove before him: a sound which tapped something primal in him, making him want to flee in terror. He shivered, but gathered his will not to move. He was a Garou, after all; his rage was his courage. After a few moments of silence, he crept forward and peeked around a large tree.

A dinosaur tore at the flesh of its fresh kill. It chewed at the bloody remains of the deer, every now and then peeking about, bird-like, to make sure nothing else was near. It stood on two legs and had sharp claws on its small forearms.

Oh shit! Evan thought. *It's one of those raptors from that movie. That means more of them must be around.* He slowly and quietly shifted to Crinos form and concentrated on his surroundings, using his near-lupine senses to discover if the dinosaur had friends nearby. But he smelled and heard nothing. The dinosaur appeared to be alone. Evan breathed a sigh of relief and backed up, turning around to head back to camp.

He heard the noise before he saw it. Only his Garou senses and speed saved him, as he jumped to the left in time to avoid the rush of the raptor. It sped past him, crying in anger and spinning around.

Evan shifted to Hispo form, the dire wolf, and ran forward, hoping to throw the thing off by attacking it. The raptor shifted to the side and slashed at Evan as he ran by. Its claws tore off some fur, but Evan's adrenaline was pumping too much for him to feel the pain.

He kept running, hoping to make it back to camp to get his packmates' help. He was afraid that he was no match for this natural predator. He heard it moving in the woods to his right, running to head him off. Suddenly he saw the Table Rock clearing ahead and put on an extra burst of speed. The raptor lunged from the trees as he sped past, then stopped dead in its tracks.

Evan ran into the open clearing and turned around to face his attacker. But it stood at the fringe of the woods, looking edgy, nervously tramping the ground. Finally it honked in frustration and slipped back into the cover of the trees.

Evan let out his breath and collapsed. After long minutes of thanking Gaia for his life, he stood up and shifted back to Homid form. His wound was only a scratch. He was also pumped up, and knew he wouldn't be sleeping anytime soon. But his guess about the supernatural nature of the clearing had been right; it did spook the natural inhabitants.

He walked over to Mari but stopped before he got to her. There was a shimmering light on the other side of the rock, growing bigger by the second.

What now? he wondered as he ran to the edge of the rock and peeked around. In the empty air, a hole had opened, silvered moonlight flowing out of it. A wolf leaped out of the hole and looked around.

Evan ducked back behind the rock and ran to Mari. He shook her awake and covered her mouth before she could speak. "There's a Moon Bridge on the other side of the rock. Someone's come out of it."

Mari bolted up. She instantly assumed Glabro form, growing larger and more muscled, but uglier and more brutish also. "Wake Albrecht," she whispered, and crept over to the corner of the rock.

Evan shook Albrecht awake, clamping his hand down on

the other's mouth before he could say anything. Albrecht frowned up at Evan. "Shhh," Evan said softly. "There's a Moon Bridge behind the rock, and a Garou came out of it."

Albrecht's eyes widened and he stood up. "What the hell is a Moon Bridge doing here? I thought they couldn't open into this realm." He drew his Grand Klaive out and went to where Mari was standing. Evan followed him. They all poked their heads around the corner and saw more strangers come out of the Moon Bridge.

There were now six wolves, each looking and sniffing about. The Moon Bridge closed up, and the shimmering light was cut off. One of the wolves seemed to pick up a scent, and it barked at the others.

Albrecht raised his eyebrows. "They've found our scent. They seem to have been expecting it."

The new arrivals spread out, three around the far side of the rock, while the other three headed for the corner where the pack was watching. Albrecht pulled Evan and Mari back.

"Who the hell are they?" he asked. "They're obviously looking for us."

"We've got to leave," Mari said. "Now."

Evan started to run back to his backpack, but Albrecht grabbed him by the shirt collar.

"No time for that," he said. "We leave now."

Evan looked disappointed, but followed Albrecht and Mari as they ran to the edge of the forest. Behind them they heard a howl which immediately became multiple howls as all six wolves picked it up. They had been seen. The chase was on.

Albrecht shifted to Crinos, as did Mari. Evan began the shift while he ran, but he was having trouble concentrating. He looked over his shoulder and saw the wolf pack nearly on his heels. Yelling out, he called on his rage. In an instant he was in Crinos form, and he took to four legs, catching up with Albrecht and Mari.

The wolves howled and barked, spreading out through the

forest, trying to overtake the pack.

Albrecht led the pack to the left, along a ridge that apparently went to the mountain pass. If he could get to a tight pass, they could fight the wolves one-on-one.

One of the wolves caught up with them and snapped at Mari's heels. Mari spun around and slashed at it, spinning back again and continuing her run. Her claws had connected: the wolf's snout had opened up, and blood sprayed onto the pine-needle blanket that covered the ground. The wolf yelped and stopped the chase, but the other wolves ran past him.

Mari's brief attack had lost her some ground. She ran after the rest of the pack, but she was off course, running to the right where they had gone left. Too late to compensate for her mistake, she yelled out to them, "Keep running! I'll meet up with you!"

Albrecht growled back in acknowledgment. He kept the pace up, slowing himself slightly when it looked like Evan might fall behind.

The wolves split up. Three of them — the wounded one among them — went after Albrecht and Evan, while the other three went after Mari.

Mari broke through a thick stand of pines and slipped down a hill, sliding on the needles but managing to keep her balance. Ahead, to the left, was a cave mouth big enough for only one person to stand in it. She ran for it, hearing the wolves still behind her. As she entered the cave, she saw a light glowing from deep within, around a far curve. She ran forward, hearing her pursuers enter the cave behind her and abandoning her plan of holding them off at the entrance. As she came around the curve, she stopped short, staring around her in shock.

The cave was gone. She now stood on a muddy field under gray skies and roiling clouds. In the distance she heard moans of pain and, farther off, screams of horror. Barbed wire snaked through the field, and she thought she saw human limbs —

hands and feet — buried in the dirt.

No! she thought. *This can't be. I've left Pangaea. This is another realm. Gaia, please let it not be what I think it is.*

She heard howling behind her and turned to see the wolves appear one by one. They stopped and stared at her, grinning evilly. Their gray fur began to change, to grow blacker. On two of them the fur began to fall off in patches, revealing mangy hides underneath. The pursuers began cackling. As the laws of Pangaea faded, they once more assumed their tribal aspects. Their ears grew to ugly proportions, with interior ridges — becoming the ears of a bat, not a wolf.

Mari growled at the Black Spiral Dancers and centered herself, ready for their charge.

CHAPTER TWELVE

Albrecht and Evan ran through the crevasse. They had managed to outdistance the wolves in the twisting, turning gully, but they still heard the howls behind them, just out of sight. Albrecht was trying to find a good place to make their stand. He didn't like the numbers they were up against. Evan wasn't a great fighter, and Albrecht didn't want to have to worry about him while he took on two of the wolves himself, leaving the other to attack the boy.

The ground was on a steady incline, and Albrecht could hear rushing water ahead. Albrecht prayed the water was a river running parallel to them; if it ran crosswise, they would have to make their stand, backs to the water.

They came out of the crevasse onto a ledge above a raging river which rushed from their right to their left. Albrecht cursed. They were trapped here. He looked around, trying to find some advantage to the ledge. Shoving Evan to one side of the ledge, he set himself on the other side. Their only hope was that the wolves would be running fast enough to have to fight to slow their momentum before they fell into the river below. Albrecht and Evan could then take them from behind, perhaps using their unbalance to shove them off the ledge.

The howls were mere yards away. Albrecht hunkered down against the rock and motioned to Evan to do the same.

The first wolf ran past them and scooted to a halt at the lip of the cliff. Before the next wolf appeared, Albrecht leapt at the first and kicked him in the back. The wolf somersaulted forward, over the lip, waving his limbs spastically as he hung in midair for a moment. He then fell into the water and was carried away by the current.

The second wolf vaulted onto the ledge and slammed into Albrecht, who had to pivot to keep from going over. The she-wolf was at his throat, sinking in her fangs. Albrecht grabbed her torso between his arms and squeezed her with all his might. That seemed to knock the wind out of her, since she let go of Albrecht's throat, coughing. Albrecht lifted her up and threw her over the ledge. She yipped and scrambled in the air, as if trying to swim back to the ledge. But Albrecht's throw had been good, and the wolf flew into the river.

Meanwhile, the third wolf had slunk around the corner and chomped into Evan's left leg while the boy was watching Albrecht. Evan cried out and slashed his claws at the wolf's neck, but the wolf lithely dodged and jumped in for another nip. Evan stepped back, dangerously close to the edge. When the wolf leapt in for a third bite, Evan stumbled backwards and fell off the cliff. At the last second, he reached out, grabbing for anything to keep him from falling. His hand closed on the wolf's thick pelt. The wolf tried to step back, but Evan's momentum took them both over and into the river.

"Evan!" Albrecht cried out, trying to catch sight of him once he disappeared under the water. Down to the left he resurfaced, struggling to stay up. He was already yards downstream and traveling faster. Albrecht cursed and leapt in.

The water was freezing, run-off from the mountaintop snows. Albrecht concentrated, knowing he couldn't allow the shock to stun him. He swam as fast as he could downstream, trying to catch up to the struggling Evan. He passed one of the enemy wolves crawling onto the far bank, exhausted.

As he looked ahead for Evan, he saw curls of white water. Rocks jutted out of the stream, and the water rushed around them at incredible speed. As he maneuvered around the boulders, Albrecht hoped the kid hadn't slammed into one of them.

Far ahead, he heard Evan yell.

"I'm coming, kid!" he shouted. "Try to grab a branch or a rock!" Then he saw Evan.

The boy was in the middle of the current, heading for a large spray of mist. Albrecht couldn't figure out what it was until he registered the great roar that drowned out Evan's yells. Albrecht shook his head, trying to deny it. *That can't be a waterfall*, he thought. *It's too quick a change in landscape. But this is Pangaea. Anything can happen here.*

He howled out in grief as Evan disappeared over the edge. Albrecht quit looking for things to grab onto, resigned now to his fate — he was going over. He steeled himself, and then he was no longer in water, but falling through air. He looked down and saw miles and miles of falling water, disappearing into a huge cloud of mist far below.

This can't be happening, he thought, as he shut his eyes.

Then he landed. It was a hard landing, on solid ground, but he knew instantly that no bones were broken.

That was not a mile-long fall, he thought. *Felt more like forty feet*. He opened his eyes and looked around.

He was sitting on a Moon Path. Water spray was all around him, and he could still hear the roaring of water, but it sounded farther off, as if there were a wall between him and the falls. It was dark, with no sun or moon, but faint light seemed to be coming from somewhere. He turned around and saw a rent in the night sky. Light and water were filtering in from Pangaea.

Then someone groaned. He spun around and ran over to

Evan, who was lying farther up the path. He was unconscious. Then, the groan again. It wasn't coming from Evan. Albrecht looked up the path and saw one of the wolves, lying mangled. One of his legs was bent the wrong way, and it looked like a rib was sticking out of his side.

Albrecht pulled out his klaive and walked forward cautiously. As he got closer, he saw that the Garou's fur color had changed from gray to black. The hide was scarred in many places with bizarre pictograms. Unholy pictograms. The signs of the Wyrm and corrupt rites.

Albrecht spat. This thing was a Black Spiral Dancer.

He looked up at Albrecht and tried to move, but he seemed to lack the energy even for survival. His eyes half-closed, he seemed to smile at Albrecht, as if congratulating him.

"Who the hell are you, and why the hell did you attack us?" Albrecht snarled, leaning over the Dancer and placing the klaive at his throat.

The Dancer took in some heavy breaths and then sighed. "My master sent us to you. An easy kill, she said. She lied."

"Who the fuck is your master and why does she want us dead? Besides us being on the wrong side and all?"

"Queen Azaera, She of the Uncracked Egg. She demanded your death or capture. She will have it. Not from me or my pack, but from others. You live on borrowed time, Silver Fang king...."

"King? Not yet, pal. Or is that why you're trying to stop me? Did Arkady put her up to this?"

The Dancer cackled. "Oh, the Duke fumes over you. And for his petty power struggle, I'm dead. Fuck him! Fuck you! Fuck Gaia! Fuck the Wyrm! FuckFuck—"

Albrecht cut him off by slicing open his throat. The Dancer still tried to curse, but empty air escaped from the gash in his throat, never making it as far as the tongue. The Dancer grimaced and died.

Albrecht walked over to Evan and examined him. He seemed all right, just knocked around a little. His leg was gashed, but that was minor. Albrecht gently slapped him in the face, trying to wake him up.

Evan's eyes slowly rolled open and he looked around. He quickly sat up. "What happened? Where are the wolves?"

Albrecht put his hand on Evan's shoulder. "Calm down. They're dead. At least, that one is. The other two aren't here. One got to shore. I think the other one missed the gate. He's probably still falling."

Evan looked around, confused. "A gate? We're back in the Umbra! Weird."

Albrecht stood up and put his klaive back in its sheath. "Got any idea where in the Umbra we are?"

Evan shook his head. "Not in this blackness. Once the moon comes up, I might be able to figure it out. If there are any landmarks. This is more Mari's kind of thing."

"Mari!" Albrecht yelled. "Damn! She's still back there, being chased by the Black Spiral Dancers!"

"That's what they were? Black Spirals?"

"Yeah. Pals of Arkady's. If we didn't have enough suspicions before, we do now."

Evan looked back at the rent into Pangaea. "We've got to go back for Mari."

"We can't," Albrecht said. "That gate opens in mid-air. It's a long drop on the other side."

Evan looked worried. "But she could be in trouble. She might need us."

"Kid," Albrecht said, taking Evan's shoulder and guiding him down the Moon Path, away from Pangaea, "She can take care of herself. She's proven that many times. We'll just have to hope she'll find us again."

Evan nodded, but didn't say anything else. Albrecht looked ahead. Far off, there was a pinpoint of light on the horizon. "What's that?"

Evan followed Albrecht's gaze and saw the light also. "I don't know. It's too far away."

"Well, looks like we got someplace to go now. Let's check it out."

"It could be dangerous."

"Yeah? We got nothing better to do." When he saw Evan's face fall, he quickly added, "At least, there's nothing we can do right now. Don't worry, we'll find her. We will."

"I know. At least, that's what I'll try to believe. Let's go to the light." Evan walked on down the almost pitch-black Moon Path, and Albrecht followed.

The Black Spiral Dancer crashed into Mari, but she pivoted and redirected his force off to the right, pushing him in that direction. She then lashed out with a quick punch to his exposed back. Bones cracked and the Dancer fell to the ground, alive but injured.

Mari turned to face the others. They were more wary than their packmate and had assumed Crinos form also. One was taller than the other and clearly female. She hissed slowly as she moved around, trying to circle Mari. But Mari backed up, allowing neither of them to get an easy opening on her. The way she had handled the first one showed them that she clearly knew how to fight. Reckless bravery on their part would only get them killed, and they knew it.

The Dancer on the ground slowly stood up. He had obviously just used a Gift to heal himself of a cracked spine. He glared at Mari, but there was a wary fearfulness in that look.

The screams came over the hill again, and they seemed to rattle even the Dancers. It was clear that they did not know where they were; but Mari did. And she was afraid.

The Dancers all turned to look at her again, and the

landscape shifted. Mari blinked, and they were no longer on a muddy battlefield, but in a dirty, garbage-strewn alley. Glaring hungrily at her, no longer in Crinos form, the Dancers were now humans in black leather with knives out.

Mari shook her head. *This isn't right,* she told herself. *Those are Black Spiral Dancers, not gang members.* She backed up and hit a wall. Looking up quickly, she saw a sign above her: *The Urban Jungle.*

She stepped back, sweating. She knew this place. It was a nightclub she used to sneak out to as a teenager. It all came back to her in a rush. The nightclub, the alley, the gang. She shuddered.

The gang was approaching her, sensing her dismay, smelling the fear. She gritted her teeth and growled. She flexed her claws and looked at her hands in surprise. She wasn't in Crinos form anymore; she was in Homid. She concentrated, drawing on her anger to shift forms. Nothing happened.

She cursed. *It's this place,* she told herself. *It's this realm. It's trying to get at you, to scare you. You can't let it.*

One of the gang lunged forward and cut her across the stomach with his knife. Not a deep cut, but a painful one. Right on the scar Albrecht had made two years ago in their fight. The one for which she had yet to repay him.

Another member, the female, ran forward and swung a crowbar at her head, but Mari was thinking straight now. She easily blocked it with her forearm — although it hurt to do so in Homid form — and followed up with a right-arm punch to the girl's abdomen. The girl doubled over, clutching her stomach. Mari continued the attack and slammed her foot into the girl's head, driving her face into the oily pavement. She then kicked her with her other foot, and the girl flew back, her neck flexing more than it should have, with a snapping sound. She fell to the ground, her neck broken.

The other two gang members grabbed Mari from behind,

and she moved to slip free. But one of them sank a knife between her ribs. Mari screamed in pain and fell over, blood gushing from her side. The thugs stood over her, laughing as she bled. Then they looked down the alley fearfully and ran away.

Mari tried to move her neck to see what had scared them, but she couldn't. This was so familiar. The damn gang members and their taunting. But what had really happened all those years ago was that she had freaked out and gone berserk before they had ever touched her. She had undergone her First Change and torn the gang to pieces. When she had come to, she had been covered in their blood. Their dead eyes had looked up at her, accusingly, and she'd run away, crying at the cold-blooded murder she'd just committed. Over the years, as she looked back, she had managed to convince herself that they had been going to rape her, that she was justified in killing the scum, that she had been cleaning up the streets.

But that was a lie, and she knew it. A lie around which she had built her whole identity. She had killed them. They had been just kids — younger than her — and not even a gang; just a bunch of kids hanging around together, out past their bedtimes. They had teased her, called her names, and she — sheltered girl that she was — had overreacted. They were dead because of her inability to control the Change. So what if she had never done it before, hadn't even known she was Garou? Did they care? They had never touched her except with hurtful words.

A police officer walked over and looked down at her. And she remembered him. She had forgotten him until now. The cop. Yet another thread in the weaving of Mari Cabrah's self. He had been the fuel behind her self-defense course fire, her attempts to teach women to fight for themselves and not to rely on authority.

And she remembered what he had done that night, when

he'd found a teen-aged girl alone in a back alley with a bunch of dead bodies.

She closed her eyes. *Give it to me*, she thought. *Go ahead and do it. The kids have already gotten their revenge, through the Black Spiral Dancers. Finish the job.*

The police officer brought his club back and swung it down hard on Mari's head. Everything went black. Mari thought one last thing: *So this is death....*

CHAPTER THIRTEEN

The moon had risen when Albrecht and Evan cautiously approached what they had realized could only be a campfire. They had even heard someone singing from the vicinity. But they were taking no chances, so they approached silently and carefully.

Their walk had taken almost an hour, during which time Evan told Albrecht about his encounter with the dinosaur. Albrecht was impressed but said he could have taken the thing. Evan fumed in silence for a while after that. He was getting a bit tired of being treated like a child. So what if he was no match for a dinosaur? Albrecht would have been clueless in Pangaia without some of Evan's suggestions. Brawn wasn't always a match for education.

Albrecht motioned to Evan as they approached the fire. He was about to whisper for Evan to cut to the right while he cut left when he heard a low, wolfish growl behind him. He turned around and saw a thin, almost jackal-like wolf standing a few feet behind him, staring at him threateningly. Albrecht could see markings — tattoos — on its fur. He breathed a sigh of relief. The symbol for the Silent Striders was burned into its haunches.

"We're friends," he said, putting his palms out. "I'm Lord Albrecht, of the Silver Fangs, and this is Evan Heals-the-Past, a Wendigo."

The wolf cocked its head, seemingly surprised. Then, from mere feet behind them, someone spoke. Loudly.

"Lord Albrecht? I've heard of you!"

Albrecht turned slowly around again and saw a short, red-haired man dressed in a Pogues T-shirt and torn blue jeans. His arms were laced with tattoos, and Albrecht recognized the Fianna symbol among them: the mark of the Celtic tribe of Garou. Albrecht's eyebrows rose. There were also quite a few honor and wisdom marks there, badges of merit. Standing behind the Fianna — towering over him in fact — was a blond-haired Crinos Garou, who eyed Albrecht suspiciously. This one carried a huge, two-handed hammer. Judging from the size of his muscles, it wasn't at all too heavy for him.

The red-haired man put out his hand and spoke in a heavy Irish brogue. "Pleased to meet you! My name's Jack Wetthumb!"

Albrecht shook the man's hand. "It's damn good to see some friends here."

"Oh? Troubles you've been having, is it?" Jack said. He looked at Evan and extended his hand to him as well. "Your name's a bit familiar also, but I can't place it."

"I'm Albrecht's packmate," Evan said.

"Right," Jack said, looking at him, trying to remember how he knew him. He wagged his finger at him. "You were that kid in the Amazon a few months back. The one the Nexus Crawler came after." He turned to Albrecht. "And you were there, fighting it! It all comes back now."

"Were you there?" Evan asked. "In the Amazon War?"

"Yeah, sure was. That's where I got all these scribbles on my arms. They give out medals like candy down there. All you gotta do is survive."

Albrecht nodded and glanced at the big guy. "Who's your

friend? And the Silent Strider?" he asked, turning around to look at the wolf, who sat on its haunches now.

"She," Jack said, pointing at the wolf, "is known as Parts-the-Water, a damn fine Theurge. Invaluable when you're hiking the Umbra. And this fella," he said, motioning with his thumb at the large Garou, "is Ivar Hated-by-the-Wyrm. I think you can figure out just by looking at him how he got his name. He's a Get of Fenris, and my best pal. Ain't that right?" he said, looking up at Ivar. Ivar didn't say anything, but neither did he deny the accusation.

Albrecht smiled. "What about your name? How'd you pick that up?"

Jack laughed. "You ever heard of Finn Mac Cool? He's our most famous Fianna of old. Once, to get wisdom, he caught this magic salmon. To make a long story short, the eating of it gave him the smarts, but he had to suck his thumb for it — the thumb where the juices of the cooking fish had burned him. Well, I found just such a fish myself, and went through the same experience. Now," he said, holding up his right thumb. "When I sucks on this weasel here, I get the smarts, just like ol' Finn."

"He's just saying that," Ivar said. Jack looked up at him, annoyed. "He didn't eat any magic fish. He's as dumb as ever when he sucks his thumb. He just wants you to think otherwise."

"Uh… don't listen to Ivar," Jack said. "He's got a cracked sense of humor. Hey! Why don't we take you to the camp and introduce you to the rest of our bunch?"

Albrecht and Evan nodded, and they followed Jack and his friends to the campfire. There was a man sitting with a guitar, smiling at them as they came up. He looked to be Indian, from the subcontinent, rather than a native to America like the woman next to him. She was dressed in a buckskin vest and blue jeans and had long black hair falling down her back and shoulders. Albrecht stared, surprised: He knew her. She stared back, enigmatically and with faint embarrassment.

"Greetings," the man with the guitar said. "And who are our travelers?"

"This here," Jack said, "is Lord Albrecht, from Central Park. Surely you've heard of him."

"Most certainly," the man said. "It is a pleasure to meet the mighty Wyrm-slayer."

"Thanks," Albrecht said.

"And this," Jack said, "is Evan Heals-the-Past. You remember about him? The boy from the Amazon who was the talk of the jungle for that one week when we had R & R?"

"Ah, yes," the man said. "The one with the Nexus Crawler problem. I am glad you resolved that issue and are here to visit with us today."

"Thanks," Evan said. "It's really nice of you to say so."

"This fella," Jack said, pointing at the man, "is Pramati, our songster and Stargazer. Weird combo, huh? It makes for some thought-provoking fireside sing-alongs."

Pramati bowed and smiled.

"And last, but certainly not least among us," Jack said, pointing at the woman, "is Mary Black Fox."

"We've met before," Albrecht said, meeting her eyes and smiling. "But I didn't know you were Garou. What tribe are you?"

She seemed uncomfortable and looked at Jack, who glanced at Ivar, eyebrows raised, as if they were sharing a private joke.

"I'm Cherokee, actually," she said.

"I meant—" Albrecht said.

"She's not a Garou, lad," Jack said. "She's a witch. At least that's what her people call her. She's more properly a Dreamspeaker."

Albrecht's eyes widened. "A mage? Really? You didn't tell me that before either. I haven't met too many of your kind."

"I… wasn't a mage then," she said. "My Awakening was yet to come. And you're lucky you haven't met many of 'my kind.' They don't like Garou. My Tradition excepted, of course. The Dreamspeakers are the only ones among our order to understand what you guys are all about."

"I've heard of Dreamspeakers," Evan said. "You're shamans, right?"

"I suppose that's the best way to describe us," she said. "We're not like the hermetic mages; or the scientific ones for that matter."

Evan nodded. Albrecht smiled at her again. She looked away.

"Well, why don't you fellas find a spot and have a sit?" Jack said, sitting down himself and eyeing Mary with a smirk. "We've got vittles here, if you're hungry. Since you don't have any provisions on you, I assume you're on hard times. So sit down, eat up and tell us about yourselves."

Albrecht and Evan gratefully sat down and ate. The meal was rich beef vegetable stew from a pot over the fire. Albrecht wondered where they had gotten the ingredients for this out in the Umbra, but didn't care enough to ask. He was too busy eating.

After they finished, Jack pulled some bottles of Guinness from a cooler behind him and offered them. They had both gratefully taken the beers and drunk when Albrecht stopped and looked at Evan.

"Hey!" he said. "Should you be drinking yet?"

"Legally?" Evan said. "No. But just try and take it from me." He took a long chug, and Jack rolled over laughing.

"The kid's gonna turn out all right," he said. "Don't worry about him. Nothing wrong with a little sip now and again."

Albrecht shrugged and drank his beer. Ivar and Parts-the-Water did not sit down, but instead stood at the edge of their circle, watching for possible danger. They listened in, however.

"So what do you call yourselves?" Albrecht asked.

"We're the Screamin' Trailblazers," Jack said. "Or that's

what they called us down in the jungle, anyway. We've been thinking about shortening it to just 'Trailblazers.' What do you think?"

"I like them both," Albrecht said.

"Well, that's no help," Jack said, leaning back against his bed roll. "All right, lads, so what are you doing way out in the middle of nowhere?"

Evan looked at Albrecht. Albrecht sighed. "You deserve to know, although I really need to ask what you guys are doing here first."

Jack frowned. "It's bit rude, since we asked first.... But you're well spoken of in Central Park, so I'll trust you have your reasons for asking.

"We're after the skin of the Wyrm."

Albrecht blinked. "The what? The skin?"

"That's right. The skin of the Wyrm. You see, we heard this story down in the Amazon from an elder who was dying. He had this nice tidbit of knowledge he wanted to hand on before meeting his maker. So he handed it to us. You see, it seems that the Wyrm, being a giant snake and all, used to shed its skin regularly, back when everything was in balance. As a matter of fact, it was this shedding of the skin that helped keep the balance. Well, things got all screwed up, for whatever reason — we all know that's a matter of debate among the tribes. Well, one of the reasons things went wrong is that the Wyrm quit shedding its skin."

Evan nodded. "So the cycles were broken. It refused to grow and die and grow again, like everything is supposed to."

Jack sat up. "That's right. It hasn't shed its skin in ages, you see. So it's getting awful itchy and scummy, uncomfortable-like. That's one reason why the Wyrm is so pissy. It's wearing a damn uncomfortable skin."

"If that's the case," Albrecht said, "then why do you want to find it? It seems to me that, if you find the skin, you find the Wyrm."

"Yeah, but we're not looking for its current skin. We're

looking for the old skin, the last one it shed. We figure like this elder in the jungle did, that if we can find it — somehow, someway — we can convince the Wyrm to shed its current skin. And if that happens, things might go all right."

Albrecht nodded. "That's quite a quest. Sounds like a wild goose chase; but if it's true and you do get the skin, it could mean a lot."

"That's exactly what we say!" Jack said.

"So, you got any leads?" Albrecht said.

"Yes," Pramati said. "There are many tales that speak of this skin. The trick is to find it. We have... some ideas."

"But you can understand us wanting to keep them secret," Jack said.

"Yeah," Albrecht said. "No problem. It's your quest."

"And what's yours?" Jack said.

"We're looking for the Silver Crown."

Jack looked confused, but Pramati whistled.

"That is a real quest," he said. "But I do not understand. Is not the crown hidden by the Silver Fangs?"

Albrecht looked down. "Uh... no. That's just a rumor. A false one."

Jack and Pramati exchanged glances.

"That's big news, you know," Jack said. "There are a lot of folks who'd be looking for it if that word got out."

"I know," Albrecht said. "I'm just going to have to trust you, with your honor badges and all, not to tell anyone."

Jack was silent for a while, looking at Albrecht. "Ah, you're a wise one. You know just where to push the buttons. I respect honor and all, and since you called me on it, I'll take up your challenge. Mum's the word, lad. At least from me and my pack. But I'll have to ask you to do the same about our quest."

"Done," Albrecht said.

Jack sat back again, smiling. "So, you got any leads on it?"

"We were just in Pangaea," Evan said. "But we got chased

out before we could really look."

"Pangaea?" Jack said. "Beautiful place! But damn dangerous. Things are primal there. So, just what chased you out? A T-rex? A smilodon?"

"Black Spiral Dancers," Albrecht said. "My... cousin... doesn't want me to get the crown. He's guaranteed to be king of the North Country Protectorate otherwise."

"I don't get it," Jack said. "What's a Silver Fang king got to do with Black Spiral Dancers?"

"He's working with them. He used them to murder King Morningkill."

"Morningkill's dead?" Jack exclaimed, looking at the rest of his pack. They all looked surprised and dismayed. "We've been in here too long. When did this happen?"

Albrecht thought for a minute. "Nine days?"

"Ah... that recent then? I'm sorry. My condolences. You are his grandkid, aren't you? That's what they say."

"Yeah. I am. Thanks."

"So who is this rat bastard who's taking over for him?"

"His name's Arkady."

"Huh. I'll have to remember that. You realize, of course, that I can't just sit on this piece of information. I gotta warn others."

"I know. Just don't talk about the crown. I don't mind — hell, I want — others knowing about Arkady."

"I get it now. You're after the crown 'cause it's the only way you can dethrone him."

"Yep."

"Well, you didn't tell us we were supping with the king-to-be! Not every day we get to hang with royalty."

Albrecht smiled but looked down. "That's assuming the crown... well, accepts me."

Jack nodded and sat back, thinking.

"Look," Evan said. "We've lost one of our packmates. Mari Cabrah. She was in Pangaea, being chased by Black Spirals."

Pramati shook his head, putting his guitar down, and said, "Why did you not say so before? We can help with that." He began searching in his bag for something.

Jack looked worried. "Hey, Pram, I don't think we should…."

"Nonsense," Pramati said. "We are with the potential king of the North Country Protectorate. Of course we can share our fetishes."

Jack looked at Evan, embarrassed. "Sorry, mate. It's just that… well, when people find out you've got neat stuff, they want to take it."

Evan nodded. "I understand."

Pramati pulled a box out. He smiled at them all and opened it. Inside was a leaf. A simple green leaf.

"What is it?" Albrecht said, leaning forward. "A leaf?"

"Yes," Pramati said. "But not just any leaf. It is a leaf from the One Tree. The first tree to grow in the world at the Dawn. It is Gaia's leaf. We were all born under its boughs. It is our center, our *axis mundi*. The tree ever calls to us."

"What does it do?" Evan asked.

Pramati took the leaf out carefully and handed it to Evan. Evan took it, holding it as if it were precious gold.

"Hold it in your palm. Go, stand away from the fire. Think of the loved one you have lost who is in the spirit world. Call out to her. Open your spirit in the calling, remember the tree. If you can do this, your friend will hear you and, if she chooses, will come to you. Distance does not matter, for the tree is always there, everywhere. It is the center. We all stand under it, even though we cannot see it."

Evan stood up and went a few yards from the fire. He looked at the leaf and thought of Mari. He thought of how she could be wounded somewhere, dying alone. He thought she might be dead already, but then stopped himself. *No*, he thought, *I won't accept that. She is alive. She is under the tree with us. She is here.*

"Mari!" he cried. "Where are you?"

He felt the leaf move gently in his hand, as if stirred by a breeze. He called her name again, with all his heart. And he looked up. Above him, towering and huge, was a tree, climbing to the heavens. On each branch were thousands of leaves, but they were all different — leaves from a million different trees on one tree. He saw a squirrel crawl down the trunk to look at him. Its nose quivered.

He heard a groan at his feet and looked down. Mari was there, lying among the roots of the tree.

"Mari! You're here!"

She opened her eyes and looked up at him. "Evan? Are you dead, too?"

"You're not dead, Mari! Just far away. Take my hand, come to where we are!" He held his hand out to her. She reached out and took it. The tree disappeared, and Mari was lying on the ground next to Evan, the light of the campfire dancing across her.

"It worked!" Evan yelled.

Albrecht got up and ran over. Bending down next to Mari, he examined her. "What happened? You're pretty beat up."

She looked at him as if she couldn't believe he was there. "Albrecht? What...?"

Jack came over. "Hello, miss. Don't worry, we'll fix you up." He waved Mary over. She got up and came to examine Mari.

"I'm going to heal you," she said. "This won't hurt a bit." She put her hands on Mari's wounds and concentrated. The wounds began to heal themselves, as if time were accelerated around them. In seconds, they were fully cured.

Mari looked at her, confused. "Thank you. I... I am surprised to be here."

Evan helped her stand up. "Come on, we'll go to the fire. You can tell us what happened."

Albrecht stepped in and helped support her on the other

side. As they walked, she seemed to find her strength, and eventually shook them off. Standing on her own, she went to the fire and sat down.

Albrecht and Evan sat themselves on either side of her, looking concerned.

"You want to talk?" Albrecht said.

"I... I remember now," she said. "I was in Atrocity."

Jack grimaced. Pramati looked very concerned. Mary put her hand on Mari's, but Mari shook her head and withdrew her hand.

"I'm all right. It was just rough, that's all. I had forgotten that the only way out of Atrocity is to die to it."

"So the legends say," Pramati said. "I have never been there myself, thankfully. It must have been hard. They say that shadows of every crime ever committed live there."

"They don't feel like shadows," Mari said. "They come off like flesh and blood. The place gets you in its grip, forces you to become an actor in its play. You can't do anything about it."

"So what happened to you there?" Evan said.

"I'd rather not talk about it. It's personal."

Evan nodded.

"Well, it's over now," Jack said. "You should have some of this stew. Strengthen you up."

Mari looked at him. "Excuse me, but who are you?"

Jack laughed. "Friends of your friends here. We'll catch up as you eat."

Pramati handed Mari a bowl of stew and she ate. She was hungrier than she could ever remember being in her life. As she ate, the other pack introduced themselves to her, and explained their quest.

When she was done, Jack told them they could sleep for a few hours, until the next night, when they would break camp and move on. Albrecht volunteered to keep watch, but Jack wouldn't have any of it.

"We've just been walking for days, lad — no real action for us. We're pretty well rested up. It's you who need sleep. So get some shut-eye. We'll wake you before leaving."

"Thanks," Albrecht said. "I owe you."

"And you better believe that, if you get that crown of yours and become king, I'll be calling the favor in."

Albrecht laughed. "All right. I'll be expecting you." He lay back on the blanket Pramati had put out for them. Mari was already asleep. *That's not like her,* Albrecht thought. *She's usually one to prowl about for danger first. Ah, she's just tired.*

Evan was soon snoring. Albrecht rolled over again. He had a feeling that they had better catch as much sleep as they could; they might not get another chance for a long time.

CHAPTER FOURTEEN

Albrecht woke in pitch blackness. He sat up and looked around. The fire was still burning, but very low now. Ivar sat between it and him, blocking most of the light. The moon was gone. It was day in the physical world, but night in the spirit world.

He stood up, stretching as he walked over to the fire. Ivar was eating the leftovers from the stew pot and nodded a greeting at Albrecht, but kept on chewing. Parts-the-Water was curled up on a blanket, fast asleep, and Jack was snoring nearby. Albrecht looked around and saw Pramati sitting a way off, watching the dark landscape around them. Mary was on the other side of the camp, also watching outward.

Albrecht walked over to her. She looked up at him nervously as he sat down beside her.

"What's going on?" Albrecht said. "You act like you don't know me. Was I such a jerk?"

"Look," Mary said. "You were a short fling. That's all."

Albrecht furrowed his brow. "I didn't have to be, you know."

"I'm... not comfortable seeing you. I've changed a lot since then. I'm a mage now. I've found an identity."

"An identity? And you didn't have one before?"

She turned and looked at him, bewildered at his ignorance. "No. I didn't. I thought that was obvious. I was a girl who'd run to the big city to see what life was like off the rez. I met those Garou friends of yours and became fascinated with them. I thought they were just urban primitives, and you were the coolest of the bunch. Of course I was attracted to you. But was I really anything more than a fling to you? When I found out about the Garou later, and that you were one of them, I knew long-term relationships weren't your style. They're not mine, either."

Albrecht looked off into the darkness. "Huh. That's quite a mouthful. All right, it was just a fling. But you're a mage now, a mover and shaker in the supernatural world. Hell, in my book, that means it would've worked out well for both of us. Me being Garou wouldn't have mattered that much."

Mary shook her head, smiling now, as if Albrecht were a child who had inadvertently said something funny. "You are a Silver Fang, Albrecht. I've talked with Pramati. I know about your Kinfolk. I'm not the breeding type. I don't want children."

"So? Who said anything about kids?"

"You are a Garou. You've got to spread your seed. Otherwise your race dies. I know that. I accept that. But I don't want a relationship with it."

Albrecht frowned again.

"You've never had a one-on-one equal relationship, have you?"

"Sure I have."

"Don't fool yourself. You're a Garou. You've got to be the alpha in any social situation. You're trying to be king, for chrissakes."

Albrecht was silent.

"I'm sorry if I come off harsh, but as soon as I saw you, I knew I'd have to rehash my past. Realize this, for me: *I don't like what I used to be*. Don't get me wrong. I'm glad I ran into your friends. They led me to this pack, which is the greatest thing that ever happened to me, short of my Awakening. But that girl I used to be.... She's a stranger now. There was never anything between you and me, Albrecht. Nothing of any substance. You tell yourself in your memory that I was special, but is that really true? Have you tried to look for anyone else, or have you wallowed in self-pity? I'm not that girl of a few years ago. You might as well forget her."

Albrecht nodded. "Fine. No problem. Look, I gotta... check on my pack." He stood up and walked away, not looking at her.

Mary watched him go. She felt sorry for him. It wasn't easy for a Garou to forge a relationship; nobody wanted to put up with that kind of rage. All someone like Albrecht had in the end was his pack. She did not envy him. She felt guilty about being so cruel to him, but skirting the truth here would only have made it worse.

Albrecht walked over to where his pack was sleeping and walked past, over to Pramati, to sit down next to the Stargazer.

"Greetings," Pramati said.

"Hey," Albrecht said. "So, where do you guys go next?"

"We are going back to our caern in New Mexico. We need to rest and plan our next journey. It will be our hardest yet."

"Well, luck and all. Say... Mary over there. Is she really fit for this kind of work?"

Pramati looked back at Mary, who sat turned away from them. "She is excellent, Albrecht. We could not have gotten this far without her. Mages have powers we can't imagine. Most helpful powers."

"Yeah? That's good. She's just... kinda young and all."

"So is Evan. So are most of us when we undergo our Firsting. Gaia does not care about age when she calls us for duty. I know you are hurting from a pained heart—"

"Wait a minute—"

"Let me speak. Please. It is obvious. It is the fate of the Garou. It is so rare for us to find a mate, we who are forbidden to breed with our own kind. Our rage drives others away. It is a scary thing for them to live with. Gaia asks much of us. Many sacrifices. But this is perhaps the greatest. Take strength in that, Lord Albrecht. Every lost lover is a sign of our commitment to Gaia."

Albrecht looked at Pramati. "You're right. I don't even know why it bothers me so much, either. I mean, she's right. We were just a fling and all."

"Ah. That is simple. It is the most common wound in the world, but also the deadliest. Bruised ego. If we had no ego to injure, just think what a peaceful world this would be!"

Albrecht put on a humoring smile for Pramati. "Uh... yeah. I guess."

"Ha, ha. I see your real face beneath that smile. Do not worry, I am not offended. You are wondering, how could I travel so far with a crude man like Jack if I have such a sensitive heart?"

"You're damn perceptive, you know that?"

"I am a Galliard. Luna pays me to notice such things. They are the stuff stories are made of."

Albrecht smiled and sat for a while in silence. Then he said, "This is kind of funny, you know? The chances of my meeting up with her now were real slim, but here she is. I've been thinking about the *Lay of the Silver Crown*, and what it means for me now. None of it has seemed to work out so far, but... I don't know. I just got the whole hearth and home thing slapped away from me. That happened to the guy in the story, too. Makes me wonder how much of this is coincidence...."

"Legends indeed live in us today. But in what way? Who can say? We may ask the Theurges, but I have a feeling that we must each find the answer for ourselves."

"All this deep-thought stuff is out of my league. I'm an

Ahroun, damn it. This is Evan's job."

"It is the job of each and every one of us. A warrior with no awareness of his place in the spiritual order is merely a raging animal."

Albrecht sat in silence for a while. Pramati watched him as if wondering whether his lesson had gotten through.

"Tell me," Pramati said. "Where do you go next?"

"I have no idea," Albrecht said. "We didn't find clues in Pangaea. I don't know where to start."

"Why Pangaea at all?"

"A friend of ours, Antonine Teardrop — one of your own — dug up a legend about the crown. Seemed to point to Pangaea. But that was centuries ago. It could be anywhere now."

"Hmm. The crown is a powerful symbol, you know. It represents all of Garou civilization. I know that will sound strange to you, but we really do have a civilization. The Litany proves that, as do our rites and traditions. It is said that civilization began in Pangaea. The Dawn Times. That is the past. We stand in the present. But what is the future? What lies in store for civilization? Where does it lead?"

"I have no clue whatsoever. Where are you heading with this?"

"We know that our ways are dying. We need to revive them. That is what the crown represents — the resurrection of the old ways, making them new again. Now, assume that the ways are not revitalized, that they become stagnant and weary. Where does that lead? We know the beginning of civilization. But what is its end? Its inevitable conclusion, if it is not continually remade?"

"Uh... ruin? Anarchy?"

"No. That is a state of chaos upon which new forms will be built. I speak of the world as it is now if it is allowed to stay as it is, without changing. Think, my friend. What lies at the heart of a meaningless life? For that is what our ways, devoid of change, become."

"Nihilism. Emptiness. Darkness."

"Yes. Emptiness. Void. It is the inevitable future to which civilization is drawn. It is where the Silver Crown, forgotten for so many years, would be drawn. It is a place, Albrecht. A real place now. Here, in the spirit world."

Albrecht looked at Pramati, his eyes narrowing. "The Abyss."

Pramati nodded. "It is where you must go to seek the crown."

Albrecht shook his head. "Then I might as well just stop now. I don't stand a chance in that place. No Garou does. Hell, it's the end of everything. You walk in, but you don't walk out again."

"Untrue. Many have survived to tell the tale."

"But they all shudder when they do. Most barely escape alive, with or without their sanity intact. That place'll chew us up and spit us out."

"Nonetheless, it is the only place the crown could be. Everything lost goes to the Abyss. Lost heroes, lost children, lost fetishes. It must be there, Albrecht."

Albrecht nodded. "It makes sense, but... Gaia! I can't drag Evan and Mari into that!"

"Are they not here by their choice?"

"Yeah, but they're doing it for me. Hell, Mari's already been through a lot of shit. Did you see her last night? Wasn't like her at all. And Evan.... He has no idea what he's getting into."

"I am not so sure of that, my friend. That boy has strengths you can't imagine. He may be your savior in this quest."

"Look, he's smart and all, but he's just a kid. His rite was barely a year ago. He's not ready for the Abyss."

"I believe the decision will not be yours to make."

Albrecht stood up. "Thanks for the advice. I really do appreciate it, but... I gotta think about this."

"Certainly. Please do not hesitate to ask me anything else you wish."

Albrecht nodded and walked back to the fire, his head

swimming. *The Abyss!* He'd be a fool to go there. But he'd be a fool not to, if that was indeed where the crown was.

He bent down and shook Evan and Mari awake. "Hey. It's getting near moonrise. I've got to talk to you guys."

Mari and Evan stood up. Mari began stretching, her morning martial exercises. Evan yawned and scratched his head.

"You... uh," Albrecht said. "You're going to have to go back to New York."

Mari stopped her exercises and shot him a mean glance. "What are you talking about? We don't have the crown yet."

"Yeah," Evan said. "It's certainly not back in New York."

"Look... I've got to go somewhere pretty fierce. I don't want you guys coming. It's such a long shot that.... Well, I don't think it's worth risking us all for. This is my quest. I gotta go it alone."

"Oh no you don't!" Mari said, stepping up to him, her face inches from his. "I am *not* turning around now! I don't care where you're going, I'm coming along, if it's to Malfeas itself!"

"Me too," Evan said.

Albrecht looked at both of them and shook his head. "You guys are great. You really are. But I'm not kidding. The Abyss is—"

"The Abyss?!" Mari said. "What got that in your head?"

"I've talked this over with Pramati. It's the only logical place to look."

"Logic is not always the best course in the Umbra," Mari said. "We could try the Aetherial Realm first. There are wise Garou there. They might know."

"Look, guys," Albrecht said. "If it were anywhere else, it would have been found by now. It's lost. It's got to be in the Abyss."

"What about the Silver Fang Homeland?" Evan said. "Each tribe has its own spiritual realm. Maybe it's there."

Albrecht shook his head. "I think Greyfist would have

known if that were the case. Besides, it's said that the homelands are sub-realms of Pangaea. We didn't have any luck there."

Mari walked off a way, thinking. Evan began pacing, thinking also.

"The Trailblazers are going back to New Mexico," Albrecht said. "You can go with them and catch a Moon Bridge from there to New York."

"Stop it, Albrecht!" Mari said. "I told you we weren't giving up on this. It is *not* an option. Put it out of your head. If we have to go to the Abyss, then we'll go."

Albrecht threw up his hands. "All right! All right! But if you go stark raving mad there, I will not feel one ounce of guilt. Because I did not choose to take you there."

"Good. I wouldn't want something like my sanity to weigh heavy on your conscience, Albrecht. Gaia forbid that!" She walked over to the fire, snarling, and sat down next to Ivar.

Albrecht looked after her, puzzled.

"I think you've pushed it one time too many," Evan said, looking after Mari. "She's been through a lot, and I guess she's sick of your condescending attitude."

"Condescending? She usually starts it! She can't get over that tussle we had a couple of years back!"

"Let's just drop it now," Evan said. He walked over and sat down next to her. Albrecht remained where he was. He pulled out a cigarette, lit it and stood there, staring out at the dark plain.

Within the hour, the moon rose over the horizon. It was a gibbous moon, a Galliard's moon. Albrecht knew they had only a few more days until the full moon. Once the full moon hit its cusp, the midpoint between waxing and waning, their quest would be over regardless of whether they had succeeded. Arkady would be crowned king then, with all the rites of the Silver Fangs, and no artifact of old would be able to change that present truth.

The Trailblazers were packing up their camp. They seemed to have an efficient system for it: They were all packed up within ten minutes, with everything distributed among their backpacks. Ivar seemed to be carrying more than the rest of them.

Jack came up to Albrecht. "Well, lad, it's been fine meeting you. I wish you the best."

Albrecht put out his hand. Jack shook it.

"I hope you find the skin," Albrecht said. "Regardless, drop me a line now and then and let me know how it's going."

Jack smiled. "You got it. I will. And let me know how it all turns out for you. You can find us at the Painted Coyote Caern, in New Mexico. I wish you could come with us. Pram told me about your talk. I don't envy you. The Abyss is... bad news."

"Don't worry," Albrecht said. "Others have done it before us."

"Yeah, that's the spirit!" Jack smiled. "Well, we're off. Oh, by the way, Parts-the-Water gave Mari a couple of electric torches. They should help you in that dark pit. They're fixed up special, with spirits and all. Shouldn't go out on you anytime soon."

"Thanks," Albrecht said. "Happy trails."

"And to you!" Jack walked back to his pack, who were standing by the Moon Path now. It glowed bright under the gibbous moon. They all turned and waved at Albrecht, Mari and Evan, then walked off down the Path.

Albrecht watched them go until they took a curve in the path and were gone behind a rise. Then he sighed and walked over to Evan and Mari.

"You guys ready?" he said.

"Yeah," Evan said.

"I've been thinking," Mari said, handing a flashlight to each of them. "The best way to get to the Abyss is to find a break in a Moon Path, and follow that."

"Won't be many of those," Albrecht said. "The moon's gibbous now."

"If we keep looking, we'll find one. It doesn't take too long to find the Abyss."

Albrecht and Evan didn't say anything, but headed toward the Moon Path. Mari followed.

They walked for the entire night without finding a break in the path, and so decided to give up for the night and begin looking for whatever haven they could find to rest in during the day. About an hour before moonset, they discovered a small, abandoned, Weaver realm.

The place resembled a city block, with office buildings rising to the sky. Strands of old Pattern Spider webs hung from them. They had not been tended for a long time.

"This appears to have once been a Glen," Evan said as they walked down the street. "Until the Weaver spirits got hold of it."

Albrecht pointed at some grass bursting through the cracked pavement. "It looks like Gaia is reclaiming the place. I wonder what drove the spiders off."

"They weren't driven off," Mari said. "Look there. They were eaten."

Albrecht and Evan looked over to where Mari was pointing. In an alleyway, the desiccated and gnawed bones of a Pattern Spider were scattered about.

"Wonder what the hell eats Weaverlings?" Albrecht said, stepping up to examine the remains of the dead spirit.

"Whatever it was," Mari said. "There's no sign that anything's been here for a while. Not enough food, I suppose."

"Then I guess it's safe to camp here," Evan said.

Albrecht nodded. "I don't think we should go into the buildings, though."

"There's an alleyway over there that looks defensible," Mari said. "The Moon Path resumes on the other side of the fence, allowing us an escape route, and the alley entrance is thin enough to keep attackers coming one-on-one."

"Good," Albrecht said.

They planted their camp in the alley and set watches. It took each of them a while to get to sleep between watches, but when they did, none of them dreamed.

When the moon rose the next night, they set off again. Another long night of travel with no sign of breakage in the path. Albrecht was tempted to grab the next Lune — they had been few and far between on the path — and force it to break up the path. But he knew that would be more trouble than it was worth. Lunes didn't normally listen to reason.

About two hours before moonset, they came across a gap in the path. The pack stopped and looked at each other. Then Albrecht took the first step forward and boldly strode into the gap, while Mari and Evan followed. The ground there was featureless ephemera. Albrecht then walked off to the right, crosswise to the path. They walked in that direction for a while.

Then rolling mists began to move in from both sides. The fog never came close enough to touch the pack, but it created a corridor leading straight ahead. The pack followed it. Soon the mist walls moved back, and they could see a crevasse appear in the ground ahead. It started small but widened with distance, disappearing into the fogbank ahead.

When they came to the edge, they looked down.

And saw nothing.

They each gasped and stepped back, looking away from the yawning gulf, the void below. They all felt drawn down, as if gravity here pulled them harder. But they resisted it.

They each shuddered, considering what they had seen. Utter darkness, and within… the end of everything. Annihilation incarnate.

They each stepped back from the edge to consider the next move.

"What now?" Albrecht asked.

"There are tales of three paths here," Mari said. "One, called the Golden Path, is fraught with danger. It is said to be treacherous going, but great treasure awaits whoever gets to the end of it. I have never heard of anyone getting to the end. The Silver Path is the most enigmatic. I'm not sure where it leads, but some say great wisdom waits for those who brave it. Now, the Iron Path, it's the easiest. It leads to many caverns lacing the sides of the crevasse. However — and this is the catch — lots of nasty things live in those caverns. Including a creature named Nightmaster."

"What kind of creature?" Albrecht asked.

"He used to be a Shadow Lord, a Garou. Now he is said to be a child of the Abyss: its avatar. He's in charge of some of the things that live down there."

"You said caverns," Albrecht said. "I hear that's where fetishes show up."

"Yes, collected by the inhabitants. But if the crown is there, it's surely guarded by someone. Or something."

"Well, time's running out here. Let's find the Iron Path and get down there."

Mari nodded. "If we continue along the crevasse a little longer, I think we'll see the beginning of the path."

They walked along the edge, although each kept well back from it. The silence of the place was unnerving to all of them. Not even the sound of wind could be heard, although the tugging of the air could be felt, pulling down toward the darkness.

Soon they came across a path that led to a ledge down the crevasse. Precious gems could be seen along the rock wall, embedded in it. Veins of precious metals also appeared, especially gold.

"The Golden Path," Mari said. "We don't want that one."

They kept walking until they encountered another ledge, leading down. A cave opened off it about thirty yards down.

"This is it," Mari said. "The Iron Path. The Silver must be ahead, but we want this one."

Albrecht headed toward the ledge. "I'll go first. You two follow. Be careful."

"You, too," Evan said, following after him. Mari took up the rear.

The ledge was wide enough for them in Homid form, but it would be tricky if they had to take Crinos form. About fifteen yards down, it began to get dark.

"Damn," Albrecht said. "Moon's going down."

"Turn on your flashlight," Mari said.

Albrecht fished into his trenchcoat and pulled out the flashlight the Silent Strider had provided him. It was painted with pictograms, but otherwise appeared to be a regular flashlight. He clicked it on, and bright light flooded out of it. He aimed it at the path ahead and began walking again. Evan and Mari turned on their lights and followed.

When he got to the cave mouth, Albrecht carefully stepped in, shining the flashlight all around first. Bones littered the floor, some of them appearing to be the skulls of Crinos Garou. The rear of the cave disappeared into darkness. Albrecht motioned the others to follow him as he walked farther into the cave.

"I think we should start here. I bet it leads down, just like the ledge. But if the crown is here, it's in one of these caves, not just sitting on the path."

"I agree," Mari said. "Proceed."

They continued on. Far ahead they heard the dripping of water, apparently condensation from the cavern walls. They walked in the darkness with only their flashlights to guide them for what seemed like hours. The cave broke off into many different passages, and Albrecht took whichever seemed to lead down. It was too dark for them to map their way, and they had no paper anyway. Occasionally Mari would scratch a mark into the rock wall at a crossroads. Except for these faint marks, they left no sign of their passage.

Sometimes they found items scattered across the cavern floors, as if someone had dumped them there and forgotten about them. These objects varied from carved wooden toys to computer screens. The detritus of many cultures gathered in the dark.

In one small side cavern, Mari turned off to investigate a reflection from her waving flashlight. In the dirt, half-buried, was an ornate klaive. She called the others over to see it.

"It looks quite old, but very well preserved," she said. "It's got some interesting carvings on the pommel...."

"Don't touch it!" Albrecht said. "It might be cursed."

Mari moved away from it. "Anything here could be cursed. I wonder... what if the Silver Crown is also cursed from this place?"

Albrecht did not respond. He continued on down the passage. Mari and Evan followed.

Soon they heard scratching noises up ahead, faint and intermittent. They moved cautiously forward, and came to a large cavern. Albrecht swung his flashlight to the right and then back again as it passed over something unusual.

In the center of the room was a cage. And in the cage was a little girl, miserably clawing at the lock with her pale hands.

Albrecht hurried forward, but Mari put her hand on his shoulder. He turned back and saw her cautious look. She didn't trust this situation. He walked forward anyway.

The girl did not seem to notice them or the light of the flashlight.

"Hey! Girl!" Albrecht said as he reached the cage.

The girl did not respond. She just kept scratching at the

lock. Her fingers were bleeding.

Albrecht shone the flashlight in her eyes. Her pupils did not respond. He turned to Mari, who was also at the cage now.

"She's deaf and blind, I think," Albrecht said.

"Be careful," Mari warned. "She may not be what she seems."

"Don't worry," Albrecht said. "Evan! Shine your light at the lock. I'm going to try to break it."

Evan did not respond.

Albrecht swung his flashlight around. There was no sign of the boy.

"Evan!" he yelled.

Mari was running around the room now, shining her light in every corner. "Evan! Where are you?"

"When did you last see him?" Albrecht asked.

"He was right behind me before we entered the cavern," she said, running back to the passageway by which they had entered and swinging her light up it. She turned back to Albrecht.

"He's gone," she said.

CHAPTER FIFTEEN

Evan stumbled along in the darkness, weak and dizzy. He felt around. The rock walls surrounded him on both sides, getting narrower. He didn't remember this place. He had come the wrong way.

He tried to calm down, to keep from panicking. He thought back, retracing his steps to figure out how he had come here. He remembered walking behind Mari, and then something had grabbed him from behind. Something which smelled awful. Its clawed hand had covered his mouth to keep him from crying out as it dragged him off into another passage, taking his flashlight from him.

He had tried to resist, shifting to Crinos form, but his abductor was stronger. Then it had let Evan go. Evan had run, back toward Albrecht and Mari, crying out for them. But the passageways weren't the same. He couldn't see anything, and was forced to rely on touch and smell. But everything here smelled the same — a musty, moist cave.

His abductor was gone without a sound or scent. Evan was puzzled. He carefully walked back the way he had come, but each step seemed to take something out of him. He felt spent, the way he did after using Garou magic, after expending his own spiritual energy.

He leaned up against a wall and thought about his predicament. He thought about the tales and legends of this place.

And then he knew. He knew what was happening to him. His spirit was being drained against his will. And he knew the person behind it.

Nightmaster.

Evan shivered, but he summoned all his courage and spoke: "I know you're there, Nightmaster. I've heard the stories. I know it has to be you."

He heard a step, not more than ten feet away down the passage ahead of him. He caught the scent again: the scent of ancient musk, of a very old animal. He heard low, raspy breathing. And then a voice.

"Who is this boy? Who calls me by name?"

Evan swallowed. "I am Evan Heals-the-Past, a Wendigo."

A grunt, mere feet away. Nightmaster was closer. "Why has the boy come? The boy knows of his enemy. Yet he has trespassed into his lair."

"We have no quarrel with you. We are just seeking an artifact."

"We? The boy has packmates. Who are these packmates? The boy will tell us."

Evan gasped as he felt hot, rancid breath against his cheek. Nightmaster was standing inches away from him now.

"Please. I can't see anything. Can I have my flashlight?"

Another grunt. "The light? The boy knows this place devours the light. Yet the boy begs for it. Begs for what is unnatural to this place. Why?"

"I... want to see what you look like."

"The boy wishes to see Nightmaster, leader of the Society of Nidhogg? Nightmaster, extinguisher of the sun? The boy has humor. Yes, the boy shall see Nightmaster."

Evan felt the flashlight being thrust into his hands. He

flipped the switch, and light flooded the passageway. Standing inches away from him, looming at least three or four feet taller than him, was a Crinos Garou. At least, it had once been a Crinos Garou. The fur was oily and the skin parched and dried, looking almost mummified. Evan looked up into Nightmaster's eyes and saw the empty chasm there, a reflection of the empty void he had witnessed outside. The end of everything stared back at him through two wolfish eyes.

"Is the boy scared? Does he tremble before the mighty Shadow Lord?"

Evan nodded, unable to speak.

"The boy will now say what his packmates seek."

"Uh... we... ah.... The Silver Crown. That's what we're looking for."

Nightmaster stepped back and cocked his head at an angle. But Evan was not sure whether that was meant as a gesture of confusion, coming from this shell of a Garou.

"The Silver Crown. The hated crown. Crown of my enemy. Crown of the wrongful kings. The crown which was created as a joke against the Shadow Lords. The crown which stole the leadership of the pack from them. The evil crown. Why does the boy want the crown?"

"To... uh... crown my packmate king."

"Packmate is a Shadow Lord?"

"No. A Silver Fang."

Nightmaster roared in anger, lunging at Evan with his snout. Evan cringed back, knowing he was helpless before the more powerful Garou. But Nightmaster's jaws stopped just short of Evan's muzzle, as he stared into Evan's eyes, a chaotic movement deep within his own. Evan stared back, seeing that raging emotion in Nightmaster's eyes.

Evan decided to take a gamble, although he knew it would probably get him killed. "You're not as empty as I thought," he said.

Nightmaster stepped back and cocked his head again. "The

boy is going mad. Seeing things. Untrue things."

"In your eyes, when you got angry. There was rage there. Not just the abyss."

Nightmaster growled low and moved toward Evan, but then stopped, confused. "Anger. Nightmaster has anger. Nightmaster always has the anger. It is part of the emptiness."

"But if you've got something, such as anger, then you can't be empty. By definition."

Nightmaster reached out and snatched Evan by the neck. He spun around and marched down the passage, dragging Evan with him. Evan struggled to breathe as the grip began strangling him. As he thrust his fingers between his throat and Nightmaster's hand, the grip loosened. Not enough to let Evan drop, though.

"The boy is wrong. The boy knows not the Abyss. The boy will know the Abyss. Like all the children. The boy will learn the Abyss. Will learn the darkness. Will be devoured by darkness. Will be a child again. Child of the Abyss."

Nightmaster stormed through passageways, jogging now. Evan was slammed into the walls as his captor hurriedly turned corners. He struggled to right himself, to get his feet under him so he could at least keep pace with the mad Garou, but Nightmaster moved too quickly and made too many surprise turns.

Then Nightmaster came to a sudden stop and tossed Evan through the air. Evan tried to twist so he would land on his feet, but then slammed into a metal cage. He yelped at the pain, and hit the ground hard, knocking the wind out of himself. As he lay there, stunned, he saw light, and heard voices calling his name....

Albrecht and Mari stood in the cavern, arguing about what to do. Albrecht wanted to pick up Evan's scent and chase it through the tunnels. Mari claimed that the scent would disappear and they would be lost; that their best hope was to wait there for Evan to reappear. As Albrecht was about to give up in disgust and take to the passageway, they heard something large and heavy hit the other side of the cage.

Albrecht ran around the cage and saw Evan lying there in Crinos form. "Evan!"

Mari came around the other side. "Thank Gaia! He's here! But what brought him here?" She swung her flashlight around the room but saw nothing.

Evan groaned, trying to speak, but he was clearly stunned and having trouble coming to his senses.

The cage door loudly unlocked itself. Albrecht pointed his flashlight toward it as the door swung wide, but no one was there. The little girl stopped scratching, although she seemed not to understand that the door was open.

A voice appeared in the cavern, coming from all directions. "The boy will get in the cage, where all children belong."

"Who the hell?" Albrecht barked.

Mari stood up, instantly in Crinos form, looking for something to attack.

Evan sat up, coughing. "It... it's Nightmaster...."

Mari's eyes narrowed and she scanned the corners of the room. Nothing.

Albrecht helped Evan to his feet. "The Shadow Lord?"

"Yes," Nightmaster said, nowhere in sight. "The true lord. Not the usurper. Not the pretender. Not the Silver Fang."

Albrecht looked around the room. "Oh, yeah? I'm not the one living in a cave, pal."

"Impudent Fang. Idiot Fang. Seeks the crown. Nightmaster will give him the crown. He will rule. King of sacrifices. Sacrificed to the Abyss."

The spirits within the flashlights screamed as the lights went out, plunging the cavern into darkness.

Albrecht drew his klaive and assumed a fighting stance. He was in Crinos form and so he opened his senses, trying to catch any sign of Nightmaster. He could see, hear and smell nothing.

A claw ran up his back, not breaking the skin or tearing his coat; but it sent a chill through him. He swung his klaive around to hit the spot Nightmaster had to be standing in. Nothing.

"The boy will get into the cage. All children into the cage. Learn the Abyss."

"You put that girl there?" Mari yelled. "You bastard! What for? She's just a girl."

"Lost girl. Wanders to Abyss. Gift for Abyss. But must be trained. Must learn to accept Abyss. Must see nothing. Must hear nothing. Must feel nothing. Must be nothing."

"You fucking asshole!" Albrecht yelled. "You don't like Silver Fangs? Well, come and get me!"

A claw slashed at Albrecht's leg, but he felt the slight stirring of the air before it struck, and was able to move aside before the full force of the blow hit him. He swung his klaive down and it struck something in mid-darkness. A grunt was heard.

"Taste of your own medicine, asshole," Albrecht said. "So the mighty Shadow Lord is not perfect. Of course not. Otherwise he would be wearing the Silver Crown himself. But then, I bet he's afraid to put it on. Aren't you?"

"Silver Crown? Give it to Nightmaster and he will put it on. Become king over more than Abyss."

Albrecht frowned. "Tell me where it is and I'll give it to you."

"No. You have it! You will give it to Nightmaster!" Something crashed into Albrecht, forcing him to the ground.

Albrecht concentrated, drawing on the power given to him by the spirits, and his fur lit up into a bright white glow, flooding the cavern.

Standing next to the prone Albrecht, revealed in the intense light of Gaia's power, Nightmaster screamed and clutched at his eyes. Albrecht slashed at the Garou's legs with his klaive, and hacked off one of them. Nightmaster crashed to the ground, trying to crawl away.

Mari ran at him from the other side and kicked him in the head, knocking him back toward the glowing Albrecht.

Albrecht grabbed him by the throat and held his klaive inches from the Garou's gut. Nightmaster blinked, trying to adjust to the light.

"Where's the Silver Crown, damn it?!"

Nightmaster looked at Albrecht, awareness of a sort dawning on his face. "The crown is here? Nightmaster has not been told! Nightmaster must punish his legions!"

Albrecht rammed his klaive into the Garou's stomach and Nightmaster screamed in pain, coughing up a pool of oily, brackish blood before he fell over dead.

Albrecht pulled out his klaive and wiped it on the dead Garou's fur. The blood was sticky, however, and did not come off easily.

"Well, this was a load of shit," Albrecht said. "The crown's not even here."

"Albrecht!" Mari cried.

Albrecht looked down at Nightmaster in time to see him get up and run off, hopping on one leg. Albrecht took off after him, but the other Garou reached the passageway first. When Albrecht came around the corner, he was gone.

"Damn it! He's got a lot of lives!"

Evan walked over to him, looking in terrible shape. His eyes barely focused. "All I know is, he scares the shit out of me. He's what we'll become if we stay here. He's probably gathering his legions now. We've got to go."

Albrecht nodded, staring worriedly at Evan before going back into the cavern. He had never seen the kid looking so ragged before. Mari was standing by the door of the cage. She looked up at him as he came near, and he saw tears in her eyes.

"She's dead," Mari said. "He cut her throat. Probably when everything was dark. What kind of sick—"

"Let's just go, Mari," Albrecht said. He turned back to the passage and walked out. Mari bowed her head and followed him, knowing there was nothing she could do. And it hurt like hell.

Evan joined them in the passage and they followed Albrecht out, his glowing fur lighting the passage for them.

"I'll say this for the Silver Fangs," Mari said. "Your spirits teach you good Gifts."

"The Lambent Flame was created for just such a situation as this," Albrecht said, marching forward. "When the First Wolf encountered the Greater Darkness to free Gaia from its clutches, the Darkness devoured him. But he learned the secret of death while in that cold embrace. And he learned how to combat the darkness with his own light. Our legends say that the Abyss is the body of the slain Greater Darkness. I didn't believe it until today."

Mari's wall scratchings helped them to orient themselves, but they took many wrong turns on the upward ascent. The passageways actually seemed to change their features at times, and Mari swore that she saw her marks on crossroads she had never been through before. These false marks invariably led them back down into the caverns. They would then have to backtrack and find those passages which inclined upwards.

What disturbed Albrecht more, however, was that he and Mari had to keep Evan from wandering off by himself down strange passageways. Whenever they stopped him, he seemed to start as if waking from a dream. Looking around, his eyes would show a despair greater than he had a right to claim for his years. Albrecht knew they had to get out of there before the place claimed Evan.

They heard noises far off, scratchings and floppings, wet

slaps of flesh on stone, as if things were moving in the walls. Scuttlings before and behind them. But nothing could be seen.

They hurried their pace and readied their weapons. They were all in Crinos form, and their nervousness had begun to tell on their self-control. Mari was jittery, and Evan shivered. Albrecht was a rock, a pillar of immovable determination. His seething anger at Nightmaster and the fact that, once again, the crown had eluded him served to focus his energy on one goal: escape.

"The Fang will hurt," Nightmaster's voice came out of the darkness, from no place, indeterminable. "Yes, he will experience much pain."

Albrecht did not stop, but kept moving forward. Mari growled. She hated this baiting by the Shadow Lord. Evan concentrated and drew upon Gaia's strength to still his nerves and allow him to think straight. His purpose renewed, he began to search through the dark for any sign of the hollow-souled Shadow Lord.

"The pack will join the Abyss. The pack will welcome the Abyss. Become empty to it. One with it. Nothing with it. Legions... attack!"

A howling erupted all around them and shapes appeared before and behind: large Crinos Garou. Albrecht didn't hesitate, but immediately tore into the three attackers before him with his klaive. Surprised at the ferocity and speed of his attack, two of the Garou whimpered and disappeared, their blood trailing into the walls. The last remaining enemy swept his claws out and scraped them against Albrecht's chest. They barely broke the skin, and Albrecht lunged forward with his snout, clamping his teeth into his foe's neck. Blood sprayed across the passageway as the Garou tried to pull out of the hold, ripping his own throat in the process. The body hit the floor with a thud, and was still.

Behind the pack, Mari faced four attackers. She lashed out with her leg, meeting one of the attackers full in the face and knocking it back into the others, who were all trying to edge past him to get to Mari. She stepped back and held out her hands, calling on her Gift. Her claws shot from her hand like wasps and tore into the Garou, who screamed in pain and whimpered back down the passageway, seeking refuge in the dark. Only one remained, panting eagerly for the kill.

Mari waited for him to come and swept his feet out from under him with her left leg while leaping up with her right. She landed on his stomach and flexed her toes, driving her sharp claws into his gut. She then twisted in place, tearing a circular gash into his stomach. He howled in pain and she rammed her fist into his snout, breaking his fangs. He crumpled, unconscious.

Evan suddenly bolted past Mari and ran after the fleeing Garou.

"No, Evan!" Mari yelled and went after him.

Evan had a good lead on her, though, and reached the Garou before she could get to him. Mari had visions of Evan becoming one of them, of Evan as an empty-eyed zombie Garou. She screamed. "Evan! No!"

But Evan did not slow down. He howled in rage and leapt onto the closest Garou, which was clearly startled at Evan's ferocity and barely got his hands up in time. It did him no good. Evan tore the limbs from their sockets and threw them behind him. He drove his snout into the Garou's chest, splitting open the chest bone and rib cage, and then savagely tore out the Garou's heart with his teeth.

The other Garou disappeared into the darkness, whimpering. Mari stopped cold, staring in horror at Evan. He was frenzying, and she knew that to stop him could cause him more harm than the Abyss Garou now could.

Evan sat on top of the Garou and stared into its slowly dying eyes. As the red haze of anger cleared, he saw a spark of emotion in those eyes. He saw fear. Then the eyes shut forever, and the Garou expelled its last breath.

Evan began to cry as it all came at him at once. The horrors of the journey had finally become greater than his ability to withstand them. Sobbing, he shifted back to Homid form.

Mari approached and put her hand on his shoulder. Albrecht slowly walked up, unsure what to think. He had just seen the kid freak out for only the second time in his young Garou life; the other had been during his First Change. A frenzy was not a nice thing to witness. It stripped a Garou of all identity, making him a bestial killing machine.

"We've got to go," he said.

Evan nodded and stood up.

"Are you all right?" Mari asked.

"Yeah. It... it just got to be a little too much. You know?"

Mari nodded.

"I know, kid," Albrecht said. "It ain't pretty, but we all lose it every once in a while. For some of us, that time comes more often."

Evan walked past Mari and nodded at Albrecht. "Let's go."

Albrecht turned back the way they had come and led them forward. "You know," he said as he walked, "Nightmaster's legion is a bunch of cowards."

"Don't be so sure," Evan said. "You didn't see Nightmaster up close like I did. The sooner we're out of here, the better."

"I agree," Mari said, flexing her now-regrown claws. "We need to keep moving."

The ground rose more quickly now, and they knew they were almost back where they had begun. They also heard a whistling noise, low, almost indiscernible. It grew in volume as they walked, and soon they felt a breeze tugging at their fur, pulling them forward, as if air were rushing out of the cave in the direction they were walking.

"Strange," Evan said. "The wind is really stirring. But there are no spirits here."

"Walk now. Talk later," Albrecht said.

They came into the first cavern, stepping on bones as they went. The brittle bones cracked underfoot, but the noise was nearly drowned by the wind. The wind was a gust now, drawing the air past them and out of the cavern entrance. Albrecht stepped out onto the ledge, and immediately jumped back in.

"Damn!" he said. "Watch your step. That wind gets fierce out there. Almost sucked me into the crevasse."

From deep in the caves behind them came Nightmaster's voice: "All are drawn in. None can escape. Silver Fang will feed the beast."

Albrecht growled. "All right. Follow me. We'll hug the wall. Move slowly and carefully."

Mari and Evan nodded, and Albrecht stepped out again. His fur whipped furiously in the wind, but he was unmoved. He slowly stepped to the side, moving back up the ledge. Evan followed, swaying for a moment as the wind hit him, but he leaned against the wall and retained his balance. Mari slipped around the corner right behind Evan, but she was well-balanced and kept her place easily.

They moved slowly up the ledge toward the top, the wind whipping about them. A horrible moaning sound rose up from the dark pit. They all shivered, unable to help themselves. The wail touched a deep part of their souls, an immature, fearful place. Almost unconsciously, Albrecht felt himself being drawn to the edge, but he fought the urge and clung to the wall, moving step by step upward. But he had caught a glance into the pit, and knew the sight would be with him forever. The sight of raw emptiness, deeper than before — a yawning, hungry gulf desperate to be filled yet devouring everything which fed it; impossible to describe truly. His mind nearly shattered trying to think about it. It was only with a great effort that he could force it from his thoughts and concentrate on walking.

He staggered forward, but gained strength with every step.

Each step got him closer to the top, closer to safety. Evan followed, looking away from the pit, hugging his face against the wall.

Smart kid, Albrecht thought. *If I'd done that, I'd have saved myself from seeing that — Shit! Don't think about it! Think about what's ahead. Only what's ahead.*

As he got to the top, the wind brought a scent to him: the smell of Garou. Many Garou. He poked his head around the corner and saw fifteen Black Spiral Dancers waiting there, all staring straight at him.

"Shit," he said.

"Albrecht!" Mari yelled over the wind. "Move it! There's a pack of Black Spirals moving up the path behind us."

"Calm down, Mari. There's a lot more up here." He walked up and stood at the head of the path, his klaive out and ready. The wind stopped as soon as he was off the ledge. Evan came up behind him.

Mari heard a scream behind her and turned to see one of the five Black Spirals fall off the ledge. The Dancers had crawled out of a cave far below and were working their way up to her. The fallen one vanished in the darkness of the great pit and his scream was abruptly cut off. The other Black Spirals stared after him in horror. One of them began to laugh hysterically, walking to the edge while his companions tried to pull him back. He fought them for a moment, then seemed to come to his senses. They began to climb the ledge again. Mari grimaced and reached the top.

A Black Spiral walked over to Albrecht's pack, holding his hand up to the others to keep them away. He was a tall man with a thin face and long black hair.

"Let's not be hasty here, Lord Albrecht," he said. "We outnumber and outgun you here. But we don't want you dead." He stopped, smiling as if he misspoke himself. "Well, to be more precise, our queen does not want you dead. In fact, she has requested an audience. Would you please come along? It would not do for the would-be king to deny the queen of a neighboring kingdom."

"You know me, but I don't know you, pal," Albrecht said.

The Black Spiral Dancer feigned surprise. "You mean Duke Arkady never mentioned me? How rude. And after all I've done for him. Well, he's left it up to me to do the introductions. I am Dagrack, war chieftain of the Dank Well Hive in the Adirondacks. We're neighbors."

Albrecht stared hatefully at the Black Spiral Dancer, but sheathed his klaive. "Don't fight them," he said to Evan and Mari. "We'd lose."

Dagrack smiled, nodding.

Mari fumed at Albrecht but then looked away. Evan seemed worried.

"Don't worry," Albrecht said. "They want us alive. At least for now."

Dagrack motioned to the path on which the pack had originally traveled into the realm. "After you. There is a Moon Bridge waiting just outside the borders of this realm."

Albrecht, Mari and Evan walked away from the crevasse. The Black Spiral Dancers, eerily silent, flowed after them.

CHAPTER SIXTEEN

More fucking caves, thought Albrecht. *These ones're worse than the others*.

Albrecht, Mari and Evan walked through a winding passageway. Other tunnels broke off from it in various places, leading off into darkness. The host of Black Spiral Dancers trailed behind them, except for Dagrack, who led the way.

The tunnels stank. Not just in an unpleasant way, but in an overwhelming, poisonous way. Albrecht had coughed up phlegm twice already, and Evan was doing worse. Mari seemed to be handling it better than either of them, although she did have a nauseated look on her face.

Throughout the tunnels, growing from the floors and walls, were giant, bloated fungi. The massive black and yellow growths seemed to pulsate at times, but it could have been a trick of the light from the sputtering torches placed along the main passage.

Far off down one tunnel, Albrecht saw a greenish glow emanating from one of the walls. He tried to hurry past that tunnel as quickly as possible. Balefire. Pure, toxic radiation. The excretions of the Wyrm, it was said.

Figures shambled along on either side of their marching

party: wretched creatures that looked like deformed Garou. Metis — the result of Garou inbreeding. Albrecht looked at them closely. He knew most Black Spiral Dancers were metis, since they found it hard to keep flocks of Kinfolk with whom they could breed. He also knew that their perverted society had a caste system: breeders on top and non-breeders on the bottom. But these things crawling along.... They must be the rejects, those born so deformed that they were barely viable. They were obviously performing the role of worker drones.

Albrecht shook his head and refused to watch them anymore. *Look too much at the Wyrm's works*, he thought, *and you might start pitying them. And that's the last thing they deserve.*

A howling and screaming could be heard from one of the tunnels ahead, along with grunting and heavy breathing. As they passed, Albrecht looked in, and immediately looked away again.

I did not need to see that, he thought. *I could've gone the rest of my life without seeing Black Spiral Dancer sex, thank you.*

Dagrack turned into a side tunnel, a larger one than most, and led them to an oak door placed at the end of the tunnel. It looked as if it barely fit the passage, since light flooded out from within through the large cracks on the sides. Dagrack slammed his fist into the door and waited.

A voice came from within: "Enter."

Dagrack pushed open the door and walked in, motioning them to follow. The room was circular and inlaid with marble. Polished marble. This room was different. Special. Albrecht looked across the room and saw why.

A woman sat on a chair on a raised dais, staring at them with glee. She was naked, and Albrecht could clearly see three pairs of breasts on her, one under the other, like an animal. She smiled, revealing her fangs. She had short blond hair and pale, pale skin.

The throne she sat on was a carved marble block with a depression large enough to fit a Crinos Garou. Albrecht shook his head. It was a mockery of his tribe. His protectorate. Many of the Silver Fangs of Vermont were marble barons, making their fortunes on the many marble deposits in the southern portion of the state. For this Black Spiral to deck her throne room out in it... it was pure insult.

Dagrack bowed on bended knee. "My queen. I have brought the would-be king and his pack."

The woman nodded. "Lord Albrecht. It is a pleasure to entertain royalty."

"Who the hell are you?" Albrecht asked.

She frowned. "Such manners for gentry! I am Queen Azaera."

"Never heard of you," Albrecht said, looking back at Mari and Evan. Mari was giving him a warning look. He frowned. She seemed to know who this lady was. Did Mari think it wasn't a good idea to insult her? *If so, I better back off*, he thought.

Azaera stood up and walked down the dais toward her guests. She was no longer smiling, but had a cold, hard look on her face. "We will stop this idle chatter, then, and come to the point. Where is the Silver Crown?"

"Why do you want it? I thought Arkady was your horse to bet on."

"Arkady does not recognize that he would only serve as a regent for me. I need the crown to cement my power, to expand my kingdom."

"What?! Are you nuts? It'll fry your head off!"

"Don't be so sure, deluded Gaialing. Your legends have lied before. Never has there been a ruler like Azaera. The crown will have to accept me. My ancestors say so. They have seen it before. They know its power."

"Your ancestors are just as cracked as you are, you freaking bitch."

Azaera walked up to him. He was taller, forcing her to look up, but her arrogance did not seem diminished by this. She ran a claw along his chest, playfully. "I appreciate pride in a king, but you go too far. I am queen here. You need to show proper deference, or I will be forced to make—" She stopped speaking as she felt the bulk of his klaive in its sheath underneath Albrecht's coat. She jumped back, screaming.

"Idiots! You did not disarm them!"

Dagrack shrugged his shoulders. "Slipped my mind. Surely they cannot threaten such a queen as you."

She spun on him, hissing as she began to shift to Crinos form, a huge, terrifying aspect. Drawing back her hand, she slashed at Dagrack's forehead. He grunted as the claw opened a gash, spilling blood down his face. But he did not move or try to defend himself.

"Churl!" Azaera yelled.

Dagrack sighed. "Yes, my queen."

Azaera seemed satisfied and walked back up the dais. "Disarm them."

"Over my dead body," Albrecht said, reaching into his coat and gripping his klaive.

Azaera turned and looked at him, eyes narrowed. "You will die, then."

"And you will never find the crown."

Azaera's eyes widened. "Ah... diplomacy. Now we are royal." She turned to Dagrack. "Take the packmates. Leave us! We speak of state secrets."

Dagrack rose and grabbed Mari's shoulder, beginning to pull her toward the door. She slipped from his grip and hit him on the back with both hands, sending him tumbling to the floor.

The rest of the Black Spiral Dancers howled and pounded toward her, then stopped dead in their tracks at a screech from Azaera.

"Stop! They are prisoners. Do not kill them. They are our *détente*." She looked at Albrecht.

He ignored her. "Mari, summon a Wyldling! Get out of here!"

Mari was standing ready to take any attack, with Evan at her back. "I can't. I can only do that from the Umbra."

Albrecht looked down. "We're fucked."

Dagrack got back up and glared at Mari. He motioned toward the door. "Make it easy on yourself and me. Just go."

Mari stepped toward the door, Evan next to her. They both looked at Albrecht as they left, but said nothing. The Black Spirals fell in behind them, and Dagrack left last, glaring at Albrecht, but then giving an angry glance at Azaera. He closed the door behind him.

Azaera walked seductively up the dais and sat on the throne, her legs spread wide. "Do you find me attractive?"

Albrecht looked away. "Not in the slightest."

Azaera frowned. "You do not know how to play the game well. So we will quit with games. You will tell me where the crown is or I will kill your packmates. No! Worse... I will make them walk the Black Spiral, dance the labyrinth. They will come to know the Wyrm as we do... as benevolent father and tortured victim of Gaia."

"Would you believe me if I said I don't know where the crown is?"

Azaera seemed to think for a minute, examining Albrecht. "Yes. But it's not what I want to hear."

"Well, I don't have any other answers for you."

Azaera looked away and seemed to be thinking to herself. "Curses. Shit. This ruins everything."

Albrecht stood watching her, wondering what weird logic was working through that demented brain.

Azaera looked at him again, smiling. "You can leave. Fly away little falcon."

Albrecht just stood there, not saying anything.

"I'm serious. Leave. I don't want you here."

"You mean I can just walk out of here? With Mari and Evan?"

"No. You can walk out of here, but they can't. Détente, lord. Détente. If you happen to find the crown, you can come back here and exchange it for them. I'll keep them around for a few days at least. After Arkady takes the throne.... Well, I think you understand political misfortunes. Don't bother coming back after that. I'll kill you then, impudent cub."

Albrecht didn't say anything. He sat there, measuring his options. He could take out his klaive and chop her up. He could then track his pack through the tunnels and rescue them, carving their way out together through a mountain of Black Spiral Dancer bodies. But he knew that was suicide. And if he did that, he would never find the crown. He had maybe two days to find it.

He felt like an ass. *Chasing after a damn heirloom rather than rescuing my packmates*. But they had known the risks when they signed onto this quest. They knew that he had to finish what he had started.

He sighed. "How do I get out of here?"

"Down the passage you came. You will recognize the Moon Bridge room when you see it. Tell the Gatekeeper that Azaera gives you leave to go. He will believe you; my Banes will inform him beforehand. Tell him where you wish to go, and he will deliver you there."

Albrecht nodded and turned to leave the room.

"Farewell, O king," Azaera said.

Albrecht did not respond. He opened the door and walked out, closing it behind him. He couldn't stand the idea of her watching him walking off down the tunnel. He marched back the way he had come, smoldering with barely suppressed rage, ignoring the crawling drones around him.

As he passed a side tunnel, he heard Mari call out. "Albrecht!"

He turned to look at her. She and Evan were being led

down the passage toward whatever fate awaited them. Evan looked scared, but Mari looked furious, ready to frenzy.

"I... I'm sorry. I can't do anything," Albrecht said, watching them be pulled away.

She glared at him. "Asshole! I should have known better than to join you! You've always been a self-obsessed asshole!"

Evan looked at Albrecht, nodding. "I... understand. Just get the crown, Albrecht."

Albrecht stood there, watching his packmates disappear into the darkness. He trembled in rage, but fought to control it. Mari's accusations he could understand. He expected that from her. But Evan.... He gave up too easy. He thought of Albrecht before himself. *That's not right*, Albrecht thought. *I don't deserve that! That kid's putting his trust in the wrong place, damn it. And it makes me feel even shittier than if he cursed me like Mari.*

Albrecht walked down the passage to the Moon Bridge room. He growled at the robed Dancer there to get him to Central Park. The Gatekeeper stared coldly at Albrecht.

"I can't," the Dancer said. "It has defenses that will not allow my pathstone to connect. Unless, of course, you could give me the proper rites...."

Albrecht growled at him. "I'll tear your head off! Don't fuck with me! I'm not in the mood. Just send me.... Hell, I don't know! To the Silver Fang Homeland in the Umbra."

The Dancer chewed his lower lip. "I can't. I can get you close, but not into the realm."

Albrecht grabbed his robe and shook him. "What's your problem? Doesn't this lead anywhere?"

The Dancer laughed. "It's a Black Spiral Dancer Moon Bridge. Do you *want* it to lead everywhere?"

Albrecht let him go. "Just open a Bridge."

The Gatekeeper began the rite. It was almost identical to the one with which Albrecht was familiar, but the names the Dancer called out to were almost unpronounceable and left a tingling in Albrecht's spine when he heard them.

A hole in the air opened up, glowing with silver radiance. Albrecht stepped into it and stepped out onto a Moon Path in the Umbra. He was in a featureless landscape under a gibbous moon. The bridge closed behind him, and he was alone.

With no idea of where to go next.

CHAPTER SEVENTEEN

When the moon finally disappeared below the horizon, dimming the Moon Path, Albrecht was still lost. He had walked for hours and had seen nothing but the path and the ephemeral barrens on either side. No realms or domains to be seen anywhere. The Black Spiral Dancer had lied. He had not put Albrecht anywhere near his destination.

Albrecht sat down on the path and put his head in his hands. He had never felt so low before. Even after the exile and during the drinking bout that had followed, he had had his youthful pride to prop him up. But now… now he felt he had used up all his luck. This was the universe's revenge for his having been a self-absorbed ass for all these years. Never thinking of others, or even of Gaia really. Always concerned instead with glory.

But glory ain't worth shit if there's no one to witness it, he thought. *It's over. Arkady's going to be king and I'll crawl back to New York, packless again. I'm going to hit the bottle again, that's for sure. This time I ain't getting back out.*

He saw a light to his left and looked up to see a Lune aimlessly floating down the dimming Moon Path. Albrecht got up and stood in its way, blocking the path.

The Lune floated toward him and stopped inches away, spinning around and around. Then it floated upwards, as if it meant to go over him.

Albrecht reached up and grabbed it, pulling it back down. "I am lost, hungry and shit out of luck. You are going to take me to the Silver Fang Homeland, do you hear me? I know I don't speak your lingo, but I think you savvy mine. All right? Let's get this over with!"

The Lune began spinning about furiously, trying to break Albrecht's grip. But Albrecht only squeezed tighter.

Light exploded from the Lune and a hole opened in the air between it and Albrecht. The Lune tugged itself away, pulling Albrecht into the hole with its momentum before he could fully release his grip. He fell into the Moon Bridge.

The hole sealed up behind him, shutting out the light, as the Lune continued its enigmatic journey down the path.

Albrecht fell. He had come out on the other side of the Moon Bridge to find himself in mid-air. Looking down, he saw the ground far below. He figured the distance to be about one hundred yards below as he plummetted toward the ground. The green, autumn-leaf-strewn ground.

The ground rippled, and became water. Albrecht crashed into it, shattering its wavy mirror and plunging in. He was swinging his limbs about wildly, trying to resurface, when the water turned into sand. His legs were buried in the white particles, and he spat out a mouthful of it.

He pulled himself out and looked around. He was in a desert. From horizon to horizon, all he saw were sand dunes, slowly shifting in a light breeze.

I'm in a Wyld realm, he thought. *That's gotta be it. A field becomes a lake which becomes a desert. What else could it be?*

He stood up and looked for landmarks of any kind. There was nothing.

I hope like hell it turns into a beautiful tropical island soon, he thought. *'Cause I'm awful thirsty already. Much more of this and I'll dry up here, king of an empty, forlorn patch of desert.*

Having nothing better to do, he started walking. The sun was bright and burning, so he pulled his trenchcoat off and draped it over his head to shade his face.

He walked like that for hours, until the sun went down and the moon rose. It was full enough for most humans to have called it a full moon, but, being a Garou, Albrecht was more sensitive to such things. He knew it was still gibbous. The full moon was his moon, an Ahroun's moon, and he knew he'd feel it in his soul when that phase took to the sky. He also knew that when it was full, two nights from now, Arkady would be crowned.

He had found no food or water. He was exhausted. Without some sustenance soon, he would start feeling the consequences. He could last longer than most humans or animals deprived of food or water, but he knew that the more active he was, the weaker he would get.

He lay down next to a smoothly rising dune and closed his eyes. In seconds, he was asleep.

He woke with a start. Something was wrong. He looked around, gripping his klaive. The landscape had changed again. He was now in a wood, surrounded by white birches. The ground was flat and even, a carpet of green grass between the tree trunks. It was eerily pure. Just the trees and the grass, in all directions. The trees even seemed to be lined up in rows, but Albrecht couldn't be sure of this. The moon was high in the sky. He had slept for at least an hour, if not more.

A voice came from behind him. "The ghosts of dead armies."

Albrecht was on his feet instantly, turning around with

klaive in hand. An old man stood a few feet away, leaning on a birch. He was thin but looked like he once had carried a lot of muscle. His white hair grew long, well past his shoulders and almost to his belt. He wore a gray robe adorned with silver pictograms — Silver Fang pictograms — representing honor, wisdom and glory. And there, on his chest, was the symbol of kingship.

"Who are you?" Albrecht asked.

"Aaron Ever Stone," the man said. "I saw you notice the trees. They are not trees. They are the ghosts of my dead army. My loyal army."

"Your name.... It's familiar. But I can't place it," Albrecht said.

"In my time on Gaia's flesh, I was king of the Esk River Protectorate in northern England. In the seventeenth century, by human reckoning."

Albrecht stood looking at the Silver Fang king, unsure what to say or do. He had never been in the presence of such a powerful ancestor before. "How... did you get here?"

The old man looked at Albrecht, puzzled. "This is my death domain. It is you who have come here. And who are you?"

"I am Lord Albrecht, scion of the House of Wyrmfoe. I was thrown into a Wyld realm. I don't even know where this is."

The old man nodded, understanding. "Ah. You are in the Silver Fang Homeland. You have passed through the Wyld zones along the edge. They come and go, but seem to get closer every few... years. If they *are* truly years, the time I reckon by the changing of the seasons. But time moves slowly here, does it not? So say the living who visit me."

"I don't know," Albrecht said. "Umbral lore was never my specialty. I can't believe I'm here. That damn Lune did send me where I wanted!"

"Why have you come?"

Albrecht thought for a minute, trying to figure out how to bring up the topic. He decided just to say it. "I'm looking for the Silver Crown."

The old man's eyes widened. "Why? Why do you seek such a thing? Are you vain?"

"No! I need it. It's the only thing that will allow me to take the crown from Arkady. Let me explain: Arkady is Wyrm-corrupt. He has allied with the Wyrm's minions. And he's set to take the throne on the cusp of the full moon—"

"Stop! I will hear no more. A king corrupt? Never! You must be mistaken. And you seek the crown? Listen to me, then: The crown is a thing of vanity and pride. It brings only pain and ruin. I know this, for I wore the crown. I was its last bearer. It was I who hid it from the world, to save the tribe from its terrible power. A power which destroys just as surely as it raises its wearer on high."

"You know where the crown is? I can't believe this! Finally, some answers. Look, you may have had problems with the crown, but I have to have it. Regardless of the consequence to me. The consequences to others will be much worse if I don't."

"You are not listening to me! Whelp! I tell you, it is an evil thing. I know this! You wish the crown? Then listen to my tale, and if the wanting of this thing is still in your heart afterwards, I will reveal its location to you."

"You've got a deal."

The old king wearily lowered himself to sit on the grass, leaning his back against a birch. He motioned for Albrecht to sit also. Albrecht went to a birch nearby the old man and sat down, leaning against it.

"I ruled a war-ravaged land. The Black Spiral Dancers, born in the fens and bogs and moors of Scotland, had their power to the north of my protectorate. Filthy place. From some deep pit in the earth they crawled forth to harry my lands, to steal our flocks and to corrupt our rivers with their filth.

"And the humans were ignorant of all this. They only knew that the border wars between England and Scotland were fierce. The border reivers were indeed a hard people, cruel and cunning, with no sense of honor or decency except to their own kin. Under the cover of such havoc as they wreaked, the Dancers raided our lands and ravaged us sore.

"I knew something had to be done. I had to get the Garou to the west and east of me to band together and take the fight to the Dancers' own lands. But they would not listen to me — Fianna and Get of Fenris. Getting them to work together against a common foe was nigh impossible. And that's when I heard of the Silver Crown.

"A wandering minstrel sang its tale, telling where it was hid, in the land now known as Pangaea. I knew this crown was the answer to my questions. It would allow me to forge an alliance of all the tribes and return wrack and ruin to the Dancers.

"So I set off on the quest with my loyal pack, the King's Own. It was a hard journey, for the Umbra was a wild and furious place in those times. Not like now. It is empty now. Devoid of life.

"We reached Pangaea with only minor wounds, and searched and searched for the crown. It was at Table Rock we found it, the holy rock. There, in a hole under the rock, the crown was hid. It took all our might to move the stone, but move it we did, for our need was dire.

"I beheld the shining crown and placed it upon my head. And I knew what I had to do. I was Falcon's chosen, the one true king of the Silver Fangs. Nothing could stop me from saving my kingdom and ending the reign of terror the Dancers had begun.

"We returned to my kingdom and the news soon spread of the crown. I sent for the leaders of the Fianna and Get of Fenris septs, my closest neighbors, to discuss a war party. They came, although they did not want to. But they could not resist.

It was as if the crown called to them to heed my request, giving them no peace until they listened and did as I said.

"Do you begin to understand the tyranny of the crown? Its power over others? Its ability to steal choice away from them, to force them unto a course of action? I did not realize this then, believing they came because they wished to.

"We supped together and I entertained them with my best Galliards. A fine evening it was. But they seemed to feign enjoyment, covering their fear of the crown. I believed they were subtly insulting me, and grew angry with them. I sent the Galliards away and commanded them to give me packs from their septs to go to war against the Dancers.

"The Fianna bowed, cowed before my authority, and said she would deliver them in a fortnight. I was pleased.

"But the Get. He steamed and shivered, fighting some inner demon. Or so I told myself. He was in actuality fighting the power of the crown. He won the battle, and cried that he would not send his packs to die for such a tyrant as I was.

"I was furious. Not only had he stained me with that insult, but he had stained Falcon also, implying that the crown had made a petty dictator. In an instant, I drew my klaive and cut him down. His head flew across the room and thudded against the chamber door.

"The Fianna stared at me in shock and dismay. She begged to leave, to return to her lands to begin the preparations for war. I gave her leave, pleased that she, at least, would join my endeavor.

"But the fortnight passed, and no sign of her packs was seen or heard. I was furious again. How dare she slight me? I knew I would have to teach her a lesson. I would have to war on her.

"I rallied the troops and led them out across the moors, to the lands of the Fianna. They were expecting us, and they put up a valiant fight. But we were masterful in war, and I was most masterful of all, for the crown bore me well through that battle. My cries and commands were as bolts of lightning against the Fianna. They could not resist my will. Eventually, they all fell before me.

"But the Fianna did not fold before my army easily. They delivered a dread accounting upon us: Only I and my pack survived. I sat upon my horse in the field of battle, surrounded by my pack, staring at the lifeless bodies of the Fianna. And at the lifeless Silver Fangs. In a fit of anger and wounded pride, I had killed the elite of two septs, the heart of a generation of Garou.

"The Dancers did not wait long to take advantage of the disaster my vanity had caused. They came down in greater numbers against the lands, the lands so newly depleted of warriors. Only the Get withstood them, bulwarked in their caern to the east.

"The Esk River Protectorate is no more. Dead. They are all dead.

"Do you see now why I warn you against this fetish? It is the cause of two septs' downfall!"

Albrecht was silent. He thought about everything he had been told about the crown. So many conflicting stories. Was the crown a gift from Gaia or a fetish like any other, but one which had become cursed over the years? Would its retrieval only doom the North Country Protectorate, as it had this old king's land?

But no, Albrecht thought. *It wasn't the crown that did this, it was the old man. It was his vanity. How can he blame the crown for backing up his commands, for lending force to them? The choice of how to use the crown was his.*

"I am sorry to hear your story. It grieves me. It is a tragedy; one which I will never forget. But... I still need the crown. I have to save my protectorate. While the crown may damn it in the end, it is the only thing which can save it now."

The old man looked at him. "It has only brought me sorrow. Deep, unyielding sorrow. Do not seek it. Stay here with me. Brighten my days with new tales of honor and glory, tales of how the Fangs succeeded without the crown. I am so lonely here, in my place of exile, with only my dead nearby…." He looked at the trees.

Albrecht felt a chill up his back. *Things are not what they seem to be*, he thought. He remembered something about this famous king, Aaron Ever Stone. Something he had forgotten, about this king's name in the tales. There was one thing mentioned in the legends: his lineage.

"I remember you now…. What royal family are you from?"

The old king looked at Albrecht quizzically. "I am a son of the House of Winter Snow."

And then Albrecht knew for sure. He stood up, stepping away from the king. "I lived up to my end of the bargain. I heard your tale. Now, where is the Silver Crown?"

The king looked up at Albrecht, exasperated. "You still want it? After all I have said?"

"Yes. You agreed to tell me where it is."

"But I would only cause your ruin by doing so. No, I cannot."

"You are going to go against your word? Where is the honor in that?"

The king looked stricken. "Honor? It has been… so long. Please, stay here with me. I can teach you much of the old ways. I even know Gifts lost to the world today. I could teach them to you…."

"No. Tell me where the crown is."

The king grabbed the birch he was leaning against and pulled himself up. "If you stay for one moon. One moon is all I ask! I will then tell you where the crown is. On my honor as a king!"

Albrecht thought. He knew he wouldn't be able to force the answer from the king by violence. The king was just an emanation, a shadow of the dead. He was a spirit. If Albrecht killed him, he would never get the answer, since the spirit would depart to reform elsewhere in the Umbra. But who knew where? He knew that time worked differently in the homeland. One moon here could be months in the real world, or only hours.

"One day then!" the king cried, his hands out in supplication. "One day is all I ask. Is this too much? I offer you secrets forgotten in the world of flesh, secrets which could empower you more greatly than the damned crown!"

Albrecht chewed his lip. He didn't know what to do. This was the only clue he had to the crown. The old king could be lying. But what choice did Albrecht have? There was no place left to go. And these secrets, these Gifts he was offered....

"You can give me something to overthrow Arkady without the crown?" he asked.

"Yes! Stay with me and I will give you all the royal rites of old, the words that are power when spoken from the lips of kings. And I will give you the Gift to win any challenge, and to call a challenge for any reason. You could return to your sept and challenge this pretender at your leisure! With these Gifts — true powers taught to my family by spirits long ago — you could rule any sept."

"How long? How long would it take to learn them?"

Aaron stood taller. "Two moons. Perhaps three. There are no spirits here to instruct your soul directly, so I must show you in the slow manner in which flesh learns. After this time, you can come and go from here freely, to return for more powers if you so desire."

Albrecht closed his eyes. He had to think. Calmly. Without the old man pleading with him. Two moons! That was too long. Arkady would be king by then. But if what Aaron said was true about these Gifts, he could march up to Arkady anytime to demand his true right. But what if it were too late? What if Arkady turned the sept over to the Wyrm on his coronation day?

Falcon! he thought. *Why is this so hard? I have done*

everything in my power here to find the crown. My packmates are in the hands of the Wyrm, probably dead by now. My protectorate is about to become Wyrm-corrupt. What else am I supposed to do? I've done everything I can, damn it! But I'm failing. It's in your hands....

He heard a screech up in the sky. He opened his eyes and looked up. A falcon wheeled above him, and let out another screech.

"No!" the old king said, looking up fearfully at the bird. "Don't heed it! It is a servant of the crown — the evil crown! Stay here! Please!"

"I can't listen to you!" Albrecht said. "I've listened to you too much already. You're lost! I recognize Harano. Your whole family has succumbed to it. Every generation! It wasn't the crown that did you in, it was your own sorrow. This isn't the tribal homeland, is it? It's some small realm somewhere you've built to house your grief. I won't be any part of it. I've got a protectorate to save!"

Albrecht looked up at the falcon. The bird flew off to Albrecht's right, and Albrecht moved to follow it.

The old king stepped in front of him. "Please! I am lonely! Carry my memory at least! Don't let my legacy die!"

"Get out of my way," Albrecht said.

"It's in the North Country!" the old king said. "I fled from my lands to the New World, and hid the crown with the Silver Fang sept there. It lies under the royal house in New Amsterdam."

Albrecht stared at the king, barely believing his ears. "You're lying! It's not in the North Country — Greyfist would have said so! I'm from North Country, damn it! New Amsterdam is the old name for New York City, and New York is not even in the North Country Protectorate!"

The old king stepped back, flinching at Albrecht's anger. "I swear! I swear that is where I hid it. I tell you, the city of humans was in North Country when I hid the crown! It was the only place far enough from home that I could get to before... before I... I was too tired to go on. The grief, you see... the grief overtook me. Swallowed me. It has left me here, all alone. Alone and weeping."

The old king began to fade, to shift shapes, but not into a wolf. He grew tall and thin, his skin becoming deathly pale, whiter than snow. He became a birch tree, silent as the rest. But not alone any longer. He was one of many birches, testaments to sorrow.

Albrecht realized that he stood in a graveyard. A graveyard for an entire royal line. A birch for every cub of the Winter Snow family lost to Harano.

He looked into the sky again and saw the falcon wheeling about, waiting for him. The falcon again flew off, and this time Albrecht followed unhindered.

CHAPTER EIGHTEEN

Fengy strolled through the park, content for once. He had just eaten a fresh fast-food meal, bought with the five-dollar bill he had found. This was working out to be a great day.

A light exploded in the air in front of him, and a hole appeared. A falcon flew from the glowing Moon Bridge, inches over Fengy's head. Fengy stared at it, aghast. This wasn't a proper Moon Bridge. It didn't open in the caern center, approved by the Gatekeeper. Was this an attack? But what could a bird do to harm the caern?

Lord Albrecht jumped out of the Moon Bridge, almost colliding with Fengy. The Moon Bridge sealed shut behind him, leaving no trace of its ever having been there.

"Watch out!" Albrecht said, running past Fengy, who was holding his hands over his head, readying himself to be run over by a pack of Garou.

Fengy looked up to see only Lord Albrecht and the bird, streaking off into the park.

"Hey!" Fengy yelled. "Where's your pack? What's going on? That wasn't a legal bridge! You're going to get in trouble with Mother Larissa!"

"Don't have time to chat!" Albrecht yelled over his

shoulder, turning down a lane and running out of sight.

"Huh!" Fengy said. "Then you don't have time for me to tell you that your friend is here looking for you?" He waited, but heard no response. Albrecht was out of hearing range. Fengy shrugged his shoulders. What did he care? If Albrecht was going to be rude, always treating him like a second-class citizen, then he could damn well find his friend on his own. Wasn't everyday someone came looking for you from North Country.

Fengy continued his walk, a bit flustered, but with a full stomach.

Albrecht had stopped running to catch his breath. He stood on a street corner, watching the falcon disappear into a closed subway station. He waited a few seconds, then bolted after it. No one was around — at least no one he noticed — so he shifted into Glabro form, tore the chain lock off the gate and ran down the stairs.

It was dark in the station, so he shifted to Lupus form and called upon one of his Gifts, honing his senses sharper than any animal's. He padded along on the cement, following the falcon. Albrecht knew this was a spirit he followed, not a real falcon, but it was still strange to see something and yet not smell it.

The falcon landed on the floor next to another fence, this one blocking the entrance into the subway tunnel. The tunnel had intermittent lighting, as if this area had not been closed off for long and the electricity not yet shut off, letting the old bulbs burn.

Albrecht shifted to Crinos and tore the fence down. As soon as it was down, the falcon took wing again and shot off down the tunnel to the right. Albrecht again assumed Lupus form and ran after it.

The tunnel went down for about a quarter mile before dead-ending. A few feet before the end, on the left side of the tunnel, was a passageway, carved into the cement and stone. Unnaturally carved.

The falcon flew into the passage. Albrecht hesitated. This was not human-made. That meant that one of New York's various supernatural residents of the sewer had carved it. He was on good terms with none of them.

He jumped into the passage anyway and ran after the quickly disappearing falcon. It was pitch black now, but his magically enhanced senses more than compensated. He could smell sewer, somewhere far ahead. But before that, he heard the falcon turn right, down a side passage. Albrecht followed. He hoped there were not too many turn-offs, since he could easily get lost down here if something were to happen to the falcon.

The passageway smelled old. He could pick up no scent on it: a sign that it had been long disused. The only sign of the falcon now was its screeches. He could not see it or smell it. The next screech he heard echoed longer than the rest. The falcon had entered a larger room. Albrecht hurried ahead, then stumbled out into the room as the passageway suddenly ended, giving him a short fall.

He heard the falcon screech from the far side of the room. From the echoes and distance, he judged the chamber was maybe thirty yards across. As he padded across the floor, he felt marble beneath him. Marble tile.

He reached the falcon, who was perched on a large, box-like object. Albrecht realized he would need eyesight here. He concentrated and lit the fires of his inner being, igniting his fur into a glowing lambent flame — the same Gift he had used against Nightmaster.

As light flooded the chamber, Albrecht looked around. It resembled an old mausoleum. The floor was marble, as were the columns holding up the ceiling. Gargoyle shapes sat at the top of the posts, staring blindly out at the room. Oddly colored dust lay along the base of the walls; Albrecht realized it was the remains of tapestries. Double doors stood open on the wall opposite the passage, but they revealed a wall of dirt on the other side. It looked as if someone had begun a digging project there, but had abandoned it before ever really beginning.

The passageway by which Albrecht had traveled was not natural to the room, but a later addition. Someone had burrowed his way past the wall and into this room.

It was obvious to Albrecht where he was: in the throne room of an ancient Silver Fang sept, perhaps the first in North America. The place had fallen pretty far from its early days of glory. No court had convened here for centuries. He figured this must be the basement of an old mansion, one that probably didn't exist anymore on the surface. Most likely, it was bulldozed and new foundations had been laid across it. He wondered what was up there now. A tenement? City Hall?

The falcon screeched and he turned back to look at it. The box it stood on was a chest. It was iron, and rusted badly, but still relatively intact.

"Is that it?" Albrecht asked. "Is the crown in there?" He shifted to Crinos form and ran to the box. The falcon screeched and fluttered off, to land on the ground next to it. The lock had long ago rusted, and it flew apart easily as Albrecht threw back the lid. He looked inside.

Nothing. The box was empty.

He looked at the falcon, which screeched and nudged the box with its head. Albrecht frowned, then understood. He shoved the box back, revealing a marble tile with writing on it.

A Garou pictogram had been carved there so long ago that it would surely have been worn down except for the box that had covered it for all these years. It was the symbol of kingship. A rite had been performed over this tile, sealing it with power. A rite of protection of some sort? Or a spirit binding? He had seen the sort before, and knew that only Silver Fang royalty could break such a seal and not suffer the consequences intended by the ritemaster.

Albrecht shifted to Crinos form and thrust his nails between the cracks. He grunted and pulled, and the tile slowly yielded. He pried it up and placed it aside, then looked at what was beneath it. The light from Albrecht's pelt shone down a small, maybe one-foot-square shaft, revealing a wooden box. A wooden box perfectly preserved, as if it had been made yesterday, except for the ancient manufacture. It appeared to be a strongbox from the Middle Ages.

Albrecht reached in and pulled it out. He placed it on the ground and examined it. There was a catch, but no lock.

Powerful, sharp jaws clamped down onto his right forearm. Albrecht screamed in pain and tugged his arm away. It slipped free of the white wolf's grip, but his muscles were practically flayed. His arm was almost useless.

He stared at the white wolf, who had come from nowhere and was growling angrily at Albrecht. The wolf shifted forms into Crinos. A black leather battle harness appeared over the huge werewolf's torso, contrasting with the pure white fur. Fur Albrecht would recognize anywhere.

"How the hell...?" Albrecht said, drawing his klaive with his left hand.

"It is mine, Albrecht!" Arkady said, stepping forward and standing over the box.

"The fuck it is! Just step back, Arkady, and I'll let you live. At least until you're banished from the tribe!"

"Shut up, you stupid cur! How dare you try to steal the kingship from me! Moving around behind my back and plotting with that traitor Greyfist!"

"Traitor? He's the most loyal Silver Fang in this hemisphere! If you've done anything to him—"

"Like kill him? Kill him for conspiring against the crown?

I have. I will kill you next!"

Albrecht stood stone-still in shock. "You... killed... Greyfist? He was my best friend in the sept!" Rage caused him to tremble and he tried to control his temper, but immediately lost the battle. He howled and lunged at Arkady, who easily jumped back.

Albrecht was like a rampaging torch as he chased Arkady across the room, the light from his fur throwing Arkady's shadow large against the wall.

Arkady drew his klaive as he ran. He slipped to the right and then spun around, stabbing at Albrecht, who was an easy target, glowing as he was. Albrecht ran onto the klaive, which went through his right lung but did not exit his back.

He fell down, coughing up blood and coming to his senses. The pain had knocked the frenzy from him. Arkady did not follow through. Instead, he ran over to the box.

Albrecht looked for the falcon spirit, but could not see it anywhere. He got to his feet and walked resolutely toward Arkady, ignoring the pain from his chest. "How did you find me?" he snarled as he walked.

Arkady, box in hand, turned to face Albrecht. He held his klaive out defensively. "You idiot! I've been here in New York for three days, waiting for you to return! Lucky I was. I did not know you would return here first. But I could not wait at the caern — wait for you to steal my birthright from me?!"

"Birthright? You forget, *I'm* Morningkill's grandson. Not you."

"But I am scion of the Clan of the Crescent Moon. We are a better family."

"I wouldn't put too much faith in this family stuff if I were you. Not after what I've seen. But you didn't answer my question. How the hell did you find me *here?*"

"The Rite of the Questing Stone, fool! Any cub could have found you. All he would have had to do was wait for you to show up!"

"Well what are you going to do now? Put the crown on? Go ahead. Put the crown on. I want to see this."

Arkady smiled at Albrecht, a twisted grimace. He shook his head. "Oh, no. I would not do something so stupid as that. This is not for me to wear. But I shall keep you from wearing it."

Albrecht growled. "You're going to have to kill me to do that." He slashed his klaive at Arkady and actually surprised the Garou, who did not parry Albrecht's left-handed attack well. The klaive sliced the tendons off his right arm. His hand went limp and the klaive fell to the ground.

Arkady howled in rage and stepped back. He dropped the box under him and crouched low, waiting for Albrecht to approach.

Albrecht moved forward warily. They were equal now. Each had only one usable arm. But he had the klaive. He knew he could finish it with one blow if he were good enough. But if he let Arkady get too close, then Albrecht would have to drop the klaive and fight claw-to-claw. And he knew Arkady was the better hand-to-hand fighter of the two.

Before he could choose his move, he heard grunting and scuffling from the passageway. He stepped back, out of Arkady's range, and stole a look in that direction.

Black Spiral Dancers crawled their way up the tunnel, toward the room, bearing balefire torches.

Albrecht turned back to Arkady. "Damn it! If you were ever a real Silver Fang, think back to that time now. Do not let them get the crown! We can fight our way out of here if we do it together."

Arkady looked at the Black Spiral Dancers, who were almost into the room, and then at Albrecht, trying to decide. He looked at the box beneath him. "No! I can't let you have the crown. The Black Spiral Dancers promised me the kingship. It is my crown."

"They want it to pervert it! You can't let that happen. Not

if you call yourself king!"

"Don't listen to him!" a voice cried out from the passageway. Black Spiral Dancers now jumped into the room and spread out to form a line, preparing to charge Albrecht. Behind them, Dagrack climbed from the passage. "He wants the crown for himself, Arkady. He can't stand the idea of you on the throne!"

Arkady growled at him. "What are you doing here? How did you find us?"

Dagrack smirked. "Oh, I've been watching you, Arkady. You can't go anywhere without my knowing about it. As soon as you entered the tunnels, I was alerted. Who do you think dug this passageway? Black Spiral Dancers — my cousins. I was but a Moon Bridge away from you."

Albrecht almost jumped past the Black Spiral leader when he saw Evan and Mari being pushed toward the room from the passageway. The line of Black Spirals surged forward at Albrecht's move, so he stepped back again.

He watched his packmates as they were pushed into the room. They looked terrible. They had bruises all over and seemed weak from hunger, but they both met Albrecht's gaze. Mari nodded at him, as if she approved of his being here. Evan actually managed a weak smile, happy to see Albrecht.

"Put them in the corner," Dagrack said. The Black Spiral Dancers pushed and shoved Evan and Mari into the far corner of the room, away from Albrecht.

Dagrack looked triumphantly at Albrecht. "I brought these two in case I had to bribe you with their lives. But I find that, after all your journeys, it is not you who have the crown. It is Arkady. My friend Arkady." He walked over to Arkady, who growled low as he approached, but did not move away from him. "Arkady who is to be king of the Silver Fangs. And this without the Silver Crown! Arkady does not need the crown. He has me instead."

"I need no one but myself!" Arkady yelled. "I am not your

puppet. I am master here! The next king of the Silver Fangs."

Dagrack stared at Arkady, and then bowed slightly. "Of course, my lord. Excuse your servant that he spoke otherwise. I wish simply to advise you in the matter of your antagonist here."

"What?" Arkady said. "What do you have to say?"

"Revenge, Arkady. It is your time for revenge. Revenge against those who wronged you long ago, who denied you and forced you out."

Arkady shut his eyes, holding down anger. "Damn them! But they matter not now! They are gone many years while I stand here, soon to be king."

"Oh, no, Arkady, they are not gone. You think that your oppressors existed in body alone? No! Their spirits still thwart you. Their servant stands before you, defiant, ready to run any obstacle to prevent you from succeeding. Lord Albrecht, scion of a royal line. He is just the same as they were, Arkady. Remember the Motherland and what they did to you there? What royals just like Albrecht did to you?"

"No. Do not warp this. He is like me — an exile. But he is wrong to defy me!" Arkady turned to glare at Albrecht. "He should have bowed down when he could. It is too late now."

"Yes, too late," Dagrack said. "He must be punished."

"What the hell are you talking about, you asshole?" Albrecht growled. "Arkady, why are you listening to him? He's a Black Spiral Dancer!"

"You will be quiet!" Arkady said. "Dagrack, fetch my klaive."

Dagrack smiled and went over to pick up Arkady's klaive, walking back to stand next to him with it. All the while, he smirked at Albrecht. Arkady concentrated, crooning low, calling on his Gift to heal his arm.

Albrecht fidgeted, uncertain what to do. Arkady was distracted; he might be able to grab the crown. But what if the Dancers did something to Evan and Mari? He couldn't decide how to act.

Arkady finished his healing and flexed his right arm. He took the klaive from Dagrack and looked back at Albrecht. "What to do with you, Albrecht?"

"Shit if I know," Albrecht said. "How about giving me the crown and letting my packmates go?"

Arkady snorted. "You will stop treating me like a fool! I have beaten you on all occasions. Bend knee and I will consider letting you live."

"My lord," Dagrack said. "I have a better punishment. One which will prove whether Albrecht is worthy to live or not."

"What do you say? Spit it out!"

"I have heard the *Lay of the Silver Crown*, the legend Albrecht doubtless followed in his quest. It speaks of a punishment placed upon the first Garou to seek the crown, a punishment for his impudence."

"Eh? What happened to him?"

"His claws were cut off, his fangs pulled and his pelt removed."

Arkady wrinkled his brow in disgust.

"Is this not what you swore to do to Albrecht? To flay his hide and hang it from a tree? I say if he survives this punishment, he can live. I will even let his packmates go free to help him crawl from the room."

"What do you gain from this?" Arkady said, staring at Dagrack.

Dagrack's demeanor did not change at all. "Why, the pleasure of helping you mete out your first royal edict and setting you on the course of kingship. You need to learn that a king must have a hard hand, lest he be dethroned by upstarts such as Albrecht."

Arkady looked at Albrecht and seemed to think on this.

"Don't listen to him, Arkady," Albrecht said. "Don't let him tell you what it is to be a king. That's your choice. Get rid of him! You know this isn't fair. My hands are tied as long as he has my packmates captive. Let them go and we'll settle this one-on-one."

Arkady sneered and shook his head. "Now who is giving kingly advice? You, who tried to snatch the throne from me! Dagrack at least helped me to get it. You must learn, Albrecht, that packmates are secondary to rulership. If you truly desire the crown, you will forsake them. Come at me! Let them fall as they may. We shall fight and decide the affair!"

Albrecht shook his head. "No. I'm not going to abandon them. I did that once already. I won't do it twice. You gotta decide: What are you going to do about it?"

"I will take my advisor's advice. I shall exact the traditional punishment for treachery against the crown. Yield your claws and fangs, Albrecht. Your pelt also. Or watch your packmates die and you with them."

Albrecht growled low.

"Arglach! Cut the boy!" Dagrack ordered. One of the Black Spiral Dancers swiped a claw at Evan's head, slicing his left ear clean off. Evan yelled and clutched his head. Mari stepped toward the Dancer, growling, but the other Dancers gathered menacingly about her. She backed up a step, putting her hand on Evan's shoulder. The Dancer who had cut off the ear picked it up from the floor and swallowed it, looking pleased.

"An incentive," Dagrack said to Albrecht. "Think hard on this."

Damn it! Albrecht thought. *What can I do?* He measured the odds against him and knew they were too much. Arkady was healed, and was more than a match for him even when wounded. Add Dagrack and his pack to that, and he didn't stand a chance against them. He looked at Evan and Mari. Mari glared at him, giving him a look he knew. It said that he would be a fool not to try to fight his way out. Evan looked at him, but he couldn't read the kid's intent.

I wish I were a Get of Fenris, he thought. *They think nothing of dying gloriously in combat as long as they can take a few bodies out with them. But I'm not a Get. I'm Morningkill's grandson, and I owe it to the Fangs to live up to my heritage.*

He looked for the falcon spirit, but it was gone. This was his choice alone. It was one thing to suffer declawing in a story: another thing entirely to have it really happen to you. He looked up at Arkady.

"Do you swear, on whatever honor you have left, that if I submit to this, my packmates can leave unharmed?"

"Yes," Arkady said. "I can be merciful also. I bear them no ill will."

Dagrack's eyes narrowed as he looked at Arkady. He obviously did not like the promise.

"Then make sure your lap dog knows that," Albrecht said.

Arkady looked at Dagrack. "You will heed me in this. If one of your mongrels harms them, I will kill you first and then all of your horde."

Dagrack nodded. "Of course. I have no need to disobey you."

"Drop your weapon, Albrecht. Let Dagrack perform the punishment."

Albrecht gritted his teeth and placed his klaive on the ground.

"Kick it over here," Arkady said.

Albrecht shoved the sword with his foot and it slid across the marble floor to Arkady. Dagrack stepped forward, drawing out a small klaive of his own. Like all klaives, it was silver.

"Please put out your hands, noble lord."

Albrecht glared hatefully at him and looked at Mari and Evan. Mari was giving him a wide-eyed "you idiot" look, while Evan was stone-faced. Albrecht turned back to Dagrack and slowly raised his arms, palms up.

Dagrack smiled, and in an flash swung his klaive down.

Albrecht grunted as the tips of his fingers fell to the floor. The pain burned him, the agonizing touch of silver. But he slowly put his now-clawless hands down and cocked his head at Dagrack.

"So fall our ideals," Dagrack said. "Like dead flesh. Now, open wide."

Albrecht opened his large muzzle, revealing sharp fangs. Dagrack pulled a pair of silver tongs from his pocket. Albrecht wondered if he had come here planning on this punishment all along. If so, he was pretty cocky about his sway over Arkady.

Dagrack placed the pliers in Albrecht's mouth and began to yank his teeth out, one by one. He grunted with exertion as he pulled the teeth, finding them hard to remove. Albrecht shut his eyes and concentrated on blocking out the pain. It was hard to do. The silver burned his gums and the blood welled up in his throat, forcing him to cough it out at Dagrack.

Dagrack smiled as the blood sprayed over him, but he did not stop his work. "Oh, I envy you in a way, Albrecht. Such an exquisite pain for those who could appreciate it. I would carry the memory of such an ecstasy with me forever." He yanked out the final fang, leaving Albrecht's blunt back teeth intact.

Albrecht spat out more blood, speaking with great difficulty. "Then why don't you give me those pliers. I'll oblige you."

"I fear I haven't the courage. I yearn so, but fear so. I envy your conviction, Silver Fang."

"Enough compliments," Arkady said. "Take his pelt. Give it to me."

Dagrack pulled his klaive out again. "I am afraid this one will hurt the most. Try not to lose control and attack me. I would be forced to kill you then. And your friends."

Albrecht stood still, closing his eyes and trying to meditate, to go deep within himself and escape the pain. But he howled loud and long when Dagrack made the first incision at the base of his throat and worked down from there, slicing through the skin of the chest and down to the groin. The Black Spiral Dancer then sliced cleanly down the inside of both legs. Albrecht nearly toppled from the pain, but Dagrack steadied him.

"Enjoying your part in the morality play, Albrecht?" Dagrack asked. "What have your morals brought you? Only this!" He carved the skin off Albrecht's foot with one swipe. "The unkindest cut of all. Do you think I chose this punishment out of sheer sadism? No, the irony is what's important here. Didn't the *Lay of the Silver Crown* teach you anything? About how important being good and cleaning your plate is?"

Albrecht growled, his eyes shut. He winced as Dagrack continued the cutting.

"Where's Gaia now? Where is your wonderful mother? The endlessly caring nurturer? Could they have lied to you, Albrecht? All those stories about the Earth Mother? She is no kind lady. I know that better than you. No, she is a cannibal with a fanged cunt. First she fucks you and then she cuts you."

Gaia! Albrecht cried to himself. *Why are you letting this happen! I have done everything asked of me! What the hell else could I do? Does it always come down to blood and pain in the end? Is that all this equates to? And Falcon! What happened to you? You ran away as soon as Arkady showed up. You abandoned me. I called to you and you ran. I'm alone in this. I guess it's always been that way.*

But the pack. I have a pack, damn it. And they are going to live because of this. This pain — aargh! It hurts! But Mari will live. Evan will live. He'll write me up in the Silver Record, won't he? He's a good kid. I'm sure he wouldn't forget me. I'll be famous for this. A martyr.

I don't want to die. Not here. Not torn up by some damn Black

Spiral Dancer. But we don't always get what we ask for....

Dagrack peeled the hide off Albrecht, starting from below and sliding the arms off like sleeves turned inside out. As the hide slid across Albrecht's raw and bloody muscles, he screamed again in pain. Only his Garou nature kept him alive. Only the regenerative power given the werewolves by Gaia allowed him to live to endure such pain and torture.

"This is the lesson of the crown, Silver Fang," Dagrack said. "No noble sacrifice. No reward for your ideals. Only a Grand Guignol of pain, humiliation and ultimate degradation. Serves you right. Serves all your kind. How dare you lecture my tribe on our ways! But where are your ways now? I'm stripping them away with your pelt. That is the moral of your damn crown! It's not about honor, you fool. It's about power. It always has been."

"Shut up!" Arkady said. "Just finish it."

Dagrack walked away from Albrecht with the pelt, which no longer glowed now that it was flayed from Albrecht's body. He dragged the wet, bloody thing over to Arkady, who took it in his hand.

Albrecht collapsed to the floor, shivering and barely conscious through the haze of pain.

"Let them go," Arkady said, signaling the Black Spiral Dancers. They moved away from Mari and Evan, who both bolted to Albrecht's side.

Evan bent down and immediately called on his Gift to heal Albrecht, but while it sealed up some of the oozing blood, it did not regrow the fur, claws or fangs.

"You sick bastard," Mari said, seething at Arkady. "You're pretty damn proud of this, aren't you? Why don't you try doing that to me? I'll carve you up!"

"Tend to him and then get out of here," Arkady said. "I am being gracious in letting you live. You conspired against Silver Fang leadership rites. No tribe will defend you on that."

"Wanna bet? Wait till Alani Astarte hears about this! She'll have every tribe turn against you. No one will recognize your rule."

"Oh? If she will not, then others in your tribe will. She is old and will die long before I leave the throne. Her successor will surely ally with my causes."

Mari fumed and bent down over Albrecht. "How is he?" she asked Evan.

Evan sighed. "Alive. But — Gaia! How are we going to get him out of here without killing him?"

Dagrack stepped in front of Arkady. "I have given you Albrecht's pelt. Now I ask one thing of you in return. A simple thing. One well within your power to grant."

"Tell me," Arkady said.

"I want the Silver Crown."

"No! You are joking! I would not dare give this to you!"

"Why not? In my hands, it is safe from any enemy to your crown. I certainly cannot use it to dethrone you. Do you think I would be stupid enough to wear it? No, Arkady. I need it to overthrow Azaera."

"Your queen? Why?"

"Why not? She is a tyrant. She uses you as a puppet. I work with you out of respect. She wants only power. If I have the crown — not even to wear it, but to possess it — the Black Spiral Dancers will come to my side. Rumor alone of the crown will bring them to me. With such an army of sycophants, I could easily overthrow the bitch!"

"No... don't...." Albrecht choked out, from his prone position on the ground.

Arkady looked at him, amazed. "Do not give Dagrack the crown? Why? Because you still labor under the illusion that you can have it? Oh, no. I will give the crown to whom I see fit. In his hands, it is at least as far away from yours as it can get."

Dagrack beamed. "Thank you, my lord! I am deeply

honored." He reached his hands out for the box beneath Arkady, but Arkady put his foot on the box. Dagrack looked up questioningly.

"You must swear to hide it away, and to let none of the tribes know where you put it. Is this clear? If I hear rumor of it from any of the tribes, I will kill you and take it back."

"Of course. I will be most occult concerning its hiding."

Arkady removed his foot, and Dagrack picked up the box.

"Mari...." Albrecht whispered, trying to rise. "Get it... don't let...."

Mari was already moving. She was next to Dagrack before he knew it, and reaching for the box. Arkady leaped in and punched her full in the face. She was knocked back, giving Dagrack time to scurry over to his pack.

Mari moved in on Arkady, but the Silver Fang placed his klaive between himself and her.

"Do you wish to be carved up as was your friend?" he said.

"No, Mari!" Evan yelled. "They've got the crown. There's nothing we can do."

Mari glared at Arkady and over at Dagrack, dropping into an attack stance.

Albrecht stood up, grunting loudly, startling everyone. "No. Don't, Mari." He swayed but kept his balance. "It's over."

Mari quivered in anger at Albrecht but then sighed, and stepped away from Arkady. "Damn you, Albrecht. I hate you for giving in."

"Sorry," Albrecht said. "I'll make it up to you later." He almost fell, but Evan caught him. Mari ran over to help steady him, concerned now. "Heh. Not too good on my feet here."

Dagrack was ignoring them now as he opened the box. A silver radiance came forth, lighting his awestruck face. "It's beautiful. It's so... noble." He reached in and pulled out a silver headband, simple and unadorned. He let the box drop to the floor.

That's it? Albrecht thought, gritting his teeth in pain. A *band of silver? No jewels or stuff?*

Dagrack turned to show the crown to everyone in the room, beaming with pride. He then turned toward Arkady and held the crown over his own head. "Power, Arkady. Power. Only cowards fear the taboos of their elders."

"What are you doing?" Arkady cried, running toward him. "Put it away! You'll die!"

Dagrack put on the crown.

And smiled. "You see. I am the true king here. No ethical retribution. No moral finger-wagging. Your stories were wrong. Your lies about the Wyrm are also proved wrong, Arkady. We are not corrupt. Just—"

He broke off into a scream as the crown began to glow brightly. It seared itself onto his head, fusing with the skin. Smoke rose from his singed fur, stinking up the room. He frantically shifted to Lupus form, trying to knock it off, but it was part of him now. He danced around, yelping in pain.

The Black Spiral Dancers stared at him, aghast, not sure what to do.

Dagrack's head was melting. The skin caught fire and burned away, revealing red and oozing musculature underneath, which itself burned away to reveal bone. The bone blackened and bubbled, cracking into shards.

Dagrack still screamed.

His eyes pooled to jelly and ran out of the sockets, smearing across his chest fur. He fell to the ground as the bone cracked away, blackened and charred, falling from his face to reveal a cooking brain, bubbling in its own juices. The crown seemed to shrink to constrict the brain, but the gray matter quickly liquefied and spilled across the floor.

The crown hit the floor with a gentle clang.

In the next few seconds, nobody moved. They all stared at the sizzling mass of flesh that once had been Dagrack's head. His body was perfectly intact.

Then Albrecht bolted toward the crown. Calling on

reserves of energy he hadn't known he had, he ran with all his might toward the crown. He was followed a mere fraction of a second later by Arkady. The Black Spiral Dancers were too stunned to react to this explosion of blinding speed from the Silver Fangs.

Albrecht reached the crown first by a palm's width. He held it up and away from the grasping Arkady.

"Give it!" Arkady growled, and dug his claws into Albrecht's exposed abdomen, puncturing the stomach wall, spilling out guts and blood.

Albrecht grunted but concentrated on one thing: dropping the crown on his head. In the moment it took the crown to settle — a measureless moment, lasting an eternity for Albrecht and Arkady, but mere fractions of a second for the others in the room — Albrecht wondered what it would feel like when his brain melted away. He prayed that he could die with more dignity than Dagrack had. *Please Gaia, let it be a quick death*.

The crown fitted itself to his head, tightening about his skull. The silver band seared into his furless flesh, causing more pain than Albrecht would have believed possible. More pain than he had known when the fur was flayed from his flesh and the teeth yanked from his jaws. More pain than could possibly exist. The silver burned into his skin and melded with it, becoming part of it, an inextricable piece of his body and being. Albrecht shut his eyes, tears flowing down his cheeks.

Visions danced in his head, images of the past. King Morningkill bent down over Albrecht, a child of twelve, and patted his shoulder. The king dipped his hand in paint and drew a pictogram across Albrecht's face. The sign of the chosen. At twelve years old, before even his Firsting, Albrecht was chosen heir to the throne. Morningkill smiled at Albrecht.

The images swirled in his mind. His first kill, a simple Bane. But it had been his first and he had done it well. The admiration of his young packmates, the other Fangs who had undergone their rites with him, becoming Garou together. The praise and cheers for the boy who would one day be king.

And the growing vanity from such praise. Albrecht saw again the scene of his exile. He dragged the Wyrm carcass behind him, beaming with pride. But Morningkill stood up on his throne and commanded Albrecht to kneel. Albrecht refused and was banished by the king. He lost his temper and leapt at his grandfather, but Greyfist pulled him back.

New York. He wandered the streets, alone. The Bone Gnawers had been pleased to welcome him, but he disdained their company. As the days passed and soon the months, he grew more and more like them, fishing his meals from garbage cans. He drank bottle after bottle of increasingly worse alcohol. Every day made him more cynical, more gutter-mouthed. He had once spoken only as a high-born Fang was expected to, but his speech soon devolved into curse word after curse word.

Then Evan ran into him, colliding with him in the street, running for his life from Black Spiral Dancers. He had his Firsting right there, tearing into the Spirals and killing them. Albrecht took him in and helped him get to the northern spirits who taught him his heritage. And in the process, he climbed out of the gutter. He had been saved by Falcon then. He had been considered worthy by the great bird. But now...?

The pain was gone. Albrecht blinked and opened his eyes.

A golden light came from behind Albrecht, and before he turned to look at its source, he heard the flapping of huge wings and the clack of talons on marble tile.

He turned his head and beheld Falcon. Not the tiny spirit that had led him here, but Falcon himself. The totem of the Silver Fangs stood incarnate in the room. The great bird emanated golden light from his shining feathers and an even brighter radiance from his eyes. He looked down at Albrecht.

And bowed his head.

Albrecht let out a sigh. He had survived. He had been judged worthy by the greatest judge of honor there was. By the totem which stood for honor, the totem which, in a deep, mystical way, *was* honor incarnate.

Arkady whimpered and withdrew his hand from Albrecht's guts. He crawled back a few feet, staring in fear at Falcon.

Albrecht stood up, holding in his intestines, and Falcon opened his wings wide. A golden glow blinded everyone in the room. The Black Spiral Dancers screamed and clutched their eyes, scuttling into the corner. When the glow subsided, Albrecht blinked, staring down at his body. At his fur and claws. He gnashed his teeth and howled for joy that he now had teeth to gnash. He was whole again, his stomach sealed and his arm usable.

He looked around the room. Everyone was staring at him. Albrecht turned to Arkady, who was still on the floor. The Garou did not meet his gaze. Instead, he stared at Falcon, trembling. Albrecht turned back to Falcon.

Falcon spoke in a deep, rumbling voice. "He is yours to command, King Albrecht. You wear the Silver Crown. You are king of the Garou, as ordained by Gaia at the Dawn. What is your command to him?"

Albrecht looked back at Arkady. He knew this was his most important moment. His first royal edict. His ruling would be a reality, no matter what Arkady wished otherwise. The crown would ensure that. It would force Arkady to do his bidding. And that was a terrible power to wield.

Albrecht thought. He could kill Arkady outright. Or worse, he could force the Garou to suffer what he had: loss of his pelt. He savored that thought. But then he realized what it would do to him if he went through with it. He would be Arkady. In many ways, they were reflections of each other already: both exiles, both royals, both contenders for the crown. But he wanted nothing to do with Arkady's style of rulership as displayed by what Albrecht had just gone through.

But was mercy proper here? Did Arkady deserve it? He had killed Greyfist, Albrecht's oldest friend and a trusted seneschal. Didn't Greyfist deserve revenge? To be weak here, to fail to dole out the proper justice.... Who would that ruling harm in the future?

Albrecht felt the full weight of the crown: not a physical weight, but one of responsibility. Arkady's life was in his hands. Arkady, who could go on to harm other Garou as he had his own sept. But Albrecht had always hated the sanctimonious leaders who so casually handed out life or death sentences, never seeming to care for the consequences of their edicts. He knew that he could not let hate rule him. He had to rule his own rage before he could rule others.

Damn it, he thought. *I don't want to become what I most hate. I don't want to be a despot. I don't want to be the strong arm of authority.*

"Get up, Arkady," Albrecht said.

Arkady looked up at him suspiciously, trembling. But he stood up, as if he had no choice. The power of the crown compelled him.

"I am not going to kill you, although you damn well deserve it."

Arkady's eyebrows rose. He stared in utter shock at Albrecht.

"But you are now an exile. Not just from the protectorate, as I was, but from the tribe. You are no longer a Silver Fang."

Arkady lowered his head. "No. Kill me. Don't make me walk alone. Kill me."

"No. Your punishment is to wander alone. Tribeless. No one will take you in. You deserve worse, you asshole. But I won't kill you. I'm not going to start playing that game. I ought to thank you, in a twisted way. You helped me shed my skin here. Literally. A friend of mine says that's what the problem with the world is: The Wyrm's not shedding its skin."

Arkady looked at Albrecht with contempt and a sneer on his face.

"And just for that grimace you're wearing," Albrecht said, "you can bow down and acknowledge your punishment."

Arkady growled but seemed unable to resist Albrecht's command. He bowed.

"Get out of here. Get out of the city, out of the state. Get out of the fucking country. Go back to where you came from."

Arkady looked up at Albrecht with fear in his eyes. "No. You can't. Not back to Russia. You don't know how things are there. You don't know the power of the Hag—"

"And I don't give a damn. Just go."

Arkady rose, all his will useless before the power of the true king's commands. He walked to the passageway, trembling with anger.

"One more thing," Albrecht said. "You are forbidden to deal with Black Spiral Dancers. Not even they can help you now."

Arkady looked at Albrecht. All the hate and anger in him had drained away. All that was left was sorrow. "You do not know what it is to walk alone, Albrecht. Even you, who have known exile, do not know the terror of the ronin. Do you think this fate I will now suffer is unknown to me? It was my life in Russia. A hard life. Only the Black Spiral Dancers offered aid. But when I arrived here, in North Country, I was accepted. No communication could escape Russia to reveal my past there. I swore never to lose that acceptance. Being king would have allowed me to keep that and eventually to betray the Black Spirals who had so beholden me to them. But you have ruined that."

He turned and crawled into the passageway. Albrecht said nothing else to him.

Albrecht looked at the Black Spiral Dancers. He then looked at Evan and Mari. "All right. You're my advisors. What do we do with them?"

"Kill them," Mari said, staring murderously at them. "Kill them all."

Evan lowered his head and said nothing, but Albrecht could see the hate he had for them, and his shame at that hate.

"I want you to go back to your caern," Albrecht said, addressing all of the Dancers, who tried to avert their gazes but could not. They were, after all, Garou, and Albrecht wore the Silver Crown. "And kill everything you see there. If you don't get killed in the process, I want you to fall on yourselves and kill each other. If one of you is left after that, that one may live. But I want the survivor to tell this story to all your kind. Let them know that they better not fuck with me. Get out of here."

The Black Spiral Dancers ran for the passageway, bloodlust already in their eyes. They were looking forward to the coming blood-bath. All except one, the last one out of the room. Arglach. He stared back at Albrecht with fury.

"I am now leader in Dagrack's place," he said. "Leader of my hive. And you make me destroy it. From one leader to another, if I survive, I will kill you some day." He then crawled into the passage to follow his grunting and howling war party back to their Moon Bridge.

When they were gone, Albrecht turned to Falcon.

"I want to thank you for everything you've done. It seems you're always getting me out of a mess."

"You govern your own actions. I only act to aid my children when all else has failed. You had to complete the quest as far as you could; but it was impossible to complete it without me. I led you here, but only you could make the final sacrifice."

"Look.... I am a bit worried about this kingship thing. This ultimate power scares me a bit."

"Have no fear. Your ability to command the actions of others is no longer a trait of the crown."

"Huh?"

"It was a test, Albrecht. As everything else has been. The

first command is the most important. It will hallow or taint your days forever after. The test is over. The crown's powers are no longer so great."

"Did I choose right, then? Should I have killed Arkady?"

Falcon was silent.

"Look.... If the crown isn't so powerful anymore, what good is it?"

"It is the symbol of Gaia's unity. One king over all the tribes. One law for all the tribes. The Litany. You wear the crown, so you must support the Litany, even when it harms your tribe. The other tribes may not immediately recognize your position, but if you rule wisely, they will learn by example."

"So all those legends about the crown's amazing powers were just tall tales?"

"No, they were true. But that was another age. The time of the king is fading, Albrecht. Gaia willing, there will come a time when all of Gaia's creatures will be able to rule themselves with no guidance but their own hearts."

"But wait a minute. The crown is from the Dawn. Everything was perfect then. Why did they need the crown?"

"Perfect? What age has ever been perfect? Things were newly born then, Albrecht. Unformed. Their purposes under Gaia had not begun to be fulfilled."

Falcon then spread his wings wide. "Enough instruction. You must return to your caern. Tomorrow is Coronation Day!"

A golden light suffused the room and blinded them all. When they again opened their eyes, they were standing on the field outside Morningkill's mansion, before the throne of the Silver Fangs.

Garou nearby sprang into action, anticipating an intruder, but they stopped dead in their tracks when they saw Falcon and his passengers.

Then Falcon raised his wings once more and was gone.

Albrecht stood there, whole again, completely healed by

Falcon. The crown was on his head, a plain silver band. He looked at the Garou, running from all over and pointing at him, staring in awe. *Well*, he thought, *this sure is a change from the last time I was here*.

Mari and Evan turned about, looking in all directions.

"Is that the throne?" Evan asked, pointing at the Grand Oak and the seat carved into it.

"Yeah," Albrecht said, eyeing it. He wondered if it were comfortable to sit in.

"All this for that hunk of oak? It doesn't look like much," Mari said.

Albrecht looked at her frowning face and started to laugh. "After all this, that's all you have to say?"

"I'm entitled to my own criticism," Mari said.

Albrecht shook his head and walked up to the throne. He sat down on it. As he sat in the seat of his grandfather, he looked out over the Garou gathering around, staring at him with expectant faces, waiting for him to speak.

And he realized that the hardest part was just beginning.

EPILOGUE

The rites had been performed. They had taken the entire day and most of the night, but they were done. Lord Albrecht was now King Albrecht, invested through the rituals of his people.

There had been a special guest for the investiture, one Albrecht had invited personally. One who had not set foot within the caern for a longer time even than Albrecht's exile. Loba Carcassone stood proudly to the right of the throne, the position of the king's chosen, his favored warriors. The Silver Fang pariah had long been ignored for her campaign against the Wyrm's child-abuse plots, but now she was honored for them, recognized as the hero she was. Albrecht knew that, if everything she said about the Defiler Wyrm was true, there would be an accounting soon — even if he had to lead the charge himself. But that was a matter for the future. For now, Loba once again stood in her tribal protectorate. The exiles had come home.

The feast lasted for a week. Celebrants were invited from all over, even from the other tribes. Antonine Teardrop was there for the Stargazers. Mother Larissa came for the Bone Gnawers. Others came, too, leaders of their own protectorates or septs: Alani Astarte, the wise old matron of the Black Furies; Pearl River and True Silverheels of the Children of Gaia, two level-headed ex-hippies; the somewhat rowdy but entertaining Riordan Cliffgrazer of the Fianna; and Nepthys Mu'at of the Silent Striders, who didn't stay long.

The Get of Fenris sent no one. Their leader, Arn Guth Stormbright, had never been a friend to Albrecht. The same for the Red Talons and the Shadow Lords, all nursing sour thoughts about the Silver Fangs in general and Albrecht in particular. The Uktena and Wendigo were also absent. They did not recognize the Silver Fangs' rule, and so stayed away.

Yet this was the first time in many years that so many tribal leaders had come together. It was an occasion for true celebration. Albrecht couldn't believe it himself. Two days ago he had been just an uncouth, prideful Garou to them. Now, they came to wish him well and to discuss the future between their tribes.

Albrecht had hidden in Greyfist's library for most of the first day, nervous and unsure of how to receive them. He had never done anything remotely like this before.

There was a knock on the door, and Evan poked his head in.

"Hey, kid," Albrecht said, pacing before the desk.

Evan walked in. "You're going to have to go out there. We told them you're still suffering from your wounds, but that you'd be out soon."

"I can't do this! I'm not a diplomat. I can't schmooze with these guys."

"You don't have to. Just be yourself. They'll respect that more."

"Oh, yeah. Right. They'll respect me for being myself? For cursing and spitting out cynical homilies at every turn? They'll love me. I'll be a hit."

"Albrecht, quit whining. You've been through much worse

than a simple party. You know how to do this. What did your grandfather use to do?"

Albrecht stopped pacing. "I remember once, long ago, when a high and mighty Garou came to see him. Bull Roarer, I think, of the Uktena. I don't know what he was doing here. But he's old and respected. Jacob stepped down from the throne and greeted him in Lupus form, which seemed to please the old wolf."

"See? You've got a good example to follow in your grandfather."

"Ha! Then there was the time, much later, when Kleon Winston came. You know, the Glass Walker Don? Morningkill made him wait out in the rain for an hour before he finally saw him. And then Winston left angry anyway. It's funny, but the electricity in the mansion didn't work too well for a month after that. We figured the Walker had left a gremlin behind for his troubles."

"So? It's still an example. It's just what not to do. You've got both angles now."

Albrecht looked at Evan. "Always looking on the bright side, huh?"

Evan looked back at him. "Even when we were getting kicked around by those Dancers, I knew you'd succeed. I don't think Mari had such faith, but I did. I knew I might die. But I knew you would succeed so you could take the throne and unite the tribes — those tribes out there on the field waiting for you. If I had died, what would you have done now?"

Albrecht was silent for a moment. "I'd have gone out there and made peace. For your sake."

"Good. And now that I'm alive, you're not going to?"

Albrecht smiled. "All right, Master Po. I'm going out there." He punched Evan in the arm as he walked past him. And then he went out to greet the dignitaries.

The feast was over. The guests had gone home, satisfied that the king was someone they could deal with. They did not universally recognize his rule over their tribes, but they did realize that he was a fair judge who could help them work through their own disputes.

The Silver Fangs of the North Country Protectorate all beamed with pride. The grandson of King Jacob Morningkill now sat on the throne. Things were as they should be. The low had again been raised high.

Albrecht sat on the throne, watching the Kin families clean up the field of litter left after the feast. He smoked a fat, smelly cigar and had his feet up on the armrest of the throne as he leaned back over the other armrest. He belched.

The party had been over for a few hours now. He had changed back into his old clothes, a T-shirt and jeans. His klaive hung from its shoulder holster on his left side. His long hair was no longer tied back, but flowed loosely down his shoulders. He hadn't shaved for a few days, and his beard was coming back. And the crown was on his head, immovable.

Seeing Evan and Mari walking across the field toward him, Albrecht sat up straight and put out the cigar. They were only his packmates, but he had learned from the last few days that he needed to clean up his act if he was going to lead the tribe.

Mari shook her head as she approached. They came and stood at the foot of the throne, looking up at him.

"We're going back to New York," Mari said.

"What?!" Albrecht barked, sitting up. "But you've got great digs here!"

"We live in New York, Albrecht."

Albrecht frowned and slouched again. "Yeah. I guess. Hey! I can visit anytime I want. I'm king, aren't I? No more waiting in line for Moon Bridges. No more greasing the palm of the Gatekeeper. Anytime! You guys can come back anytime, too. Sure."

"Of course we will," Evan said. "We are packmates. That hasn't changed."

"Speaking of which," Mari said. "I don't know if I'm comfortable with this king thing of yours. You're already getting an ego about it."

"Hey! Hey, now. I've been a perfect gentlemen here. We are a pack, Mari. We are equals."

Mari shook her head. "For now. But how soon till you start trying to pull rank? A male does not boss around a Black Fury!"

"Whoah! I won't. I don't even rule the Black Fury tribe. Alani Astarte made that clear. But she does recognize my position as a unifier. The Furies still make their own decisions. I'm just a figurehead, really."

"But an important figurehead," Evan said. "We're not humans. Symbols mean something for us. And that's why you're important, Albrecht. Don't let the other tribes tell you otherwise."

"Don't worry. I'm not going to push them around, but they're not going to push me, either. I *am* the king of the Silver Fangs, after all. Like it or not, the other tribes need to recognize our precedence."

"Hmph. This is just too weird," Mari said. "But don't you ever forget that I can kick your white-furred ass around this field. You just got lucky the last time."

"Luck?! Luck, was it? I don't know about that. I got in a pretty good lick—"

"Stop it!" Evan said. "What is this? A sitcom? You guys return to normal at the end of the episode? Haven't you learned anything from this?"

"I still owe him for this scar," Mari said, pointing at the scar on her belly.

"I'm sorry already!" Albrecht said. "How many times do you want me to say it?"

"Mari, you did attack him first, you know," Evan said.

Mari fumed silently for a moment. "He was trespassing in my territory. But I guess I overreacted."

"Well...." Albrecht said. "I guess I should have watched where I was going. But I didn't expect you to attack me."

"Wait a minute," Mari said. "You told me you didn't know it was my territory."

"Uh... well, I might have lied."

"You bastard!" Mari yelled, stepping toward him.

"Will you two stop!" Evan said, stepping between them. "I am getting really sick of pulling you off each other!"

"I'm sorry," Albrecht said to Mari. "I've said it before. What do you want? A free shot at me?"

"Yes," Mari said. "I'll take that as an apology."

Albrecht tore his shirt in half down the front, revealing his chest. "There. There it is. Go for it."

Mari stepped up, but then stopped. She looked at the ugly scar on his right pectoral, the one Arkady had made with his klaive. The wound was healed, thanks to Falcon, and the lung had already grown back, but the scar would be permanent. She stepped away.

"It's too easy," Mari said. "I know I can take you. I don't need you to sit there for me. It's over."

"Apology accepted?"

"Yes."

Evan smiled. "Thank Gaia that chapter is over! Well, Albrecht, we'll catch up with you soon. But we've really got to get back home. Mari has classes to teach."

"I know, I know. You just get going. Maybe I'll drop by next week, once things have calmed down here."

"Good," Evan said.

"Farewell, Albrecht," Mari said.

"Good-bye, Mari," Albrecht said. "And thanks for your help. I couldn't have done it without you."

Mari smiled. "I know. You would have failed miserably

without me. What else is new?" She turned around and walked off.

Albrecht's eyes narrowed, but he smiled. He waved at Evan as the boy followed Mari.

The new king sat back on the throne and watched Eliphas open a Moon Bridge for his packmates. When it closed and they were gone, he sighed. It was kind of lonely here. The only person he really knew anymore was Eliphas. With Greyfist gone, he had few good friends here. Regina was all right, but he barely knew her. His family had lightened up toward him considerably, although he knew some of that was simply kissing up to the king. Sutter still wouldn't speak with him, though.

No, it was going to be a lonely place. He'd have to bridge back to New York now and then just to stay sane.

He saw two people coming toward him from far across the field. And he knew then that it wouldn't be too lonely.

His father walked with young Seth. They were coming over to him, and his father waved. Seth waved also, beaming at his uncle, the king.

Albrecht smiled and waved back.

LEXICON

Airts: The magical paths within the spirit world (e.g., Spirit Tracks, Moon Paths, etc.).
Apocalypse: The age of destruction, the final cycle, the birth of death, the everlasting corruption, the end of Gaia — a word used in Garou mythology to describe the time of the final battle with the Wyrm. Many consider this time to be the present.
Auspice: The phase of the moon under which a particular Garou was born; commonly thought to determine personality and tendencies. The auspices are: Ragabash (New Moon; Trickster), Theurge (Crescent Moon; Seer), Philodox (Half Moon; Judge), Galliard (Gibbous Moon; Moon Dancer), Ahroun (Full Moon; Warrior).
Bane: Evil spirits that follow the Wyrm. There are many different kinds of Banes: Scrag, Kalus, Psychomachiae and more.
Bawn: A boundary area around a caern, where mortals are watched.
Breed: The ancestry of a Garou, be it wolf, human or other Garou.
Caern: A sacred place; a meeting spot where the Garou can contact the spirit world.
Celestine: The greatest spirits; the closest things the Garou have to gods. Examples are Luna (the Moon) and Helios (the Sun).
Charach: A Garou who sleeps with another Garou or has done so in the past. Often used as a word of anger.
Concolation: A great moot, wherein many tribes gather to discuss matters that concern the Nation of Garou.

Corruption: The act of destroying, devolving or debasing life; also, the often overwhelming effects of the Wyrm's actions. In the present age, it often specifically refers to the ecological ruin humans wreak upon the environment.
Crinos: The half-wolf, half-human form of the Garou.
Delirium: The madness suffered by humans who look upon a Garou in Crinos form.
Domain: A mini-Realm in the Umbra, usually connected to a larger Realm in the Deep Umbra.
Flock, The: All of humanity, particularly those humans from whom the Garou recruit their members.
Gaia: The Earth and related Realms, in both a physical and a spiritual sense; the Mother Goddess.
Garou: The term werewolves use for themselves.
Gatekeeper: A Garou who is in charge of the spiritual and magical defense of a caern, including the opening and closing of Moon Bridges.
Gauntlet: The barrier between the physical world of Earth and the spirit world of the Umbra. It is strongest around technological (Weaver) places, weakest around caerns.
Gift: A magical ability, taught to the Garou by spirits of nature.
Glen: A small realm or domain of Gaian energy in the spirit world. Glens often appear as lush forests or jungles.
Harano: Inexplicable gloom, inexpressible longing for unnamable things, weeping for that which is not yet lost. Some say it is depression caused by contemplation of Gaia's suffering.
Hispo: The near-wolf form of the Garou.
Homid: A Garou of human ancestry. Occasionally used disdainfully by ferals (e.g., "That boy fights like a homid.").
Klaive: A fetish dagger or sword, usually of great spiritual potency and nearly always made of silver.
Litany: The code of laws kept by the Garou.
Lodge of the Moon: One half of a Silver Fang court. This

organization tends to the spiritual affairs of the sept. There are three positions: Shaman, Steward and Squire.

Lodge of the Sun: One half of a Silver Fang court. This organization tends to the material affairs of the sept. There are three positions: Shaman, Steward and Squire.

Luna: See *Celestine*.

Lunae: Realms which sometimes appear at the crossroads of two or more Moon Paths. They are almost always guarded by resident Lunes.

Lune: An enigmatic spirit allied to Luna. Lunes guard the Moon Paths.

Lupus: A Garou of wolf origin.

Metis: The sterile and often deformed offspring of two Garou. Generally reviled by Garou society.

Moon Bridge: A gate between two caerns; it most often appears during moots.

Moon Path: See *Airts*.

Moot: A sept or tribal conclave that takes place at a caern.

Mule: Slang for metis.

Near Umbra: The spirit world surrounding the Gaia Realm.

Pack: A small group of Garou bound to each other by ties of friendship and mission as opposed to culture.

Pictogram: The Garou possess a written language of pictograms, many of which are quite ancient. They may appear to the uninitiated to be mere claw marks, but there is an "alphabet" of elaborate symbology.

Penumbra: "Earth's Shadow;" the spirit world directly surrounding the physical world; many, but not all, terrain features will be the same.

Protectorate: The territory claimed and patrolled by a pack or sept.

Realms: The worlds of "solid" reality within the Tellurian. Earth is referred to as the Realm.

-rhya: "Greater in station"; a suffix appended to a name.

Rite: A magical ritual.

Ronin: A Garou who has chosen or been forced to leave Garou society. It is a harsh fate to become a "lone wolf."
Seneschal: A Silver Fang king's second-hand man and closest advisor.
Sept: The group of Garou who live near and tend an individual caern.
Silver Record, the: The sacred "bible" of the Garou, a collection of their most treasured legends and deeds from all the tribes.
Stepping Sideways: Entering the spirit world. Most elders consider this term flippant and disrespectful.
Throat: To best another in ritual combat. Used as a verb (e.g., "I throated his sorry butt!").
Totem: A spirit joined to a pack or tribe and representative of its inner nature. A tribal totem is an Incarna, while a pack totem is an Incarna avatar (a Jaggling equivalent).
Triat, The: The Weaver, the Wyld and the Wyrm. The trinity of primal cosmic forces.
Tribe: The larger community of Garou. Tribe members are often bound by similar totems and lifestyles.
Umbra: The spirit world.
Urrah: Garou who live in the city; also, the tainted ones.
Veil, The: See *Delirium*.
Warder: A Garou who is in charge of the martial defense of a caern.
Ways, The: The traditions of the Garou.
Weaver, The: Manifestation and symbol of order and pattern. Computers, science, logic and mathematics are examples of the Weaver's influence on the material plane.
Wyld, The: Manifestation and symbol of pure change. The chaos of transmutation and elemental force.
Wyrm, The: Manifestation and symbol of evil, entropy and decay in Garou belief. Vampires are often manifestations of the Wyrm, as are toxic waste and pollution.
Wyrmhole: A place that has been spiritually defiled by the Wyrm; invariably a location of great corruption.

ABOUT THE AUTHOR

William Bridges, who is the line developer for White Wolf's **Werewolf: The Apocalypse** roleplaying game, has written many sourcebooks for White Wolf, including **Croatan Song** (a **Werewolf** graphic novel). He is also the co-scriptwriter for Viacom New Media's horror interactive game **Dracula Unleashed**. He graduated from the Virginia Commonwealth University with a degree in Filmmaking and a minor in Philosophy, and currently lives in Atlanta, Georgia.

FREE RAGE CARD REDEMPTION FORM

This form entitles you to a free Rage promotional card based upon this novel, **The Silver Crown.**

How to get your card: Fill out the order form below. Enclose it with a S.A.S.E. (*that's a Self Addressed Stamped Envelope*) and send it to:

The Silver Crown Rage Card
White Wolf, Inc.
Suite 100
780 Park North Blvd.
Clarkston, GA 30021

Allow 6 - 8 weeks for delivery. This card is a free promotional offer and is subject to availability. Requests that do not include a Self Addressed Stamped Envelope will not be filled.

First Name:____________ Last Name:____________

Address:________________________________

Street:_________________________________

City:____________ State:____ Zip Code:_______

Phone Number:___________________ Age:_______

Are you familiar with White Wolf products?_________

Have you ever played a White Wolf game before?______

If yes, which ones?___________________________

Describe in detail your favorite pair of shoes:_________

____

____

THE SILVER CROWN